QUEEN OF SACRIFICE

THE BLOOD MOON PROPHECY

BOOK ONE

SUSAN PERSON

PERISEK
PUBLISHING

For my father, this book would not exist without you.

QUEEN OF SACRIFICE

ONE

We all lived on Earth, but we definitely didn't live in the same world. Adrenaline coursed through my veins in anticipation. Hunting vampires might not be the best thing about being a witch, but it ranked pretty high on the list. I stepped out of the cab into the cool October evening. The lights flickered like the heightened pulse of downtown Dallas. The skyscrapers stood like statues, shrouded in a slight haze of dampened air. Tonight, I hunted my enemy.

I drew in a deep breath, begging it to cleanse and focus me. The cigarette smoke, already clinging to my hair and clothes, coupled with the stench of trash, refused my request. The tepid temperatures translated to perfect hunting conditions. Vampires visited Club Red often and in particular on nights when the mild weather delivered people in plentiful fashion as it did tonight. Disheveled patrons stumbled out of the over-packed club any decent

Fire Marshall would shut down. I shook my head and walked to the front of the line.

My lips curved into a smile for the doorman, Ian. He winked and moved the deep red velvet rope aside for me to enter, bypassing the line wrapped around the corner. I smirked at the sighs, groans, and whistles. The arched cherry wood door opened by way of bouncers the size of wrestlers on either side. *Would the humans thank me for my services if they knew witches and vampires existed?* While I loved the hunt, I considered what it would be like to trade places with them in their normal lives. There was something appealing in the habitual regularity of their day-to-day activity.

The bartender poured a shot of liquid courage for me before I even made it over to him. "Women in leather are always trouble. Who's the lucky guy?" Rob smiled and handed me the small glass.

Humans and their small talk equated to distraction. One a hunter couldn't afford. Like most of my kind, I kept the humans at arm's length. A witch and human friendship opened up a vulnerability the vampires could use against a hunter. I fiddled with my necklace, running my hand over the intricate old-world scrollwork until I found the hidden vial of Vampire Death.

"I don't know yet," I said with a wink and a laugh. "Has my brother been in tonight?" The sting of the vodka slid down my throat to warm my belly. The burn awakened my senses.

"No, he mentioned a birthday party tonight." He hesitated, setting a second glass in front of me. "Aren't y'all twins?"

I smiled to hide my inner wince. Today wasn't our birthday, but Grandmother suggested we celebrate the night before given it was a birthday ending in a seven. Tomorrow, my twin brother and I would be tucked away in our safe spots at the time of our birth.

"We are." I nodded. "We like to celebrate differently." I slung my head back, taking the shot.

"Well, happy birthday, princess." He leaned over the bar to give me a quick peck on the cheek.

My lips turned up in appreciation. Rob had always been kind, and his good looks garnered lots of attention from the human patrons. If I weren't a hunter, I'd have taken him to bed, but there wasn't a chance of that tonight or any other night. I pivoted to take in the crowd and pressed my back against the bar. I focused my full attention on the dance floor. With closed eyes, I inhaled the perfumes and colognes mixed with the sweat of the people. The vampires, scattered throughout the club, found a dinner buffet filled with humans who had enough alcohol in them to loosen their inhibitions.

Many of the women danced on each other to entice the men. It was almost a ritual in this club as well as in others. I'd seen it again and again, and hunters weren't always able to save them. My gut twinged at the thought of failure. What humans didn't know and what we were forbidden to tell them was many of the men were killers. Not to mention a fair share of the as lethal women. My senses came to life with the rapid beat of the music and the anticipation of the pursuit. Magic came alive under the surface of my skin as my intentions settled on the hunt.

I moved my hips in rhythm to the drumming beat while I made my way through the crowd and up to a redheaded bombshell dancing alone. Her friends left her and were hanging out at the bar. She would be easy prey for the killers present in her inebriated state, and my empathy for her distracted me for a moment. It had been a club much like this one where I found myself cornered by vampires. The night had been meant for a fun night of teenage freedom with fake IDs, but my memories of the night and the following two weeks were splintered. I turned my back to her and faltered. My eyes locked with emerald green ones staring back, and I stood frozen in place. My hearing followed my breath's lead, leaving me deaf and unable to inhale. The only sound audible, my own heart beating in a rush. A warmth foreign to me passed through my body, followed by a dizzying bout of déjà vu. His face contorted, distorting his chiseled features for a moment. The connection broke. Music and voices once again filled the space around me. I gasped and grabbed my neck, rubbing my necklace. The gorgeous man across the room with the gaze penetrating me was a vampire. *Shit!*

I spun on my heels, trying to catch my ragged breath. Again, I met his gaze. This time in the mirror on the other side of the dance floor.

He looked me over, starting from my knee-high black leather boots and regarding my exposed thighs before moving over my leather dress. I pressed my thighs together. He lingered at the heirloom necklace given to me by my grandmother. My fingers caressed the hidden vial. I fell into the abyss of his gaze, twisted and entwined in its depth. His expression softened, most noticeable in how his jaw relaxed. The eyes reflected didn't look like the normal killers I encountered here. His were familiar and warm. The shoulders gave him away. His still carried tension he couldn't hide. I forced my eyes closed to break the connection and turned away to reopen them.

This shouldn't happen. Not to me. I shouldered my way through the sweat-soaked crowd and headed for the back door, desperate for the cool air to clear my head.

He managed to surprise me, which never happened, especially not while I hunted. *How could I be so stupid? Figures I'd have an attraction that powerful with a vampire. Exactly my luck with men.*

Perplexed, I clamored into the alleyway. Training and instincts had taught me better than to come out the back door without being prepared. *Yet, here I am like a newb.* "Eff!"

The pungent bouquet of fresh blood and trash from the dumpsters hit me. Even through the fog hanging in the air, the eyes of a killer sought me out. He lurked in the corner where the concrete block wall met the wooden fence that concealed the dumpster. The vampire paused the greedy assault on his meal to look at his dessert. A hiss escaped his lips.

"Thanks for reminding me why I'm here, asshole." I pulled out one of the stakes concealed in my boots and hurled it at his chest. It found his heart with no difficulty. A pile of dust drifted on the wind through the darkness, leaving no trace of his presence. Satisfaction pulled at the corner of my mouth.

The vampire's meal looked at me with a dazed expression. Scarlet trickled down her neck. The smugness of the kill faded away at the sight. I touched her head with a gentle hand. *Home. Sleep.* The woman wandered down the alley to the street in front of the club. The further away, the safer she would be. I watched to make sure she cleared the corner. She would have a nasty headache in the morning, and she'd assume she drank too much.

To be human and have a normal problem like a hangover enticed me, but I had little time to dwell on a human life I'd never have. The career I envisioned for myself as a child didn't involve killing anything, even vampires, but that was from a time before I encountered the cruelty firsthand. It did little good to deny the high that came over me when I ended one. Soft steps from behind alerted me to more vampires. My hand slid over the vial on my necklace.

"You're a witch. What did you do in there? Try to cast a spell on me?" His amused tone sent shivers down my spine.

The melodic voice demanding my attention belonged to the green-eyed vampire. I didn't have to turn around to confirm. *Had he followed me outside and why did part of me hope he had?* Even as my senses prickled, his voice drew me to him with familiarity. I let out a soft breath. His presence didn't threaten me. *But it should.*

I lowered my voice. "No, I don't have to cast spells." I

slipped a hand in my boot for another stake and pivoted to face him. The softness in his face caused me to pause. The thought of killing him held no appeal like it should, but I didn't get the chance to find out. In a blur, he caught my wrist and sparks ignited from his touch. The stake dropped to the ground in the middle of the alley as my defenses came to life, ready for a fight. I gazed at how tiny my hand looked in his. He held it in a lax grip I could, without question, break.

My gaze followed the line of his arm to meet his eyes. The connection between us drowned and consumed me. His almost human scent differed from other vampires. He lacked the rot of death I had become accustomed to smelling with his kind. The draw between us caused a new sense of closeness for me. His forehead wrinkled and his eyes darkened as they had inside the club. The sight woke me up from my trance. *Stupid, Brie. So Stupid.* I chastised myself, unsure if I was angry at me or him.

"I think you're the one causing the issue, vampire." I jerked my hand from his, hearing a sizzle from his fingertips.

He glanced at his fingers and rubbed his thumb over the pads.

My oath to protect humankind from them was planted in my mind, and I would do my duty. A whiff of burnt flesh assaulted my nostrils. Once again, the thought of killing him seemed hollow and wrong. I hesitated.

Singed fingertips brushed my earlobe as he ran his hand across my cheek. In my years as a hunter, a vampire never touched me with such a soft caress. *I'd have turned them to ash if they had tried.* His thumb traced my eyebrow, and my eyes fluttered. I fought the urge for them to close. He took a step back and dropped his hands to his side. I wanted the sparks again, but moreover, I wanted to know what it meant. The confusion on his face matched the twisted mass inside me.

The gentleness in his gaze set him apart from the other gorgeous vamps' cold brutality. His eyes carried concern in them by and large reserved for humanity. The softness of his touch mimicked a human and not the deliberate acrimony of vampires. The warning in my head, ringing like the Liberty Bell, reminded me vampires played games with their prey. Some were more gifted than others.

"I assure you I have no intention of hurting you." His voice was like velvet, soft and rich.

Why did I want to trust him? God. I wanted to believe him. Had he gotten into my head? He must have. But I didn't want him to go.

Droplets of mist glistened on his thick, black hair. He ran his hand through without acknowledging them. I wondered what it would be like to slide my fingers into the dark mass and shook my head to clear the thought. *Come on, Brie. You know better than to fall for vampire tricks.*

"You drink blood." I lifted my chin in defiance.

"I do," he said. "But I give you my word I will not drink yours tonight." The words flowed from his mouth, and I comprehended his honesty in the way he didn't deny what he was. Other vampires would lie to gain trust. "I want to talk. That's all."

The flicker of humanity in him tugged at me. I swallowed hard, taking a step back.

"I'm supposed to believe a vampire?"

"Yes." He took a small step towards me, taking time to raise his hand to my face. Danger stood head-on in front of me, but I stood paralyzed, not from fear but mesmerized by him. He leaned in, bringing our lips close together. The sweet vanilla aroma of a rich whisky on his breath enveloped me. Déjà vu left me dizzy again. My eyelids fluttered in anticipation of a kiss I desired. He lingered. His thumb brushed back and forth across my cheek in a slow rhythm, causing my breath to occur in a broken cadence. He licked his lips. Energy coursed between us, unlike any of my previous experiences with a human, warlock, or vampire.

The vibration in my boot interrupted the moment. I sighed at the unwelcome disruption and debated answering the call. After a long moment, I reached for the phone. In one blink, a breeze brushed my cheek and tousled my hair. I knew before I looked his unnatural speed carried him away from me, leaving the faint malty scent of whiskey hanging around me like a cologne. The distance gave me clarity, and my focus returned. *Except I wanted him here.*

"Hey, Brandon." I greeted my twin, breathless from the encounter.

"Are you ok, Brie?" he asked, his voice uncertain. "I had the strongest sensation you were in danger. You're not hunting alone, are you?"

I winced, hating I worried him. Our twin sense meant

the other knew when something was amiss with their twin.

"I'm fine. I needed to blow off some steam."

His voice relaxed and hinted at disappointment. "Mom really hoped you'd be at the party tonight."

My stomach rolled. We had this discussion many times, and it never seemed to lessen the sting of betrayal. "Brandon, I'm not you. I can't just forgive her. It's different for me."

"She loves us both, Brie. She made a mistake trying to keep us safe. Can't you let it go after twenty years?" He asked, his tone boyish but firm.

"She bound our powers to steal them with no intention of ever letting us know." I paused, rubbing between my eyes. Resentment for my mother I buried deep resurfaced. Tears pricked my eyes. I was in no mood for this conversation. "I need to go." It was almost midnight. "Happy birthday, brother. I love you." I jabbed the end button with my finger before he could reply.

I couldn't take my anger out on him. Brandon wanted to find the good in her, but I lacked the faith I ever would. If she had succeeded and captured our powers, our seventh birthday would have been a common birthday. We would have never known the world where humans are hunted by vampires and our kind hunted the bloodthirsty creatures. Normalcy, in the human sense, didn't exist for us. Brandon could let it stay in the past, but the outrage for my mother sat underneath the surface for me. *Was I angry about her failure? For her attempt thrusting us into the spotlight?*

Maybe both. Hunting defined me. *I'm a hunter. That's my normal.*

By the time I turned the corner away from the club, my thoughts dove into the past, almost too deep to notice a tingling sensation rippled up my neck. *Vampire.* A fight tonight of all nights excited me, and the potential release after I end one of them enthused me. I drew both hands to my chest and whispered, "Cloak." Sliding into the dark archway of the building, I waited. My heart pounded in anticipation. *Only one?* The vampire got closer. Magnetism pulled me to him before he came into view. The sight of the green-eyed vampire caused my mouth to go dry and my palms to sweat. *He followed me.*

I chastised myself for being too consumed by thoughts of my mother's treachery to pay attention to the world around me. His expert vampire vision sought me out in the darkness. Unlike human eyes, vampires could locate me if they tried hard enough. I glanced up and down the deserted street, realizing a quick kill was the best option. I reached for the vial of Vampire Death from my necklace. My high tolerance to the poison made a few days of illness from the potion a small price to pay for the kill.

"I can sense you are here," he said in his lyrical voice.

His voice familiar, pulled deep in my heart and melted my usual protective bitch mode away. *Did I know him? I couldn't. Could I?* My hand dropped to my side. I longed to hear someone speak to me with such softness. My chest tightened, but I said nothing and held my breath. Pain pinched at my temple as I tried to rectify the comfortable cadence when he was near.

Blood trickled from the corner of his mouth, and I watched in awe as he lapped it up with his tongue. The vampire's actions should have repulsed me, but tonight it caused something to stir in me I couldn't altogether explain.

"There is something different about you. About us. I know you noticed it too. I fed, so there is no danger to you."

He fed. He took a human life so he wouldn't be tempted to take a witch's life? If I'd ended him earlier, he would have... *I should stake him for harming or worse, killing a human. Should.* I had noticed something different with him, but distance had helped clear the fogginess of our first encounter. While I couldn't make myself end him, it would take more than his charm to persuade me to uncloak.

I tried to think straight when the heat took over. *Damn it to Hell.* This cannot be happening now. My birthday wasn't until tomorrow. *After midnight. It's today.* A tremor ran through me. *The transformation should happen at 11:57 tonight. The exact time of my birth.* The cold, cracked cement sidewalk was not the place for this to happen. This spot left me too exposed, but it was too late.

A rush of energy passed through me. The cloaking spell retreated. The electric charge caused me to stumble. My body glowed as the power exerted itself. It was like the Fourth of July inside me. When the transformation finished, exhaustion took over, and I could no longer stand. My knees buckled. The ground came closer. *This is going to hurt.* But the pain never came. Nor the crash into the pavement. Instead, powerful arms wrapped around me, carrying me away. The sweet vanilla scent of whiskey wafted in the air. *The vampire.* I couldn't keep my eyes open. Sleep took over.

)) ● ((

WHERE THE HELL AM I? Everything looked fuzzy. I blinked through muddledness. The room came into focus and the memory of being caught as I fell last night. *Was that a transformation last night? It wasn't time for it.* This bedroom was in the vampire's refuge. *Fuck me. I need to get out of here.* My necklace was still secure with the small dose of Vampire Death attached. I glanced around the room for other weapons, but curiosity took over. It looked like a normal bedroom. I took inventory, through sleepy eyes, of the two nightstands, both appointed with lamps, and a dresser with a mirror. Decorated with tones of gray and black, which left the room cold. *Interesting.* The coldness didn't fit with the warmth from him last night. But vampires weren't known for their kindness. *Vampires are killers, Brie.*

I sat up from the nest of pillows on the bed and shuffled to the mirror. He'd fed before he tracked me, but that didn't mean he could pass up witch blood. I checked for bite marks and found none. Satisfied he kept his word to not harm me, I readied myself to face him. My duty required this meeting to end in his death. I prayed for an alternative, but I was sworn to eliminate the vampire threat. If I didn't fulfill my oath, I could be expelled from the hunters or ostracized from the coven. I'd never not done it, and I'd already let him escape once last night. Except he scooped me up amidst the transformation last night. *Didn't I owe him for that?* My body ached from fatigue as if it agreed with my decision to let him live... today.

The delicious aroma of Italian spices lured me through the apartment. I spied the front door and considered sneaking out, but the aroma drew me toward it. *A vampire cooking? This I had to see.* The living room view told me we were in a high-rise building. I placed my hand on the bottle of Vampire Death, just in case. I paused in the doorway of the kitchen. The sexy vampire stirred a red sauce on the stove. If the clock on the wall was correct, I had been out for a couple of hours. I wondered if the vampire planned to let me go.

"I figured you would be hungry," he said, without turning around. I'd never seen a vampire cook, but I tended to put a stake in them before they could demonstrate their culinary skills. It'd be easy to use the vampire death vial on him from this distance, but my senses didn't even tingle on alert. *Strange, with a vampire so near.* My stomach growled the answer for me. "Have a seat at the bar."

"Why did you bring me here?" I asked.

"You were glowing. I couldn't leave you on the street. You'd have been taken."

Or worse.

He glanced over his shoulder. The relaxed grin along with his answer warmed my heart, and I relished it for an infinitesimal moment. *You cannot be attracted to a vampire, Brie. Not even one this sexy. Not even if his smile makes you want to go to him.* And I did want to go to him. I wanted the kiss promised last night.

"Why would you care if I was taken?" I raised an eyebrow. If other vampires had seen me glow, they would have been tempted by my witch blood, or they would have taken me to a high-ranking vampire as a gift. I shuddered at the idea of being a prisoner to them. *Death would be a thousand times better.*

"Because I do. Now, eat up." He placed a plate in front of me with spaghetti and meatballs. *My go-to.* I looked up at him, unable to hide my smile, and took a small bite. "It's not poison. I promise. Why would I bring you here to turn around and poison you?"

He had a point. Famished from the drain of the transformation, I dove into the plate without further discussion.

"This is my comfort meal," I said and shoveled another fork of spaghetti.

The corners of his mouth curved up. When I finished, he took my empty plate and set it in the sink. The skin on his hands and forearms was marred by pink marks, still fresh. *Because of me.* I shifted in the seat. Carrying me while I was transforming would have been excruciating for him. Why would a vampire help a witch?

"Who are you, vampire?"

"My name is Nicholas, but you can call me Nick. And your name is Brie," he said with a triumphant smile. His name swirled in my head, and I pressed fingertips to my temple to calm the swimming it caused.

"How do you know my name?"

"I overheard part of your phone conversation as I left the alley." His answer seemed genuine. *It's not like I whispered when I talked to Brandon.*

"You are an unusual witch, Brie. I am typically repelled by witches." He rested his elbows on the counter and brought himself eye level with me. "Yet, I find myself attracted to you, as I am sure other vampires are. It should be the other way around, considering you hunt our kind."

"Of course, I hunt your kind. You kill humans and witches alike." *I can't hunt him, though. Regardless of the consequences I will face. At least not until I understand the connection and why I'm attracted to him.* He was hiding something. Of that, I was sure.

He smiled. "You are both brave and stupid, young one. We must get you home." His tone amused, he held his hand out.

Young one? Seriously? Is he really letting me go? I slipped my palm into his, unsure if I wanted to leave. Warmth radiated from the touch, but my magic didn't burn him this time. I studied our hands as he helped me from the bar stool. *What caused this kind of charge?* I'd heard of vampires being caught in castings. Maybe being so close to me when I transformed had a lingering effect on him. *And what the fuck was up with the transformation coming early?*

His expression changed. He let go.

The absence of his touch left me cold. *Had he been stunned by it, too?*

He led the way to the door. I turned to shake his hand, not ready to leave but knowing I couldn't stay.

"I'm taking you home, Brie." His voice held a hint of amusement in it.

Not much of a chance someone from the coven would see him at my apartment, but it was better if we parted ways here.

"What makes you think I am letting a vampire take me home?" I left my hand extended as a courtesy. *Please let me feel the zap again.*

He took it and whirled me into the elevator, and the touch rewarded me with the connection I craved. His movements prevented me from observing his reaction. *Damn.*

I grabbed hold of the rail to steady myself and cursed the giggle bubbling out of me. *Giggling, Brie? That is not me.*

"You picked the wrong witch for dancing," I said, through my laughter. It was one thing to gyrate in a club, but I didn't dance any other way.

He leaned in close like he had in the alleyway and looked me in the eye. The jolt of the connection made me gasp.

"I don't think so." He traced my jawline with his finger. He punched the button for the garage and leaned back against the metal wall.

I rested my head on the cool surface. *What am I doing? This is crazy. I'll let him drive me home. He will leave, and it will be done.* The ride down was silent except for the mechanical noises of the elevator.

He grasped my hand again as we exited. The current flared with renewed strength, and I looked up into his green eyes. He moved fast. Bewilderment possessed me. I tried to reach for the last stake in my boot. My body pinned to the rough concrete wall, I realized the precarious situation. This vampire was strong. Stronger than any other I'd encountered. He didn't move, though. His hard body pressed against me, but not one muscle moved. I intimidated most men, whether or not they knew I was a witch. The vampire didn't appear intimidated at all. He dominated the situation. *Dominated me.* A thrill shot through me. *This is what it feels like to be alive. Really alive.* Our erratic breaths were in unison, and I locked in on his gaze.

He kept his eyes on mine. I hadn't yearned for a man's touch in several years, and I wanted Nick's hands on me. He pinned me to the wall and leaned in close, so close his breath brushed over my face. I hadn't kissed a vampire since I took the oath. Our lips touched. Sparks, stronger than a static shock, flowed from his body into mine and from mine to his. He let my arms fall free. His hands sunk into my hair.

My arms found their way around him and pulled him closer. He slid one hand behind my back, pulling me tightly to him. My lips parted. His tongue explored. He tasted of whiskey, and it roused me. His movements became more urgent as my body stirred awake.

The moment engulfed me. My tongue slipped along

one of his fangs. The delicate touch drew not more than a drop of blood.

He pulled back and turned away, muttering something I didn't understand. His lips were like velvet and awakened need deep inside me. I ran my fingers over my lips. *His lips on mine. I wanted it again, and I'd pay whatever price from my coven to have it.*

His hand slid around mine, and he dragged me to his shiny black Lamborghini. He opened the doors with a button on the key fob. I rolled my eyes.

A slight smirk emerged on his face. *Typical bloodsucker.* His smug smile both irritated and amused me.

"I could stake you," I said under my breath, pressing my lips together to hide my smile. He spun around in front of me, still grinning. I shouldn't trust him. My training said not to trust him, but something inside me said I could. It overrode everything.

"But you won't." He opened the door, and with an extended hand, guided me into the seat.

I crossed my arms across my chest, creating an invisible barrier to close off what I knew would never happen. *Couldn't ever happen.*

He coaxed my hand free, breaking the invisible barrier between us. His fingers pressed against mine in a soft squeeze.

I studied our entwined fingers. They fit together. A small flash of memory came to me. I tried to focus in on it, but my head pounded.

"You're going to need to tell me where you live." The quiet, controlled sound of his voice made me wonder if he struggled not to take my blood after such a small taste.

"Sorry. I'm a couple of blocks away. Turn right at the next light." He shot me a quick glance. My chest tightened a little. I'd never brought a vampire home before. "My building is on the right. There." I pointed to the turn-around in front of my high rise. He didn't say a word as we pulled up. *Just walk away, Brie. You're letting him live. Leave it at that. But that kiss...*

"Well, thanks for the ride home." I reached for the handle to open the crazy door. Nicholas squeezed my hand, drawing my attention.

"Brie, I'd like to see you again, but I'm not sure it is a good idea." He looked from my hand to my eyes, and we shared the powerful connection again. My heart quickened each time our eyes locked, and I wanted to stay in the moment forever. I could see good and truth in him, even if he didn't have an aura. My urge to lean over to kiss him was hard to ignore. I sighed as I blinked away the closeness.

"Nick, I'm a witch, and you're a vampire. We are natural enemies, and to most humans, we don't even exist. No one from either of our kind would believe we spent the evening together without one of us killing the other. I know it's not a good idea for us to see each other again," I said before I lost courage because, despite my training, I wanted nothing more than to spend every possible second with him. He released my hand.

I stepped out of the car without either of us saying another word and turned around, expecting to see him drive away. Instead, he took several determined steps toward me and placed both hands on either side of my face. His ardent goodbye kiss wandered through my body, finding its way to my most private areas. He made no move to stop, even with the doorman as the audience. My entire body tingled awake.

He broke the kiss and left me breathless as he walked to his car without a word. I shielded my eyes from the sunrise. Rooted in the driveway, I watched him drive away, wondering if I would ever see him again. He faded into the horizon. Only then did the fine linen card in my hand with his contact information come into focus. *A witch, especially a hunter, cannot be with a vampire. Period.* I promised myself not to contact Nick, no matter how much I wanted him.

CHAPTER
TWO

⟩ ⟩ ● ⟨ ⟨

The blessing of a birthday was more of a curse the day after, and even though this one had come almost a full day early, like an unwanted period, the effect was the same.

Late morning sun beamed through the window. Unable to blot out the light, I gave up on my resolution to sleep till noon and swung my legs over the side of the bed. The warmth stirred memories of last night, but my toes curled against the cold floor. I pushed upright off the bed, and my head ached in retaliation. The two shots of vodka at the bar couldn't take the blame for this hangover. The power surge through my body and the new gifts it bestowed deserved all the credit. On my seventeenth birthday, I gained the ability to see auras. *Can't wait to see what it brought this time.*

I rubbed my neck on the way to the bathroom. The side of the tub served as a seat while I started the water. Steam billowed through the room, and I watched my reflection disappear in the mirror. One dropper from the vial on the back of the tub provided wafts of lavender. The water caused my skin to flush, and I had to ease into it. My toes reached the controls and turned on the jets. The soft fragrance and healing waters coaxed me into relaxation mode.

As my body mellowed, the night's events played like snapshots in my mind. Nicholas' good looks made him attractive, even by vamp standards, but he was still a vampire. I chalked the enchantment between us up to the weirdness surrounding my twenty-seventh birthday, but the urge to trust him took it to the next level. His card taunted me from the vanity chair it fell on when I changed clothes earlier. Water trailed from my arm when I grabbed it from its resting spot. My eyes studied the simple print. Just his name and telephone number. A calling card.

"Why am I even contemplating this? I'm not calling you, Nick."

The corner of the card softened where my damp fingers held it. I flung it across the room. A pang of regret tapped on my heart, and I held up my hand to guide the card down on the counter. My eyes closed tight to block out the world. The more I tried to forget last night, the more I wanted to pick up the phone.

"Ugh." I dunked my head under the water. *Grandmother. I'm supposed to go see her today. How am I going to face grandmother and her all-knowing self?*

❱❱●❰❰

THE FAMILIAR SCENT of sugar cookies and bacon wafted through the air at Grandmother's house. She cooked for an army, whether there were two or two hundred people there. I hugged her tight as I stepped inside her home, scoping out the delicious food.

"Happy Birthday," she pulled back and studied me.

"Thank you." I smiled.

"Brie, you look tired. You know how important it is to rest up for this birthday. I would have given you the potions to help." She took my arm and guided me to the table. "I'll give you some for the event tonight."

Brandon thought I favored her. She and I were the same height and close in build, but her hair was dark versus my blonde. She had a silver streak in the front, and it had grown over the last few years. Of course, my current shade of pink hair color didn't exactly fit into the family tree, but it worked for the clubs I frequented as a hunter. My hairstylist tried to talk me out of the pink, but I liked it.

"The transformation came early," I said. "It happened last night. And the potions mask more than the pain."

"Early?" She raised one brow. "For both you and Brandon?"

"I haven't talked to him yet," I said. "I went out in the city alone, and it hit me when I left the club."

I regretted saying it, knowing I should tell her about Nicholas, but not ready to let my secret go.

"What is the new strength you were blessed with?" She placed a plate of fresh bacon next to the toast and boiled eggs already on the table. The greasy aroma of the bacon filled the kitchen.

"I have no idea. I haven't figured it out yet." Ten years ago, the strength showed itself right away, and this time it remained hidden. It frightened me a little. It was always a seven birthday. No exceptions. "Maybe it just strengthened one of the existing powers."

She folded her hands in her lap. "I doubt it. That's not how it works for you. You need to meditate, and then it will come to you."

Her advice tended to come from a vision which made me curious if she knew the transformation would happen ahead of schedule. "Something is different about you." She studied me. Her hand rested on the side of my face. "You've met someone, Brie Danforth."

Fuck. I knew I wouldn't be able to hide it from her. My cheeks burned at her revelation.

"Ah. He's special to you."

I let out a nervous bark of laughter. "Attracted. Infatuated maybe. It's not going anywhere." My attention returned to my breakfast. *Please let it go.*

"Who is it, Brie? Something seems out of kilter with you. Is he human?" With her gaze soft, she studied me.

"It's no one. I ran into a guy last night while I hunted." *And the allure of him was incredible. Not like anything I've ever experienced.* I'd never lied to her, and it wasn't a total lie. She wouldn't hand me over to council for kissing a vampire, but she would be disappointed.

"May I?" She held her hands out for me. Any efforts to tell her no were futile.

I built a mental wall around Nick's identity, what little I knew from our brief time, and set my fork down and placed my hands in hers. Grandmother's soft hands cradled mine.

Her eyes closed as she concentrated. "This attraction confuses you."

No shit.

"You are in danger, granddaughter," she said, her voice anxious. "A powerful vampire seeks you out. Who is this stranger from last night? I cannot quite see his face." As she probed, energy churned in my body.

"Grandmother, please stop. I'm going to surge." I pulled my hands back, but she refused to let go.

"I need a moment longer," she said. I yanked my hands. She squeezed her hands around mine until my fingers meshed together.

"Grandmother—" I couldn't stop it. My body sent a jolt out to her. She drew back.

Tears pricked my eyes. I didn't want to hurt her. *Damn uncontrollable defense mechanism.* I reached for her hands, but she rubbed them together.

"He is the vampire!" Disgust in her voice, she pressed her thumb to one of her palms and then the other.

"Sorry about the shock. I tried to stop it, but you know I can't always control it. Yes, the guy I met last night is a vampire." *No need to deny it now.* She'd been in my head. It felt like a hemorrhage to say it out loud, broken and leaking.

"You were drawn to this vampire?" Both her eyebrows shot up.

"Yes, and he is to me. I never surged when he held my hand or-" My voice trailed off before I divulged the kissing or that I was at his apartment and rode home in his car.

"Brie, tell me about last night." She studied me, her face harder than before. *Disappointment.* Mother had the same look.

I blushed at the memories. *So embarrassing.* I never really talked to her about my love life. Not that there was much of one to talk about the last few years.

"I was scanning the room for vampires. When my eyes met his, I couldn't move. It was like it entranced us with each other. He thought I cast a spell on him, which I hadn't. I didn't even realize he was a vampire. Not until he had the expression cross his face they get when they're hungry." I stopped there, not wanting to divulge the intimacy of the attraction. I needed to know what it was before I let it seep out to anyone else.

"There is something more here. You know you are more powerful than the average witch." She pursed her lips.

She and the coven tended to forget my twin and our bond. The irritation oozed into my voice. "We are. Brandon and I."

"No, you are, Brie. Brandon is strong, but his strength comes from his tie to you. You're the one who possesses the bulk of the power, and it's why this vampire is drawn to you instead of fleeing. The power draws vampires like a moth to a flame." Her voice, full of concern, delivered a clear warning. She paused, getting up to stand behind me. Her hands rested on my shoulders. Even after my body's reaction, she still trusted me. My eyes burned, and I placed a hand over hers. "Stay away from him. He brings unequaled danger to you."

A vampire meant danger, but my head and my heart conflicted over Nick. I'd resolved to not see him again, but I didn't believe he would hurt me.

"Not a problem. I have no intention of calling him." The words were meant to convince me, though the words sounded less confident. I touched my chest against the pang at the thought of not seeing Nicholas again, and I wondered if it affected him the same way.

My phone buzzed in my pocket, and my twin sense told me Brandon waited on the other end before I even looked at the display. Grateful for his timing, I punched the button to answer. "Hey."

"What is going on with you? I woke up from a glorious dream with the sensation you are in pain," he said, his voice groggy with sleep.

"Ewww. I'm at Grandmother's house. She wanted to make sure I felt ok after last night, and I accidentally shocked her." I winced a little at the thought.

"Really?" He sounded skeptical. "It seemed a lot worse than a little jolt, and I thought you were fine when we talked last night."

Damn it. His twin sense worked overtime these days. He'd probably try to track Nick down like he did the warlock I dated, loose use of the term, our senior year. *Poor dude.*

"It's all good, brother. How are you this morning?"

"I'm fine. I'm a little tired from the partying last night, but I'll be ready to do it again tonight." He laughed. The transformation, always worse for me, left me weak. A good night's sleep and he returned to normal. It exhausted me well into the next day, whether or not I slept. *Could grandmother be right about our powers?*

"That was weird getting the transformation a day before our birthday," I said. "Do you know what you got yet?"

"What are you talking about? I didn't have a transformation last night." The line was quiet. "Was that what happened when I called you? You should have told me. I would have come and got you."

"No, it was after that. I'm surprised you didn't feel it," I said. "And I had help."

"Help?" He laughed. "Did you finally get a man? Do I need to kick his ass?"

"No, nothing like that." I rolled my eyes. "Do you want to hunt tonight?" I asked, desperate to change the subject to something less awkward. Hunting made me strong and in control.

"What's gotten into you, sis? Go out and have some fun. We're young. We don't always have to hunt," he said, his yawn audible over the phone.

"Are you telling me to get a life? And you'd be right." I would hunt on my own like I did most of the time as of late.

"I'm going back to bed. Love ya, sis."

"Love you too," I said.

Grandmother watched me hang up the phone.

"He sensed something else, more than the little shock

you gave me." She looked at me down the bridge of her nose. "You need to go meditate."

I gave in and walked to the meditation room. The quiet contemplation often brought insight, but the revelations from it might not be what I expected, and going in with an unclear head made it harder to discern.

>>●((

I CAME AROUND from meditation to a lightness I hadn't felt before. The music came into focus, and I opened my eyes. My head was about a foot from the ceiling. *Levitation.* I dropped to the mat below with a hard thud. "Umph." *What the actual fuck. I don't even know of any witches who can levitate.*

Grandmother hovered outside the door. Her shadow passed back and forth in the space at the bottom. Confusion bubbled around me. I had no more answers about Nick than when I walked into the meditation room. I still didn't understand why I developed this attraction to Nick, but I found it difficult to focus my thoughts on anything else. The familiarity of him came in waves as if I had known him my whole life. The only time any vampires got close enough to me to remember was a time when my stubbornness and rebellious tendencies led me down a dark path of self-hatred. I wanted to forget those years, but they reminded me of where I never wanted to go again. Nick's actions differed from other vampires. He acted in kindness. *Almost human. Almost familiar.*

I tried to focus on what was familiar about Nick, but

the strange light-headedness came over me like it had several times since we met. Pain mixed with trust, mixed with recognition. But I don't know him. *So why do I feel like I do, damn it?*

Grandmother's steps took her away from the door of the meditation room. Strength to reach for the doorknob eluded me as long as she paced. I reached for the knob. The door opened in silence. Her footsteps softened as they carried her to the living room. I inhaled several deep breaths and contemplated dashing out the back door to avoid talking about it. Grandmother deserved more respect than that. My courage gathered I followed her. She sat on the couch with her hands clasped in her lap.

"Well, let's talk about the time spent in introspection." She unwound her hands and patted the seat next to her.

"I'm not sure what to think." I sat beside her.

"We'll break it down like we always do." Her smile comforted me.

"I can levitate now. When I opened my eyes, I had floated six feet in the air."

She cocked her head to the side. "Apart from my mother, I haven't heard of any who could levitate for generations." She paused. "What about the vampire?"

My breath hitched in my throat. I knew it was rare, but I didn't know it had been so long since anyone had the power of levitation.

She waited while I sorted through my thoughts. *Why had so much time passed since the last person could levitate? And it was my great-grandmother. Did it have anything to do with what I saw while in the room?*

"I don't know. It's all so confusing. I saw two futures. One showed me with him and we had kids, which I know is impossible. The other showed me without him. It's like I mourned him in the second one." Everything in meditation was subject to change. The scenes rarely came to fruition exactly as seen.

She gasped. "There is no future with a vampire, Brie." She stood up and walked to the window. "There are no children with a vampire."

I'd never even considered children until I saw that possibility. *Would I even make a good mother?* "I know. It would be nice if I could stop thinking about him for two seconds."

"You don't know." She cleared her throat. "My mother fell in love with a vampire, but she ended the relationship to marry her betrothed, your great grandfather. The vampire came back to claim her as his after she gave birth to me. His anger at her refusal drove him to kill her and my father. No one knows why he spared my life." Shock rippled through me. My chest tightened. A whimper escaped her lips, and tears filled my eyes. I scooted over on the couch and wrapped my arms around her. She had told us they died fighting vampires, but never the exact circumstances. I rubbed her back. *Did mother know?*

"Grandmother, I'm so sorry. I never knew." My stomach twisted and cramped. "I can feel your pain." She wiped my tears away. It must've been one of the new strengths. To experience others' emotions as they do. More intense than my twin sense with Brandon, but without the same connection. It was like being empathic times a hundred. *This will be tricky.*

"Well, you'll have to learn to control this new gift. It could be challenging. I've never told anyone the truth about their deaths. Not even your mother. The elders were the only ones who knew." She squeezed my shoulders. "You need to make sure the truth is something you want to hear before you draw it out of someone." She smiled at me, and her hands rested at her side.

This gift is going to be a big pain in the ass.

The truth brought enlightenment to me. She'd expressed a particular disdain for vampires over the years. It never went away, and I understood the hatred she carried more now.

My phone buzzed with a text from Brandon. I texted him back right away to let him know I had a heart-to-heart with Grandmother and discovered a new power. He seemed less than thrilled with this one. *Sorry, bro.* Another text from a number I didn't recognize waited in the inbox.

> Hi beautiful. How does dinner tonight sound?

I racked my brain trying to figure out who this could be when it came to me like a punch to the gut. *The blood-sucker. Nicholas.*

> Is this Nick?

His response came quickly.

> Who else?

Damn. I shouldn't see him, but the longing over-whelmed me. *No, I can't see him.*

> How did you get this number?

A vampire murdered Grandmother's parents, but that vampire wasn't Nick. He protected me last night. *Is he dangerous? Yes, he's a vampire. Is he dangerous to me? I don't think so.* Nick was different. I sensed it. His actions showed it.

> I have my ways. You are not the only one with a trick or two.

I giggled and shook my head at his response. He could flirt. I would give him that. Dinner was a meal. *We can share some food in a public place... as long as it doesn't involve blood.*

> Ok. Pick me up at my place at 7:00.

I had a nervous pit in my stomach as I sent the text.

> See you then. :)

A smiley face? Vampires use smiley face emojis? I smiled at it until Grandmother brought me back to the present.

"You look happy now." She smiled back.

"I guess I am." *It's just dinner. Nothing more.*

Grandmother and I spent the next hour talking about my great-grandparents. She was too young to have memories of her own, but she shared stories the elders had told her of what great hunters her parents were. No matter how great a hunter a witch was, the potential death by vampire loomed over us.

I stayed busy the rest of the day, milling around the city, observing humans, until the time came to go home and get ready for my date. *A date with a vampire? What was I thinking saying yes?* I pulled out my phone to cancel, but I'd forgotten to charge it. The battery was dead.

My nerves made me a wreck by the time seven o'clock rolled around. My palms were sweaty. I put deodorant on twice, and I wasn't sure it was enough. To make matters worse, my feet slid around in my shoes, because they were sweating too. I all but jumped out of my skin when the doorman buzzed to tell me my guest had arrived. I stopped the elevator halfway down, itemizing reasons to chicken out. Huntresses fear nothing, so I took a few deep breaths to gain my composure and hit the release button to travel down to the lobby. The floors ticked past in a countdown, and I wiped my palms on my dress.

The sight of Nicholas in a suit blew me away. He looked hot, even for a vampire. His black hair matched his suit, and he wore an oxblood red tie. *How appropriate for a bloodsucker.* I shook my head.

"Nice tie." My fingertips trailed down the dark red material like I was smoothing it. I met his green eyes and found my reflection there.

"You are beautiful but exceptionally so in this dress,

Brie." He kissed my cheek and handed me a single red rose. The sweet floral drifted up, tickling my nose. I applauded my choice of a black backless dress tonight over jeans.

"Thank you, Nick. You look handsome yourself." I smiled at him as he took my arm and led me across the lobby and out to the car.

"Where are we going?" I'd been so flustered earlier, that I hadn't even thought to ask. A hunter should know better, but my defenses seemed to get lost around him. *That's a bad thing, Brie. Just dinner. Then this is done.*

"The nice steakhouse on Maple. I have a private room reserved for us." He glanced at me from the corner of his eyes. He didn't sound as sure of himself as he did before. *Do vampires get nervous on a first date, too?* It flickered of humanity and was adorable.

The restaurant came into sight, and the car roared to the stand by the entrance. The valet jumped from his stool and stumbled over his own feet to open my door. It seemed to have more to do with the car than with me. As someone trained to blend in, I was glad. Nick tossed the keys to him, and the young man's face lit up. The other valet opened the front door for us.

Inside, the host seated us in a romantic private dining room full of fresh lilies and a chilled bottle of champagne. Nick's shoulders relaxed, and my nerves settled.

"I'm impressed you could get a private dining room on a Saturday night here." I gave him a playful wink.

"It's not so hard. I'm half owner." He winked back with a lopsided grin.

"Half owner? Of a steakhouse?" I sipped the champagne. "Interesting choice for a vampire."

"It keeps in touch with human life," he said, his voice quiet.

"What are you going to have? Vampires don't eat real food. Do they?" I'd only seen them drink blood.

He laughed a loud belly laugh at my questions.

My cheeks burned, and I covered my mouth with my hand.

"Most vampires do not eat 'real' food, as you put it, but I've never lost the craving for it." He smiled and devoured me with his eyes. "I still need blood to live, but I enjoy a good meal."

The smoothness in his voice sent ripples through my body. The overwhelming familiarness came to me again along with the dizziness that accompanied it. He could almost be human if it weren't for the bloodlust thing. My senses weren't all haywire. They were dead on with him.

THREE

◗ ·◗· ● ·◖· ◖

"Nice ride," the valet said. Nick handed him a generous tip. He sidestepped Nick on his way to open the door for me. The valet offered his hand to me.

I slipped into the seat.

"Beautiful woman, too."

What the... I pulled my hand back. "Thank you," I said, intentionally curt.

The words were just out of my mouth when a low growl came from the left. The doors shut, and we were moving.

I stared at Nick.

"What?" The word clipped compared to his usual kindness.

"Are you part werewolf too? Why did you growl at the attendant?"

"He was hitting on you." He chuckled and ran his hand through his hair.

"He paid me a compliment, and here is a newsflash. I do get hit on." *Did he think he was the only one that found me attractive?* I might not be a beauty queen, but I got approached enough.

Nick chuckled again. "I have no doubt you do." He smiled, jaw relaxed. His mood changed. The tight grip he had on the steering wheel loosened.

"You need to get a grip." *So insulting to think no one else would be interested in me.* I shifted to look out the window. *Or maybe he wants you for himself, Brie? Have you been out of the game that long girl? Geez.*

His fingers trailed along my arm until he found my fingers. He coaxed my hand into his. A gentle humanlike motion. My urge to trust him took over. I relented and let him hold my hand. The simple act generated warmth. His body released all the tension. My body responded in the same way.

"I have one." He gave me a weak smile. "A grip, that is." His eyes darted to the rearview and then to the side mirror. "Hang on." He dropped my hand and switched the car from automatic to manual. The car roared and picked up speed. He turned the steering wheel to the right and left. Both of his hands grasped the wheel and shifted the gears using the paddles. His quick movements maneuvered the car through traffic.

"What's going on?" I peered in the passenger side mirror, unable to ignore the pit in my stomach. Not the tingle from a vampire, but pure dread.

"A car I noticed earlier at the restaurant appears to be following us." He negotiated the street with swift reflexes.

My hand touched my neck where the necklace of my ancestors should have been, but I opted not to wear it for the first time since it passed to me. It was too much with the dress, and the silver heart had looked better. I didn't think I'd need it tonight. *Stupid choice.* A vacancy filled my chest as the reality of how vulnerable I'd made myself set in. I swore under my breath.

My eyes closed. My thoughts focused on the task I needed to perform.

"Cloak," I whispered. My concentration engrossed on the car and us.

"We will be invisible to human eyes, but only more challenging for vampires. Whatever you are going to do, you need to do it fast," I said through gritted teeth. Cloaking two people and a moving car took every bit of my attention.

Tires screeched, and the odor of burnt rubber penetrated my nostrils.

"You can release it now, Brie." He placed a hand on my knee.

I opened my eyes and surveyed our location. *A parking garage.* I let the cloak go with a deep breath. My fingers covered my nose. The only notable side effect of using my power was a small drop of blood from it. *That should have drained me. I'm getting stronger.*

"Is that what you did the other night when I followed you?" Nick's quiet voice drew my attention. He held his handkerchief out to me and took my free hand.

"Yes." I dabbed at my nose. The blood stopped.

"Do you know how remarkable you are?" The corner of

his eyes turned up as he smiled at me. "You're truly one of a kind."

He crooked a finger under my chin, lifting it with gentle care. His lips brushed across mine. He moved to my forehead, his breath tickling my skin.

"If they have my license plate, there's a good chance they'll be able to find my place. Can we go to yours?" His low voice pulled at a place deep within me.

"Yes," I said, embarrassed by my lack of hesitation. My cheeks flushed.

He smiled and shifted the car into gear. We pulled into the parking garage of my building in moments.

The doorman greeted us and pressed the elevator button. My friends, as few as they were, would come over to my apartment, but dates didn't make it this far. After I decided to change my pattern, I swore off men for a while, and two years had flown by while I focused on my duties to the coven. Nick marked the first date and the first vampire to ever enter this apartment with me.

The ding of the elevator jarred me from my thoughts.

"This one is mine," I said, digging my key out of my purse.

I showed him around my thousand square feet of home. He lingered on the balcony. It lacked the grand view of his, but it was my safe place. I stepped back and admired his muscular physique. His looks constituted most woman's fantasy of a movie star. Except he had fangs and drank blood, of course. I imagined some human women would find the danger enticing. He turned around as if he heard my thoughts. His hand slipped into mine and led me to stand next to him on the balcony. He'd removed his jacket and tie and unbuttoned the first few buttons of his shirt. The sight of his somewhat exposed chest made my breath catch in my throat. Our arms rested on the railing, and we stared at the busy Friday night in Dallas.

"Not as spectacular as your view." I glanced up at him.

"It's much better." His focus on me, not the skyline.

"I haven't been able to stop thinking about you since last night." He shifted his eyes to the city. "I tried to push you out of my mind, but I can't."

I wrapped my fingers around the top rail like a life preserver. Grandmother's warning rang through my mind, and tears threatened from the turmoil of my thoughts. Duty. My oath. "This can't happen, Nick. We can't happen. You and I both know there isn't a happily ever after ending for a witch and a vampire."

"I can't stay away from you, Brie." His frame drifted closer, and he turned to face me. "I've lived long enough to know this."

I shifted my body and lifted my chin to look into his eyes. The green seemed brighter in the moonlight. Our connection flowed. The power of it filled me. Did it feel this way for him, too?

His hand slipped around my waist. "Whatever our endings were, they have changed now." He brought our lips together. A gentle touch at first.

My lips parted, ready for the urgent assault he led. The resolve to deny myself anything with him faded. If this was all of him I was allowed to have, I'd take it. Never having a piece of Nick sounded like torture. I reached for the remaining buttons on his shirt, but his hand steadied mine in place. My eyes fluttered open to look at him.

"We have more than our share of time in this world. Let's take it slow and enjoy it." His actions went against the nature of vampire characteristics for lust of both blood and sexual wantonness. He caught me off guard from beginning to end.

"Are you saying you want to wait?"

"Not exactly." He tucked a stray piece of hair behind my ear. "I'm saying we have no need to rush." He pressed his lips to my cheek. They responded to his touch. Heat built in them.

"You know the elders will not allow this to happen, Nick. Your kind and my kind will make sure of it. This one night is probably all we can have."

He put his hands on either side of my face, searching my eyes. "They don't get to decide whether we are together. We do," he said, keeping his voice low.

I pulled away and wandered through the door to the living room. The dizziness hit me again as I tried to figure out the familiarity. I dropped onto the couch. He sat beside me and leaned on one arm to stare at me.

"Let's talk about something else for now. How old are you?" A safer subject to lighten the mood, except a wave of dizziness shot across me. I massaged my temple.

"Are you asking from my human birth? Or how long I have been a vampire?" He draped his hand over my shoulder.

"Both I guess." I laid my head in the crook of his neck.

"I became a vampire at thirty human years, and I have been vampire for two hundred and fifty." His arm wrapped around me and pulled me closer.

"I've always been attracted to older men." I giggled.

He chuckled and kissed the top of my head.

A tremor shook through me. *Fuck.* "What time is it?" I looked at the clock, but my vision blurred.

"It's almost midnight."

Damn it. "11:57?"

"Yes."

"It's my birthday," I said. "The exact time of my birth." I thought it wouldn't happen because of last night. A silvery glow like moonlight cascaded off of me and out across the room. I dropped down on the couch.

Nick knelt in front of me.

"Don't touch me. I don't want you to get burned." This differed from the three times before. There was no heat in me. It was a coolness like lake water before the Spring temps in Texas heated the water. Magic reached for me. *A powerful ancient caress.* The power swirled around and seeped into me. The other transformations were like awakenings of power. This was more like a transference. *What did it mean, and why now? I'd never heard of it.*

Nick's emerald-colored eyes came into focus. His forehead creased, and he placed a hand on my knee. Exhaustion claimed me, and I sank into the back of the couch.

꜠꜠●꜡꜡

THE FIRST RAYS of the sunrise poked through the blinds, and it highlighted the time I'd been out. Nick's hand held mine, and I followed the line of his arm up to his eyes.

"Good morning," he said.

"Morning." I ran my free hand through my hair. "I would offer you breakfast, but I don't have a blood bank in here.

He laughed. "I'm not hungry. How about you? Shall I fix you something?"

"I doubt there is anything other than a muffin and tea in there," I said. "I can handle that."

He leaned against the corner of the kitchen island while I made a cup of breakfast tea.

"So, does it happen often? What happened the last two nights?" He asked.

"No, usually only on certain birthdays. I thought maybe it was something like Leap Year with it happening last night. I didn't expect to have another one last night." *And what was up with the silver glow?*

"You didn't tell me it was your birthday." He pulled me between his legs and wrapped his arms around me. "Now, I have to wish you a happy belated birthday."

I sipped my tea. "I don't celebrate them. Not a lot of good memories for me."

"I'd like the opportunity to change that," he kissed my forehead.

The sun had risen high and shone brightly in the sky. A vampire bursting into flames from the sun occurred so seldom it hadn't happened in my lifetime. Some had an extreme reaction to it. More often, it manifested like an allergy or an aversion to them. There were still some who weren't bothered by it at all. Nick seemed to be the latter type.

"I've stayed too long. You need to rest." He pulled me with him to walk him out.

I let out a breath. I wasn't ready for him to go, but I needed to find out what happened last night with the transformation.

After a lengthy goodbye and a promise to see each other tonight, I leaned against the closed door, grinning like a schoolgirl. Grandmother had nailed it as usual. I had feelings for a vampire. I smiled all the way to the shower.

)) ● ((

My phone buzzed on the bathroom counter. I turned the shower off and grabbed a towel.

"Hello?" I answered with a hoarse voice.

"Brie, I had a vision you were dead, and you rose up as a vampire." My mother's voice came through the speaker like a Screech Owl.

"Mother, I assure you I'm no vampire. Have you been talking to Grandmother?" I eyeballed my reflection in the mirror, rolling my eyes. She and Grandmother talked often, after all.

"I've spoken to her, but it has nothing to do with what she saw. The Seeing Elder had a vision. It showed a terrible future for mankind and witches. They have asked all royal families to convene with them. We must be there by dusk. I'm sending the car for Brandon. I'll have it stop by for you, too." The line went dead before I could protest. I thought of running away, but I would have to face it all when I returned. The Seeing Elder's visions were subjective like mine. If Mother hadn't embellished it, this one sounded dire. I sighed and went to the closet to pick out something to wear to the meeting.

)) ● ((

I CROSSED the living room towards the door. The hair on the back of my neck stood up, stopping me in mid-stride. I turned to see Nick on my balcony. I smiled at him as I opened the glass door.

"What are you doing here?" I asked.

He placed the gentlest of kisses on my lips. "We have plans. Remember?"

"Oh. I've been. Rather, my family has been called to the Elders Council. I'm sorry, Nick. The summons distracted me, and I didn't text or call." I searched his eyes. "In my defense, I didn't expect you to be by this early."

"I couldn't wait to see you." He kissed the tip of my nose. "It's nothing serious, is it?"

"I really am not sure." I couldn't bring myself to tell him we were most likely causing the damn apocalypse, according to my mother's ramblings, anyway.

Nick brushed the hair out of my face and brought our mouths together. My lips parted, welcoming the dance between us. He pulled away, but my body was already stirring. Lifting my hand, his lips caressed each of my fingers.

"I'll have dinner while you take care of your witchy business," he said with a smile. "Call me when you are home."

He jumped from my balcony. My heart sank. I raced over to the railing to confirm he landed without harm. A breath escaped as I saw him walk down the sidewalk. *He's a vampire, dumb dumb.*

The elevator stopped at almost every floor down to the lobby, like slow torture. *Come on. I want to get this over with.* I hurried across to the main doors. The town car waited in view on the other side of the glass to take me to the Great House. Dread, like I had last night, inched forward. *Did the families really believe the apocalyptic vision?*

Brandon waited by the car. His dark hair spiked up, he stood a few inches taller than me. He held out his arms. I hugged him with a tight grip, needing some extra strength to prepare me for the Elders. I didn't know how I got so lucky to have an amazing brother like him. Always there when I needed him most.

"I thought I was going to have to come get you. What happened? I had a sinking feeling in my stomach." He touched his belly.

Sometimes I wished we could turn off our twin sense, and I didn't have to speculate he did too. We had both learned more about each other than we wanted to know, but Grandmother taught us some techniques over the last few years to control it to some degree. However, their effectiveness waned the last few months before our birthday, as it forced us to feel each other even when we didn't want to. I shook my head.

"I saw something on the balcony, but it's fine." I slid into the car. It wasn't a lie, but it wasn't the whole truth, either. *A bad habit to form. I'll come clean with him later.*

He climbed in next to me. "Must've been a big hairy spider. A giant spider is about the only thing that scares you!" He chuckled and wiggled his fingers across my arm.

I batted his hands away, but I couldn't control my laughter. I wanted to tell him the truth, but I thought the less he knew going into the Elders Council, the better for him. If the meeting was about me and Nick, then he wouldn't be implicated. Instead, I sunk into the leather seat of the car, inhaling the distinct scent.

)　)　●　(　(

THE MANSION HOUSING our history intimidated me less than normal as we arrived. The newfound peace might be stupidity on my side, but I was over my mother's fear-mongering. Brandon's wide eyes and nervousness told me he wasn't as calm. Mother looked polished with her sleek shoulder-length dark hair and power suit. She and Grandmother were both waiting for us just inside the massive wood doors. The grand marble entryway with a wide staircase led up to the next level. My stillness intact, we headed to the council room, which contained the largest of ballrooms in the mansion. It had two other ballrooms, so one off-limits went unnoticed by those not privy to the witch culture. The trail of thin light smoke and the sweet spice of white sage from the smudging of the room served as a guide down the corridor.

Mother's eyes bored into me, but Grandmother put her arm around my shoulder. They led us down the hallway past coven pictures. Many were our ancestors. The power buzzing in the air increased as we drew nearer to the room. It pulsed as if it were alive. The sensation was similar to last night's transformation. We were the last of the royal families to arrive. The royal families were those who had a pure bloodline. Long after Mother divorced him, Brandon and I figured out the man who raised us for five years did not share our blood. The knowledge we were a royal family served as further proof of the case we built for ourselves. Mother's ex-husband lacked the defining quality, of not being a warlock. Being a member of the royal families of the coven required two parents of pure bloodlines. Members whose heritage at any time included a human got labeled as a halfling. To the outside world, he might have been our father, but the coven never acknowledged him. They sheltered a secret there no one would share, but my determination to find the answers grew each day.

The doors swung shut behind us and locked. Sealed with a spell, they would only open with magic once closed. The smell of the air turned stale in the room, and the stench of rot permeated my nostrils. A heaviness descended into my stomach.

I looked from my mother to Brandon, but they did not seem to notice. I directed my gaze at Grandmother, and she nodded her head at me, then to the council. Someone on the council teetered towards death. *Was this why they called us here? To appoint a new elder?* My mother's delusional tirades were beyond crazy this time. Even for her. She'd made me paranoid about Nick. The coven followed a long-standing practice of convening the families to announce the choice for replacement. I stilled, letting the relief sink in for a moment. *No, Brie.* Someone was sick. *This is not the time for relief.*

The announcement and ceremony were some of our most protected practices. Witches' persecution as products of Satan forced us to hide. The best-known event to the humans was the Salem Witch Trials, which drove us underground into a secret society. During the time period before the witch persecution, we lived in full view. Many humans thought we were angels, both heavenly and fallen. We were always devout believers in the Goddess. We relied on our belief in the higher power, and according to our history, we were her chosen protectors of the human race. The persecutions we faced forced our protection to come from a secret place. While we aren't quite human, she gave us the same choice of free will. If we were to share our powers with humanity, we would face maltreatment again. Few humans had the knowledge we existed. Our truth remained hidden from the vast majority, such as the man who claimed he was mine and Brandon's father.

"Silence!" the man, standing beside the large half-moon-shaped wooden table where the elders sat, called out even though the room had already gone silent. I'd been absent, hunting alone, when he was chosen to call the meetings to order. His command meant for us to quiet our minds as they evoked the elements. The elder's table was placed in an elevated state and overlooked everyone. They wanted to show power, but I no longer feared them as I did as a teenager. Brandon took my hand and squeezed it. I squeezed back to assure him all was well. Fear and anticipation flowed through him, and I sent calm energy his way.

Cecily, Queen of the Witches, stepped forth to perform the ritual to evoke the elements. A stillness came over the room. I watched her command with intensity and strength. She wasn't known as the oldest witch, but she had power considered great even by witches' standards. She had yet to name a successor, and the gossips shared in hushed hallway conversations about how it troubled the council. Not much of a gossip myself, I ignored them.

"Air," she called and turned a quarter turn to the next. "Fire." Another quarter turn. "Water." One last quarter turn. "Earth." The space around her glowed and spread out to the room.

"Authentic revelations are what we seek today. Grant us your wisdom." Her voice boomed off the walls despite the vastness of the room.

The elements swirled around us as she bound us all in a circle of truth. The circle would ensure there were no hidden secrets. No witch or warlock could lie while bound to it. Once the ritual concluded, she gazed around the circle and stopped on me.

Fuck me.

I fought the urge to squirm under her gaze and lifted my chin. All eyes in the room turned to me. Brandon's grip on my hand tightened into a death grip, and I squeezed back hard to get him to loosen it.

Her gaze made me uncomfortable as if she pierced me and knew all of my dirty secrets. My heart pounded a rhythm to match my shaking hands. The queasiness in my stomach built. I wondered if her next move would expose me to everyone for cavorting with the enemy.

FOUR

☽ ☽ ● ☾ ☾

"Brielle Katerina Danforth, I call you to step forth to the center of the circle." Cecily's powerful voice reverberated through the room. *Double fuck me. This is it. I'm going to have to confess in front of the entire coven that I'm hot for a vampire. I'll never be allowed to hunt again. Maybe even face banishment.* I entered the center and looked her straight in the eyes. I refused to be afraid. "Brielle, are you a faithful servant of our Goddess, and believe it is your sworn duty to protect humanity?"

"Yes, I am a faithful servant, and I believe we are here to protect the humans," I answered without hesitation before giving her a confused look. All hunters and huntresses took the oath professing their faith and to protect humans during their final ceremony. There should not have been a question as to whether I had sworn to uphold the oath. *Unless she knows about Nick.*

"My death is upon us, as the sickness of age has seized my body. I declare you as my successor. Your reign will not be easy, as you will lead the witches through a great war." I swallowed so hard my throat ached. *Her successor? I'm not being punished?* She motioned for me to join her behind the table. My body stiffened, making it hard to walk. I surveyed the crowd of shocked faces.

"Brielle will be from here forth known as second to me until my death. The Seeing Elder has glimpsed many challenges over the years, but there have been none as grave as what we will face with the vampires. They gather their forces to attack us. They seek to eliminate any witch who will not succumb to them. The council will now meet with you while Brielle and I discuss our future." She gestured for me to follow her. Everyone bowed as she left the room. My head spun. *Successor? I'm not a leader. I'm a hunter. That's who I am.* We walked into her most private office.

What the hell just happened?

"Don't you need to close the truth circle?" I could hear my grandmother's voice echo in my memories from when I was fifteen, telling me witches never leave a circle open.

"An elder will close it." She shut the door. "Shall we sit by the fire, Brielle?" Her voice became calmer and quieter.

"Brie, and yes, the fire would be fine." My insides shook in the worst way, and I hoped it wasn't visible. *How would I tell her no after a public declaration like that? I do not want this. I'm not queen material.*

"Brie," she said with a smile.

The warmth of the fire, coupled with the seasoned wood scent, wooed me. We sat in the two chairs closest to it. Her face softened like she'd removed a mask.

"Brie, you have long been known to possess great

power. Michael, the Seeing Elder, told me when you were born you would lead us to a significant victory. The time is upon us for your leadership and power to save our race." She studied me. Her gaze wasn't intrusive, but it was insistent. "Not only our race but the humans you protect daily."

She had the wrong person. *Does she realize that?* I'd do almost anything for the coven, but they needed another queen. That wasn't me. I had no intention of accepting the position. *A little liquid courage could go a long way right now.* "Do you have any vodka?"

"You must be fully aware and fully focused on your journey," she said with a slight smile. "Your family has always had great power in their veins. Your great-great-grandmother held the title of queen. Did you know that?"

Shock set in for me as I realized she said my great-great-grandmother was a queen. Another secret the coven had kept from me and my brother. *How many family secrets could one family have?*

"No, but I think you already knew that. What if I don't want this?" Grandmother never mentioned her mother had been a queen when she told her story.

Cecily laid a gentle hand on my arm. Her kindness surprised me.

"No witch ever wants to be the queen. It is a right and a curse all in one magnificent sacrifice we make. When the call came to you last night, did you not feel the power of your ancestors choosing you?" She leaned back in the chair. "This is your fate, Brie. You will be a great leader for our kind. A much-needed leader in our darkest time." She stared into the fire.

That's why it was different last night. The knowledge didn't offer me much comfort or encouragement.

"I'm quite sure I'm not the right person. My brother is a much better negotiator and leader than I am." I didn't mean to throw him into the lion's den, but it was true. It came so naturally to him. People followed him. He'd led many successful hunts.

"No, you should have more faith in yourself and your path," she said, her gaze came back to me. "Your destiny is not only our security but the security of the human race. You have the entire world in your hands."

"Like the path of the witches who exercised their free will and were tortured during the Salem Witch Trials?" I angled my body away from her. Even with my protests, I knew I'd take on the task if there was no one else. *Is that what she is telling me? Surely I'm not the last hope.*

Cecily stilled. "They made an egregious error, letting humans know what they were. There is a reason our laws exist. Your leadership will ensure those laws are enforced as you lead our people through the coming battles."

Upholding laws like no fraternization with vampires. "It's like I am in a nightmare or someone else's life," I said under my breath.

"I assure you, this is no dream. This is your life now." She lowered her voice. "We can discuss many things in the weeks to come, but there is one urgent matter which cannot wait. The vampire boyfriend must be cast away. To continue to see him would ensure our loss to them.

Michael has foreseen it. You can have no more contact with him."

My heart sank into the pit of my stomach. *They were having me followed. Nick and I had no future.* Not that I hadn't known, but to hear it out loud from the queen of the coven was like a knife digging into my chest. I connected to him, and I wanted to explore it. But Cecily, Grandmother, and Mother all told me I must give him up. I pushed up out of my chair and headed for the door to get some space and clarity.

"I need some time on my own to consider all this." I grabbed the doorknob. She sidestepped me, holding the door shut.

"I can understand how you must be feeling. Remember, this is your duty. I will send a car for you in the morning."

"I have a job," I said without looking at her. "I'm a hunter."

"No longer. Your job is my second in command." She released the door.

I cast a sideways glance in her direction, unable to stop my brow from arching. If she thought attempts to control me would work, the response would not end in a positive way. I walked the path I chose, and it accounted for a significant part of what made me an expert hunter. The authority figures never took well to my refusals of compliance, and I presumed she would have the same reaction. I stormed past the room where everyone gathered and found my grandmother waiting for me in the lobby.

"Well, Granddaughter, you've had an exciting night." She smiled full of pride and winked, opening her arms for me. I hugged her tight to me. "Go. Sort through your thoughts. My driver will take you." She released me. She knew me well enough to know I would not accept this new role with ease, if ever. The glint of silver in her black hair caught my eye. It seemed more pronounced than usual. I kissed her cheek as I headed straight to her car, submerged in my thoughts.

> > ● ((

THE KEY CLICKED in the lock to my door, and the unadulterated relief of being home washed over me. The relief was replaced in an instant by the hair on the back of my neck standing up. Someone was in my apartment, but I saw nothing. *Cloak.* I moved through the darkness until I saw a figure on the balcony. *Nick.* I sighed. Relief drove out some of the tension. As if on cue, he turned around, and I dropped the cloak. He flashed a sideways smile, shaking his head. I gave him a weak smile back. We had too much to discuss to pretend like nothing was wrong.

He greeted me with a tender kiss I would have thought impossible for a vampire. Warmth sparked between us, and I refused to believe it meant terrible things to come.

"You have something on your mind," he said.

"You are a perceptive vampire."

He pulled me to him and held me tight. My head rested against his chest. *Brie, you have to tell him. The longer you wait, the more it will hurt.* He kissed the top of my head.

66

The affection between us grew and radiated, convincing me it came from both of us. It would have been easier if it had been in my head.

"Do you want to talk about it?" he whispered in my hair. I turned in his arms where I could lose myself gazing out at the evening bustle in Dallas. The weekends offered sounds not heard on a weekday. It calmed me.

"Not really. It's not a conversation I want to have, but we need to have it." I sighed.

"I don't particularly like the sound of that," he said beside my ear before nibbling on it.

The touch sent a shiver down my body I refused to ignore. I tilted my head back and reached my hand behind his head, pulling his face closer. My fingers gripped the back of his neck. I took his mouth as if I conquered it. *I wanted him. I wanted this. Could I have him and be the successor?*

He picked me up in his arms without breaking the kiss. His firm grip secured me and he dropped to a soft landing on the couch. Our eyes locked together. The connection stirred and his fingertips stroked my cheek, bringing our lips together again. Our mouths moved together in a soft dance. Desire led the dance into a rush of impatience as our kiss deepened. The familiar vanilla scent on his breath enveloped me like it had the first night. My hands drifted over his chest and around his back until I reached the bottom of his shirt to pull it from his waistband. In a quick movement, he sat up, pulling me with him.

"Brie, don't misunderstand me. I want you in a way I'm not sure I entirely understand myself, but there is something amiss with you. You're trying to bury some-thing." His eyes locked on mine.

I nodded, straightening my blouse. Using sex to bury things I didn't want to deal with was a pattern I thought I broke until today. I didn't want that baggage between us.

"It's something I was told at the witches' council meeting," I said, unsure what I should keep to myself and what parts to tell him. The urge to tell him every-thing dueled with my sense of loyalty to the coven. They could put me to death for telling a vampire our coven secrets. The succession would be harder for the coven to keep confidential than the war visions. *Life is never fair, Brie.*

"We can talk about it if you want. You don't have to vent it out through our passions," Nick said, and he was right.

Our circumstances required honesty, and his words struck deep in me. I had used sexual activity to vent my anger in the past, and it always ended in a mess. I didn't want it to be that way with him. I refused for it to be in any other way than love. *Love? Is that what this could be the beginnings of? Is this the start of love?* Whatever this was, it was too special to treat like the others before him. We were too special. I wanted more than sex from him, even if the council disapproved.

"I received advisement telling me I have to end this with you. There is an expectation placed on me which will require most of my time. I have to stop hunting and focus on it, and I can't associate with my 'vampire boyfriend' at all." I used air quotes to let him know they phrased it the same way to me, and I hadn't made an assumption about us.

He stiffened next to me. "You are ascending to the council, and they don't approve of a council member associating with a vampire even though they are charged with keeping the peace between the species," he said, his voice low. "Did you tell them how you feel about me?"

I don't know how to put it in words. He felt right for me. He felt like he belonged in my life. He felt a part of me. How do you explain that? Even though our blood meant we should be enemies, I wanted to spend more time with him.

"That's not exactly what happened, and I was too shocked to say much of anything except to be a bit of a bitch. Besides, I honestly am not sure what this is between us." It came out worse than it sounded in my head.

Nick chuckled. Even his laugh intoxicated me, but I raised my eyebrow not seeing the humor in it.

"You spoke back to the council?" he asked with a broad smile, showing his white teeth and his fangs.

I snickered.

"More like Queen Cecily. I had a private meeting with her." *Son of a bitch. I did. Goddess, help me.*

His eyes widened.

"Evidently, my bloodline has set my 'destiny' in their eyes." I couldn't resist air quoting destiny. I never believed in destiny. At least I didn't until I met Nick. Visions are not set in stone, so our path in life shouldn't be, either. *But was it? Am I someone meant to lead?* The transformation last night was different. Cecily knew it. I knew it.

"What do you mean?" Nick's face dropped.

"My adult life has been about being the best vampire hunter, and I haven't exactly followed the traditional roles. The coven hid something from me, but they decided now is the time for it to come to fruition." I paused my ramble, not wanting to say the words. My stomach knotted, and the words came like vomit. "Queen Cecily has chosen me as her successor, and she has forbidden me to see you anymore." Words I wanted to say stuck in my throat. I wanted to say it didn't matter, but we both knew the truth.

"You will be the next Queen of the witches, Brie?" He had a shocked look on his face and spoke slowly.

"Yes." My loyalty to the coven won out over my trust in him, and I left out the pending war part. If the war with vampires happened, we would both have to choose a side. I'd never choose his side, and I couldn't ask him to choose mine.

"Brie, do they know I am the vampire boyfriend?" he asked.

"I'm assuming so. They never said your name." I studied him, unsure why he asked. Maybe he was concerned for his own safety. "Before we worry about what they know, we need to figure out what we are and if we are going forward despite their opposition."

"I am the vampire boyfriend," Nick said, smiling.

I laughed at the amusement in his voice. *Boyfriend.* I'd dated, but I'd never had someone I considered a boyfriend as an adult. My heart expanded in my chest.

"I guess I'm the witch girlfriend then," I said, my voice light and bubbly.

We both laughed. The weight of the world was still there, but this one decision built a barrier that lifted it some.

"Brie, I am enthralled with you. My mind drifts to you constantly. I refuse to surmise what life without you would be like." He brushed my cheek with his fingertips and tenderly touched his lips to mine.

"You are the one true thing I have that seems real. Everyone has lied to me my whole life. I'm not ready to give up on where this is going."

He looked into my eyes for a long time before bringing our lips together.

"I need to tell you about who I am." Nick traced my jawline. "I'm not just any vampire, which is probably why the council has a heavy amount of concern."

"Well, they will not like any vampire, but what do you mean?"

He cleared his throat and stared at the ceiling. When he looked back at me, his eyebrows were pinched together in a tight line. I had the urge to rub the space between his brows to relax him. "I'm the son of a powerful vampire, and he sent me to the club that night to spy on the witches based on rumblings of war."

"What?" I gasped, pushing away from him. He reached out to take my hand, and I jerked it away. My stomach ached, and I tasted bile. He was a spy. I was a mark. Words might not be the only vomit tonight.

"You were not part of the deal. I didn't even know you were here until I saw you at the club." He stared straight into my eyes. I saw the agony in his words. He could have told me this from the beginning. *He should have told me.*

"But you knew who I was? How can I believe you? I trusted you, and I told you I'm going to be the next Queen of the Witches. They could condemn me to death for telling you. What have I done?" My voice strained to barely above a whisper. A surge powered up in my core. My haywire emotions driving it no doubt. "You need to go."

"Brie—"

"Go now, Nick, before I decide otherwise." I wouldn't have staked him, but I wasn't sure how long I could control the massive power building inside me. He stared at me for several long moments. He chose the door instead of the balcony and lingered there. I glanced away, unwilling to allow the connection. My refusal to hold his gaze sent the message. The door closed, and I gave myself permission to look up.

I allowed myself to believe for a moment I could find happiness, but I found another liar instead. Tears blurred my vision, and I fumbled with the lock on the door. I headed for the bedroom but collapsed into a mess of sobs in the doorway. My tears fell for what seemed like hours before I picked myself up off the floor. I washed my face and stared at the person in the mirror. Blue eyes rimmed in red looked back at me. They clouded with sadness at the betrayal of so many in my life.

A dizzy spell took root far worse than the others. My fingers clinched the edge of the sink. Snapshots rolled through my mind. That's why Nick is familiar. Flashbacks flooded my head from a dark time, and I shuddered with pain as the memories passed like a movie in front of me. He'd helped me escape a situation when I thought I would die. My knees sunk to the ground. *Why hadn't I remembered before? After eight years, could it be him?*

CHAPTER

FIVE

$$) \cdot) \cdot \bullet \cdot (\cdot ($$

Morning came too soon for my taste. After the double gut punches last night, I dwelled in a foul mood. I walked out to the balcony, which normally brought me comfort. Instead, I hurled several f-bombs at the sun. I reached my hand to the sky without concern, and the clouds swirled. *Stop.* The sky returned to normal. I'd never seen the clouds react so ominously, and it unnerved me. I shook it off and got ready for the day I dreaded immensely.

The driver arrived promptly at eight o'clock, which I found insanely early for witch, vampire, or human. I wouldn't be mistaken for a morning person. My mood had not improved from the foul depths it hit yesterday, and I had a bit of pity for the driver who tried to make polite conversation. He would have a lovely story to tell his friends about the future queen.

"There you are, Brie. Are you ready to begin your new life?" Cecily greeted me warmly with a kiss on each cheek.

"Not really. My old life worked fine for me," I snarked to Queen Cecily. I regretted being obstinate right away. She stepped back, and emotion flashed across her face. I couldn't fully read it, but empathy for her came to the forefront courtesy of some of my new abilities. I pushed it away.

"I had planned to save this for when you completed your training, but I think you may need some enlightenment now. Come with me." She headed down the dark hallway past her office to a door locked by magic. She waved her hand in front of it, and the door opened for us. Books upon books lined the room. If she expected me to read a lesson, she had lost her ever-loving mind.

"What is this room?"

"It's the room of all that was and all that is in the world of witches. The birth, life, and death, of every single witch is recorded in these journals. Your ancestors are all listed here." She paused. "Even your father."

I moved to stand directly in front of her. "My father is a human. Why would he be listed here?" I matched her tone and forced acknowledgment of a secret we all knew but never spoke about. I wanted to hear her say it out loud.

Her eyes narrowed on me, but her tone remained even. "You know the truth. You were not born to a human father."

My chest tightened. I knew we couldn't be royalty with a human father. I had always known, but my mother prohibited discussions about it. The confirmation from our queen made it real to me.

Cecily looked from me to the group of shelves, her tone

solemn. "Your biological father is one of the greatest sorcerers to ever live. A warlock completely unmatched in strength. His power grew so great he feared it would consume him and turn him dark. He lived a life of seclusion and chose to not practice magic. See for yourself." She gestured to a shelf midway up with books bound in beautiful red leather. "You will need to look for Vladislav. Danforth is not your surname."

The animosity I carried washed away to wonder over the new knowledge. A gift the queen bestowed on me. I moved to the bookcase to retrieve the book for Vladislav. Adrenaline rushed through me. I ran my fingers down the rows of books, inhaling the old leather smell until I came to the right section. The book resided on a shelf much too high for me to reach, but Cecily had left when I turned to ask where I could find a ladder. I considered climbing the wall. *Oh, screw it.* I threw my hand up in the air, and the book flew into it with force. My emotions were running wild. As Grandmother taught me from a young age, calm held the key to control with power. I breathed in and let it out.

I leaned back in one of the leather wingback chairs and opened the book. It glowed with a soft inviting light, recognizing my bloodline. The pages flipped on their own until they came to the section where my father's story begins. The story of Sorin Vladislav leaped off the pages to me, and the images flooded me. I needed to know everything. To see it. To touch it. I had to fight to control the speed at which the depictions came as I read.

The book contained an extraordinarily detailed history

about him. He had lived a vast life, and my brother and I never knew anything about him. His power was unprecedented in strength, especially for a warlock. Witch strength typically passed through the maternal line. Powerful male witches were rare, like giant diamonds. The stories didn't read as if he had emotional outbursts like I did. *So much for that being genetic.* That part must be all me. His story read of someone who exercised control. Even when he turned to the dark, he was in control enough to go into seclusion, where the stories abruptly ended. The details were sparse as he entered seclusion. Either the elders stopped, or he hid from their view.

I closed the book and stared at the leather. He'd turned dark. *What had caused that choice? Why had he never come for us? Texted? Called? Wrote a damn letter?* My mind raced with questions I wanted to ask him. *If only he were here.*

꒱꒱●꒰꒰

CECILY STOOD RIGHT in front of me. I hadn't noticed her enter the room. Didn't know how long I'd been curled up in the chair with the book, opening it again and again. Drained and exhausted from Sorin's story, I studied the last page. If she was waiting for me to divulge everything, it would be a while. Something told me she already knew more than I did, anyway.

"I still don't understand why my father needed to leave my mother. They were both from pure families and royal by right. He could have bound his powers. He certainly possessed enough strength, according to these accounts." I broke the silence between us, expecting an avoidance.

"He did not choose his power any more than you have. He feared what others might do to his family if he remained." She surprised me with her honesty.

If he left to protect us, there had to be a point over the last twenty-seven years where it was safe to see us. But he didn't, and that made my chest hurt. I closed the book and laid it on the table next to me.

"You sound like you knew him." I cocked my head to one side.

"I did," she paused. "I do." She looked towards the books and back at me. "Sorin is my brother." She met my gaze with firm acknowledgment.

I could read the truth there. A gasp escaped me. Tears pooled in my eyes. All these secrets. *No wonder witches are so fucked up and have trust issues. My father is alive.*

"What? All this time? Where is he?" The questions rolled from me, and I heard thunder matching my mood.

She walked to me, placing a gentle hand on my shoulder.

"Calm," Cecily said. My heartbeat returned to a normal rhythm. I let go to her control, not because I wanted to but because I couldn't control my power myself. She sat in the chair across from me. "Sorin did not want you to know anything about his side of the family. He thought the less you knew, the safer you would be. He knew when you were born exactly how powerful you would be."

"Did my mother know all of this?"

"Yes, she was aware."

"And he still left me with her." I rested my elbow on the arm of the chair and covered my mouth with a finger. I shifted my focus toward the window.

"She wasn't trying to take your powers for her own glory, Brie. She didn't want you to meet the same fate as Sorin." I cut my eyes in her direction. The tears in her eyes mirrored my own.

"Why didn't she tell me this?" My voice thickened. I glanced around like I would find the answers written on the walls.

"It was Sorin's wish, and her love for him bound her to keep the secret. So, they divorced, and she married a human. She chose one who would be a good father, but she didn't love him. Humans need love, and he left her." Cecily said.

Witches need love, too. Not just humans. "Where is Sorin now?"

"I don't know. When he visits me, he is in control, and he wipes anything from my memory that could be used to find him."

A strong desire to avoid the question burning in my mind was overtaken by my need to know the answer. "So, he does practice magic. Does he ask about me?"

"He does only the bare minimum required to keep his identity hidden, but he asks about you."

My temper shortened, and heat rose in my body. I wanted him to tell me why he didn't come back. Ever. "I can track him. If I am as powerful as everyone says, I can find him."

"I'm not sure it's a good idea. He's kept you at a distance for a reason, and it's for your safety," she said in a pragmatic tone.

Up until today, I didn't know my father's name or that he was even alive. There was no way this didn't end with me looking for him. "Thank you for your honesty. I need some time alone, though." I got up from the chair.

"Of course," Cecily said. "I'll have the driver pick you up at the same time tomorrow." She wrapped an arm around my shoulder, walking me to the door.

"Ok," I said, drifting to what I planned on doing next. Scrying was an option, but I could tap into my blood to locate him. Not here with all the noise of witches practicing spells, but I could from my place.

Cecily's driver waited for me by the car. Settled in the back seat, I thought about the future. My destiny included me replacing my aunt as queen. It sounded so medieval. But did it have to be that way? Did it have to be me?

)) ● ((

THE HAIR on the back of my neck stood up the moment I stepped through the door of my apartment, distracting me from the plan I had devised on the drive. I didn't sense Nick and took cautious steps forward. Should I give away my awareness that someone was here? I cloaked myself. What idiot breaks into the apartment of a hunter?

"Hello, Brie." A man's voice called to me from the living room. *Who the fuck is this?* I didn't recognize it, but it seemed familiar to me all the same. Blue eyes stared back at me from a tall, muscular dark headed man. *Sorin.* No doubt stood in my mind. The man was my father.

I thought I would feel relief at his sight, but his presence, here in my apartment, vexed me.

"Hello?" I uncloaked, trying to suppress the confusion building in me. All the years gone by without a word, and he could have come here. I'd lived alone for three years in this apartment. *If he came here today, why not before?*

"Won't you have a seat so we can talk quickly?" He motioned to my couch.

I nodded, taking a seat.

"You read my history today, and the connection came alive. I assumed you would try to search me out, so I came to see you. You have questions, but we can't discuss them here. I will send for you when I am sure it's safe. Until then, do not try to contact me. Understand?" He looked into my eyes. I saw concern in his face.

He was right. Did I have questions? Probably more than he wanted to answer.

"Yes. Are you my father?" I knew. I could see the resemblance, but my head or my heart, maybe both, needed to hear it.

He stood.

I moved to block his way with my body. I wanted his answer.

He said nothing, but nodded and wrapped his arms around me, kissing the top of my head. Tears stung my eyes. It was an answer validated without words.

"Oh, and no vampires. Stay away from all of them."

He vanished, leaving me alone. He wiped most of my

memory like he did Cecily's. Hunter training taught us to recognize the missing pieces. Sometimes we would recover them later, but mostly, they were blank spaces like black spray paint covering a camera lens. My head spun, and it pissed me off. He'd been there, but a considerable amount of the context was lost in nothingness. I wanted to call Cecily, but uncertainty stopped me. I tried to restore the memories, but I only got pieces. He left me with only what he allowed me to keep. A clap of thunder jarred me to attention and reminded me to settle down.

I took a deep cleansing breath, and a familiar draw came as I let it out. Nick had arrived, and the excitement of seeing him flowed through my body. Hurt and anger dwelled in me over his confession, but I was ready to talk. He smiled through the balcony door as I let him into the apartment.

"You could use the front door. You know, like a normal person?" I fought the smile at the corners of my mouth. I was still angry, but I was ready to talk.

"You want me to be normal? Or human?" He chuckled.

An abrupt laugh escaped me. I wanted to tell him I remembered how he saved me when I was nineteen, but I wasn't sure he did. "Neither. About last night—" I started, but he didn't let me finish.

His hands rested on either side of my face, pulling me to him. He let his fingers slide through my hair as our lips met.

Passion smoldered in me, ready to ignite at the next touch. My heart screamed I was falling in love with this vampire even though my lips couldn't. He'd saved me twice now, eight years ago, and when I transformed on the street. My eyes fluttered open.

He epitomized what I had been searching for in all my escapades. The way he could talk until the sun came up on anything and everything. He had a gentle touch, yet he could draw every ounce of passion in me to the surface to bend at his will. His touch left me burning for more. But he had concealed part of himself from me. He came clean when he realized the situation.

"Come. Let's sit and discuss us." Nick took my hand and led me to the couch. "I want you to trust me, Brie, which is why I am going to tell you all about me. Then you can decide if we are worth fighting for in this world." He took a deep breath, showing his nerves. He wanted us too, and it meant something to me.

"Start with your last name, Nick."

"Domenico. I am Nicholas Domenico." He squeezed my hand when I gasped.

It was him. Eight years later. He's here. The Domenico vampires were the ruling vampire family. They were all ruthless. The entire clan. Except for the one I met when I was held captive.

"I am the second son of Stefan Domenico," he said in a regretful tone.

I looked into his eyes and waited for him to continue, trying to process the realization of how high he ranked in the vampire world. All the witches knew the story of Stefan Domenico's rise to power. Stefan was not the first son of Marku Domenico, but he was his favorite. When Marku decided he had lived long enough and wanted to be done with the world, he chose Stefan over his elder sons. A bloody time for the vampires followed his decision, and many of the other sons died an ultimate death. Stefan had no sons, but he quickly remedied it. There were rumors of dissension among the brothers, but no one ever confirmed it. Most people thought he had those executed who tried to rise up.

"And brother of Gaius?" I asked, softly. I clenched my teeth against a tremor.

"Yes," his voice matched my softness.

"Nick, this is why the council doesn't want us together. We're both too powerful. If we were lower in the pecking order, they wouldn't care," I said in a rush.

"Or maybe this is our chance to bring peace between our people?" He brushed his free hand against my cheek.

I had a death grip on his other hand. Peace seemed like a fairytale and an outcome I never considered between vampires and witches.

"What exactly were you sent here to find out?" I asked, even though I feared the answer was related to me or my family.

He shifted on the couch. "My father sent me here to find out if the rumors of the pending war were true, and I am to take measures to delay it in order for him to build a bigger army."

"Are you delaying the war by pursuing me? Am I part of the plan?" I tried to keep the bitterness from my voice.

"No, I swear to you. We did not know of Cecily's illness or your ascension to the throne," he said, his voice sincere.

The air in the room seemed lighter. I believed him.

"Okay. Then I need to tell you what I know." I swallowed hard. "Apparently, our being together will cause this war, according to the elders, and I'm not sure if my succeeding Cecily has anything to do with it. It has more to do with the power we yield, but I can't be sure. They are limiting the information they give me, but it was enough for my father to show up." A sharp pain pierced my gut. My father made it difficult for me to speak of him. *Asshole.*

"What's wrong?" Nick searched my eyes for answers.

"Evidently, someone has put a gag order on me," I said in a clipped tone.

His forehead wrinkled up tightly, like a prune.

"Sorry." I reached up and massaged it. "Relax. I can handle it."

He turned to my hand on his cheek, placing a kiss on the palm.

"Here we are. Secrets spilled. Are we worth the challenge we will face?" He looked me in the eyes, searching for an answer.

But were there more secrets? It wouldn't be an uncomplicated relationship and we had a lot of people to convince it didn't mean the apocalypse. We both wanted us, and that had to mean something. After all, love could change the world, so why couldn't ours stop the war versus starting.

"I believe we are. Just so we are clear. We agree the challenge is to figure out how to be together without causing the demise of the humans, witches, or vampires?" I needed to hear his confirmation to know he was on the same page with me. If he wasn't, we didn't have a future.

"Yes, the vampire boyfriend agrees with you." He smiled at me.

"It's creepy to refer to yourself in the third person, but the witch girlfriend is glad we agree." I smiled back.

"You are right. It is creepy, but my witch girlfriend is very sexy, so I will let it go." He chuckled, pinning me to the couch. He brushed his lips across mine. I welcomed the fire as it coursed through my veins.

"There's something else I need to tell you, but it might be easier to show you," I said, breathless from the kiss.

He leaned back, giving me room to sit up.

My fingers rested on his temple, and I closed my eyes. "Remember," I whispered.

I let the movie from eight years ago play through our minds. Gaius had tricked me into coming to the vampire mansion. It was more like a castle but modernized to the tastes of the current century. My youth and naivety, coupled with my desire for danger, led me into the situation.

"I told you to be ready when I got here," Gaius screamed as the back of his hand met my cheek. The sting didn't compare to the bruises on my arms from last night's punishment. Weakened by the lack of food and beatings, I contemplated taking my own life. "Get dressed. Father will be waiting." He said, shoving me to the bathroom where a dress had been placed earlier for me to wear. At least they didn't feed on me like some of the other *witches.*

In the ballroom, I stood beside Gaius. My head cast down, looking up only for a place to escape. I resolved to take my own life if I could not find a way out. A tap on my shoulder made me jump. Emerald green eyes met mine. The only kindness existing in the castle came from him.

"May I?" he asked me, ignoring Gaius' look.

"Get your own," Gaius grumbled, but he didn't stop him from taking my hand.

I nodded as he led me to the dance floor. The room was modern, yet medieval. The king had a penchant for the old ways but enjoyed contemporary amenities. Large banquet tables surrounded the room, and the royal table sat on a platform so they could look down on everyone else. Gold and reds filled the room, and the vampires openly consumed blood from the humans.

They didn't drink from me. Gaius enjoyed keeping a witch weak and at his service. He preferred to withhold food and beat them. Wielding magic took strength. It was a muscle that needed exercise a witch couldn't do in shackles.

"I can get you out tonight," he said in his melodic voice.

I sighed, leaning against him. He was the only one who challenged Gaius, and he'd been my only reprieve in my weeks here. "Why do you want to help me?" I looked up into his green eyes and melted inside.

"You don't deserve this."

"And the others do?" I held his gaze.

"No." He dropped his head. "I don't care about them, though," he whispered, his breath brushing over my ear. A quiver ran down my spine. "Let's get you something to eat.." He took my hand and led me through the hallway to the expansive kitchen. I glanced over my shoulder, but Gaius had a female vampire in the corner.

"You don't have to keep feeding me, you know."

He slipped the bowl of spaghetti in front of me.

"Did you not say this was your favorite?" He smiled.

"I did." I scooped up a forkful of the spaghetti.

"I'll come to your room tonight and lead you out myself. Do not trust anyone else." He studied the bruises on my arm. When his eyes met mine, they were a mix of sadness and anger.

"Got it." I gave him a small smile back, trying to convey my gratefulness.

Gaius came to my room and beat me for leaving the party early. His prize needed to be on display, and I had deprived him of the moment. He derived pleasure from breaking a witch, and he broke my nose in one swift motion. My powers weren't strong or dependable then. *My body was too weak for my defenses to do much other than burn small circles where I pushed him.*

When my only friend came for me, he found me battered. My spirit broken, I sobbed uncontrollably. I inched away when he tried to touch me. He grabbed my chin, forcing me to look at him.

"You will remain calm and never return to this place again." His eyes locked on me with laser focus. His words filled my mind with peace and calm came over me.

Nick scooped me up and carried me through the shadows of the castle and away. There weren't many options for a vampire to take an injured witch. He left me at a club in the path of vampire hunters. He slipped away in the dark of night, and I was home at my grandmother's that night as if it had never happened.

I didn't expect him to remember how he'd helped a

naïve nineteen-year-old witch who thought she could hunt on her own. While my memories of him were suppressed, I remembered moments of my captivity, and that is what drove me to be the best at what I do. Nick's gift of freedom gave me that opportunity. I would have died if I'd stayed, and I owed Nick my life.

My hand trembled against Nick's cheek.

He pulled my hand away from his temple and pressed his lips to my palm. His eyes glistened.

"I never forgot, Brie." He kissed my fingertips. "I knew it was you as soon as our eyes locked in Club Red, but I wasn't sure you remembered." He shook his head. "I wasn't sure if you could or wanted to remember. The one thing I couldn't do was protect you within the lair, and my interest in you only made Gaius want to hurt you." His eyes fell away from my face as he stared at the floor.

"I remembered little. I blocked out what I could, trying to fill my empty heart. Turns out it froze and needed to be thawed." I didn't voice the shame always bubbling under the surface for the years afterward where I lost myself. "I must have done a better job than I thought."

"I would erase it all forever if I could," he said. When his eyes met mine, I could see the red tears pooling in contrast with his emerald green.

"I wouldn't want to erase it because you were there. You kept me alive with your kindness. You saved me by getting me out of there."

"It was love," he said. "I didn't realize I had fallen for you until you were gone. Your absence in the house was suffocating."

I'd left a string of broken relationships in the years since our stolen moments in the vampire lair, and I wasn't confident I could love him the way he needed or deserved.

"The emptiness without you there was my punishment for not protecting you," he said. A streak of red ran down his face.

My heart pounded. I kissed his cheek. "I had to learn to protect myself. It's a witch thing."

The warmth of his touch thawed the ice around my heart. I'd searched for this devotion and never came close. His lips awakened the need for love in me. He was the missing piece I needed to fill my heart.

CHAPTER

SIX

☽ · ☽ · ● · ☾ · ☾

The alarm clock's rude repetitive buzz woke me. *Goddess, I hated that thing.* I stared at the sun shining in my room, remembering the intense make-out session Nick and I had last night. I did not want him to leave, but we couldn't risk being caught. If we didn't handle our relationship in the right way, they could deem us traitors, and a traitor's death would likely follow. We needed to become public on our terms, but it had to be in a way the coven accepted. *And the vampires.* I wasn't certain how the witches or the vampires would react to the news, but it would be better to let Cecily know as soon as possible. Hearing it from someone else would break trust, and I needed her on my side. My thoughts meandered through how the conversation would go as I dressed, and as bad as I thought it would be, I decided to tell her right away.

I arrived in the lobby right on time, but the driver wasn't there. I walked around outside looking up and down the street, but he was nowhere in sight. *Well, hell. Did she give up on me already?* A black Mercedes pulled up next to me with dark tinted windows. Through a window cracked only a fraction, I heard my name.

"Brie, please join me in my car. We will drive you to the Great House today." The voice belonged to Sorin.

My neck stiffened, and I rubbed it, letting my hand settle on my necklace. After yesterday, he showed up again. I wanted to get to know him, but not if he planned to wipe my memory again.

I hesitated, still not sure if I trusted this man or the power he wielded over me.

"Please, I assure you, it is safe." He opened the door and scooted over, straightening his suit.

"Are you going to erase our conversation if I do?" I asked in a contemptuous tone.

"No erasing of conversations will happen," he said.

My blood sang at my silent call to validate his words, and the answer was he told the truth. It was one of my inconsistent powers. Sometimes it answered and sometimes it ignored my request. I conceded, sliding into the seat next to him.

"I'm not very happy with you right now." I peered out the window.

"I can see that. You tried to speak of me?"

"Yes, but you already knew that. Dick move by the way." I was unwilling to look at him, afraid my anger would soften.

"I told you to stay away from vampires."

I cut my eyes toward him. He caught me off guard and piqued my curiosity. What had he done to me...

"I cast a protection spell only meant to prevent you from divulging knowledge of me to vampires," he said in a direct tone.

My anger grew.

"You had no right." I turned my face toward the window and closed my eyes to rein in my aggravation.

"I had every right. The vampires are plotting against humans and witches alike."

"How do you know? You abandoned this life and the witches." My venom-filled words were accented by a rumble of thunder. *You abandoned me. Fucking asshole.* I screamed the obscenities in my head not wanting him to know how deep it hurt. I turned to study him.

"Now we get to the heart of your anger. I did what I felt was best for my family. You may not agree with it, but I'm sure you will understand one day." He gazed out the window.

I snuck a better look at his profile, and it struck me how much Brandon looked like him. My brother was a younger version of our father, even if Sorin hadn't actually done more than a nod to acknowledge it.

"It was not a choice I made lightly, but it was the only way I saw to keep you safe. When Cecily told me her time approached its end and it was your time to rule, I needed to come back to guide you. You have much to learn about your legacy. The responsibility on our shoulders is as great as the power we share. I declined the throne to prevent the war, which seems unavoidable now. Cecily's rule kept the truce intact for so long we all became comfortable." He looked at me, and I saw a heaviness in his eyes. It was the kind of heaviness one gets from carrying secrets too long.

He declined the throne. I opened and closed my mouth, unable to form a sentence. I wouldn't be the first to refuse it if I did, but I wouldn't do it if it meant dumping it all on Brandon.

"The vampire who has found your favor is powerful."

"Yes, I know," I said, keeping my voice even. My stomach tensed. Sorin knew who Nick was in the vampire order.

"He was sent here to gain our trust, and he will betray you."

"No. He won't," I said, looking Sorin in the eyes. He said what I expected others to say, and I prepared myself to defend Nick.

"How can you be so sure?" he asked, his voice earnest, not pretentious.

"Because I trust him. He has been honest with me." Maybe not from the beginning, but I hadn't been either. Nick opened up and confessed to me, and I to him, but I couldn't share that intimate conversation with others.

"You love him. He will use it to his advantage." Sorin sighed. "He is known for his many skills of betrayal."

"You know nothing about him," I said, my anger growing by the second. My magic brewed under my skin, and it took more focus to keep an emotional eruption at bay. I inhaled a deep breath, like Grandmother had taught me for meditation, and let it out slowly. He didn't know the Nick I do, and he didn't know Nick had saved me more than once.

"Don't mistake my candor for maliciousness. You have difficulty controlling your emotions, which can cause problems with your magic. You'll need to learn to focus better."

Was reading minds one of his gifts, or was my lack of control that obvious?

"We're here." He waited for the driver to open the door. "Come. Let's get started. Our time is short." His hand extended out to me.

A pit grew in my gut. I wanted to ask if he meant Cecily's death or the war or both, but I refrained.

"Cecily," he said, kissing her cheek. She smiled at him as if she had been expecting him.

"Brother. I've missed you," Cecily said in an affectionate tone.

They greeted each other with the comfort of family whose bonds were tight. Each exchange they made was like an old wound being reopened for me. The pain returned to my heart for the missed time with my birth father. I wanted to know him and have a bond like they had, but my chance had been taken away from me.

"Brie, I'm glad to see you. I worried you wouldn't return after yesterday," she said. Her voice portrayed kindness, but we all knew not returning wasn't really an option. "Let's get started. Shall we?" She gestured down the hall.

"Cecily and I agree the most important thing we need to teach you is control over your power," Sorin said. It sounded rehearsed to the point I almost laughed. Cecily placed a hand on his arm.

"We should tell her the whole truth. She needs to understand," Cecily said, almost too soft for me to hear. Sorin nodded in agreement, and they both looked at me. Once again, there was a spotlight on me. Sweat beaded on my forehead.

"Have a seat please," Sorin said, rather than asked.

I dropped into the chair.

"Our family is unique, even among witches. We are not just a pure bloodline, but we are the descendants of the first of our kind. Being who we are means we inherit special gifts and the strongest of powers. We can control the elements and perform spells which would kill others. These powers, also, make us desirable to power-hungry witches and vampires alike." He paused, looking away. Tears were building in his eyes. The dampness gone when he turned back to face me. "Power can consume you and lead you to the dark path. The vampires will come for you at your most vulnerable to use you in the war. When they do, you will be forced to make a choice as to which path you will follow." He stopped, turning to Cecily, who took it up from there.

"As the days pass, you will encounter changes in yourself as part of the successor bond. As my power dwindles, yours will become stronger until the transition is complete." She looked at Sorin as if she was asking permission to continue.

"You turned down the throne because you knew this

would happen." I looked at Sorin as the words left my mouth. He dropped his head.

"Yes, the Seeing Elders predicted a great war, and a leader who would save us. The vampires hunted me when they heard of the prediction, but I wasn't the leader the Seers saw in their vision." He looked at me, and I shook my head. "Yes. They saw it before you were born. Despite our attempts to change the future, we have only led ourselves directly to it."

Desperate to be anywhere but here, I stood and headed for the door. Destiny, something I hadn't believed in, slapped me in the face.

"Brie, I know it is a lot to take in, but the time is short."

I spun on my heels, looking from him to Cecily.

"Not Cecily's death. The vampires are amassing their forces. We have little time to prepare you for the battle."

"Seriously? You expect me to lead the witches in a battle against the vampires when I have never been anything but on my own? I don't know the first thing about leading. Everything I've ever done has been on my own." I crossed my arms and waited for his answer.

"Not a battle, Brie. A war. There will be many battles within it. This is within you. It is your destiny to save not only the witches but the humans," his voice cracked. He expected me to lead, but I was a hunter, not a leader. I didn't have the first clue how to lead a group, much less an army.

"My destiny is to save the witches and the humans, but what about the vampires?" I asked, squaring up to him. "What about the truce and promise of peace for them? Shouldn't it be peace for all?"

He looked away before facing me.

"Many will die, and you will have blood on your hands. I would not expect this would be much of an issue for a vampire hunter," he said. "I suspect your concern for the vampires is really for one, Nicholas Domenico."

Fire burned through my body when I heard him say Nick's name with such vitriol. Anger built in me. I closed my eyes to gain control, but a wave of energy ruptured out of me. A thud caused me to open them. Sorin slid down the wall. Cecily rushed to him, but I froze in place. He seemed unscathed, and he stood to brush himself off.

"Do you see why you need training? You have a great power within you."

The power coursed through my veins. I was much stronger than I cared to admit. My phone chimed with Brandon's ring tone, which was a welcome distraction. As I dug in my purse for it, Cecily and Sorin whispered just out of my earshot.

"Hey Brandon, everything is okay. I got mad at our—" I paused, not knowing what to say.

"Brie, are you sure you're okay?" he asked, his voice concerned.

He deserved to know the truth, too. "Actually, I'm not. Can you come to the Great House? I need to tell you something important."

"I'm on my way," he said and hung up.

Sorin stared at me in disbelief.

"You need to catch up with your son like you have with me." I maintained eye contact.

"Telling him now will only put him in danger, as he has his own destiny," Sorin said in a worried tone.

"No. Keeping secrets from us has put us in danger. Hiding away from your family put us in danger. Putting everything out there will at least give us a fighting chance," I said, the anger building again. He'd never have my trust the way I trusted Brandon or Grandmother. I took a deep, cleansing breath and centered myself.

Brandon arrived right away, and I made sure I was the one who greeted him at the door. I studied him for a second, seeing how much he favored Sorin. I imagined Sorin looked just like him at this age.

Guilt pitted in my stomach for dragging him into the drama, but he had a right to know.

"Hey Sis, what's wrong?" He wrapped me in an awkward hug.

I fought tears as I pulled away. We'd wondered about this moment as kids. "You need to meet someone." I took his arm and lead him to the room where Cecily and Sorin waited.

"Okay," he said, bewilderment in his voice.

When we stepped into the room, Brandon exchanged looks with Cecily and Sorin. He looked at me, waiting for me to say something.

"Brandon, this is our—" I barely got a few words out when he interrupted me.

"Hello, father," Brandon said, his words clipped.

I let go of his arm and stared at him. "You knew?"

Wind howled outside as I fought to control my emotions. My world moved out of my control.

"I found out when mother got drunk one night. She begged me not to tell you, and I stupidly obliged."

I could feel his pain and hate deep within me. "Well, aren't we just one big happy lying family?"

"Mother only fears she will lose us both and blames our father." Brandon placed a hand on my shoulder. His remorse came in waves at me.

"Were you aware Cecily is our aunt?" I asked, my resentment faded away.

"No, but I am really not surprised." He shrugged his shoulders. Our twin sense betrayed his confusion to me alone.

I filled Brandon in on the war and my destiny. I sensed his emotions as I shared the whole prophecy with him. He gave a look to Cecily and Sorin with eyes narrowed. It was the same look he gave the girl who cheated on him when he told her to go straight to Hell. I wished he would tell them both to go to Hell the same way.

"What I haven't told Brie yet is you are her Protector. The Protector is bound to the Queen in a ceremony, but you two were bound at birth. The Seers foretold you would be born as well, and your destiny is to make sure your sister stays alive to succeed in hers. It's why the bond is so strong between you two. Your strength comes from her channeled in the bond," Sorin said to Brandon. "I tried to figure out how to prevent this destiny for you both."

My internal lie detector refused to help me, but my stomach felt like the bottom fell out. Brandon had been protective of me our entire lives, but this was on another level.

"You are my brother, and I don't expect you to be my Protector," I said. I shot Sorin my own Hell fury look. Brandon placed both hands on my shoulders to force me to look at him.

"We have always known you were the strongest, and I'd gladly give my life for you regardless of whether it is my destiny. You should know this already, Sis," Brandon said. One thing in our strange twin bond stood out. Acceptance.

My body tensed. "And I would you, and you should know that too." I gave him a feeble smile.

"We've saved each other many times since we began to hunt. I trust our bond." He squeezed me before he let go to turn to Sorin. "What do I need to do as Brie's Protector?"

I fought hard against the tears coming from the terrible pit I had rolling in my stomach, making me nauseous.

"The first thing is to never ask or expect Brie to give her life to save you. It is your job to save her for the good of all," Sorin said, tears in his eyes when he glanced at me. "You must train separately from her to learn how to best serve her."

"Separate? How can we work in tandem if we train separately?" I asked.

"Tandem is not how you will fight. Brandon must defend and protect you. He can't learn to fight for you if he trains with you," Sorin said.

I almost felt sorry for our father with the tears welling in his eyes. Almost. Brandon and I trained separately the last few years, but when we trained to become hunters, we practiced together.

"All right. When do we begin?" Brandon asked Sorin. His conviction to our destiny seemed easier than my own.

"We can begin today," Sorin said, his voice quiet with restraint.

I tried to read him, and where he stood, but his aura blocked me.

"Brandon, you don't have to do this. In fact, I would prefer if you didn't." A tear rolled down my cheek. "I'm begging you not to do this."

Despair built within me, and it was like falling into a bottomless pit. Brandon hugged me, and I held him tight, not wanting to let him go for fear of what it meant. Thunder rolled in the distance, an emphasis on my disagreement with his decision.

"It's okay. I want to do this. You were the one with the passion for hunting, but I would feed off yours. I've searched for my place for so long, and this answers questions for me. I want this," he said softly enough only I heard. "I love you, Sis."

"I love you, too." I wiped away my tears as he let me go. He followed Sorin out of the room to his destiny, with his head held high.

SEVEN

"Let's begin," Sorin said to me, but I wondered what my brother was doing, distracting me from my own tasks. He trained with Sorin in the mornings while I was with Cecily, and I had my sessions with our father in the afternoon. "Brie." I looked at him.

"If your power is like mine, then you know all I have to do is think it." I stared him down.

"There is more to it. Learn to focus and control your emotions." He reset his hands into position.

"And how do I control my emotions when I have people I thought gone show up randomly?" I raised my voice to the point of embarrassment. Days of meditation, sparring, and casting went by, but he avoided answering questions about our family.

"Let's deal with it, Brie. I told you why I made the decision. What do we need to do to resolve the bitterness you feel?" Sorin asked in an impatient tone.

"I don't know," I answered honestly. "I'm so angry

with you for leaving us and bringing all this on us. We knew he wasn't our father. We knew even though no one talked about it. Why didn't you come to see us?" My knees buckled from the baggage of the years he was gone. I didn't like showing weakness in front of him, but my strength was in short supply after the last few days. Sorin dropped to the floor, wrapping his arms around me, and I sobbed into his shoulder.

"I wanted to. Believe me, I did. I couldn't chance leading the vampires to you," he whispered.

"There has to be more to it than what you're telling us. It had to be safe after a while," I gasped out through the sobs. The release made me feel lighter.

"Yes, you are right, my perceptive daughter." He sighed. "I turned dark, Brie."

I'd read the stories, but the impact of hearing him say it made it real.

"I was trying to eliminate the threat by any means necessary, and I was dark for a long time." His voice broke from his tears. "I found my way back a few years ago, and I stopped practicing magic. It was too late for me to come into your life as a father, but then Cecily called. I came back to prevent you from following my same path. The Seeing Elders didn't just foresee one future, but they saw a fork in your path. You will face darkness, and there will be no coming back from it if you choose it. I'm here to guide you down the path of good."

My time in captivity was dark, but Sorin spoke of something even darker. It scared the hell out of me, and I put that fear in a small box deep in my head.

We lamented together. What seemed like a long time passed, but the act cleansed us of our sins and past, at least in my eyes. The vision from my meditation never far from my mind showed two futures, too. I had a pretty good idea of what it meant now. The handle to the doors jiggled and a rapid knock nearly took it down.

I jumped up from the mat.

"Brie! Brie! It's me! Answer the door!" Brandon's voice was frantic as he pounded on the door. Our twin link had him in a panic.

"Brandon, I'm okay," I called through the door as I stood.

"Answer the damn door!" Brandon's forcefulness surprised me.

"Really, I'm fine." I opened the door.

He pushed through, nearly knocking me down. He checked me over and saw my tear-stained face. I could feel the anger rising within him. Without asking any other questions, he formed an energy ball and flung it at Sorin.

I threw my hand out, freezing it in place. I sent my energy out to stop his, and I noticed our energies were no longer the same color. Brandon's was still light blue, like our eyes, but mine was now a deeper blue, almost purple. My energy absorbed his, and they disappeared in midair. "I said I am fine." I stared at him with my lips pursed.

"You sure as hell don't feel fine," he said.

"Stop," I said, calm and quiet. "Open up to feel where I am mentally now."

He closed his eyes, and his body physically relaxed.

"You are calm. Resolved." He opened his eyes. "What did he do to you?"

"We hashed out the past. It might be something you'll want to do when you are ready," I said, squeezing his arm.

"We'll see." Brandon's eyes narrowed, giving Sorin a dirty look. "Are you ready to go?" He turned back to me.

"Yes." I faced Sorin. "Thank you." He nodded at me. Confusion dizzied me leaving him like this, but I would not force the issue between him and Brandon. Mental exhaustion had taken over, which was never a good thing when it came to control over my powers.

"How can you forgive him so easily?" Brandon asked when we were alone in the car.

"You could feel my pain. It wasn't easy, but it's his story. I don't feel right being the one to tell it, and I haven't forgotten. I understand why, and that allowed me to forgive," I said, tempted to give him more information but following my gut to allow him to find the answers on his own.

"Why can't you forgive Mother, then?" he asked.

I thought about it. Mother stopped asking for forgiveness from me, but Brandon had told me she still mentioned it to him.

"I might be able to now." If I could forgive Sorin for leaving, then I could forgive Mother. Her actions weren't any worse than his.

"Really?" He sounded shocked.

"You can tell if I'm telling the truth."

"Yes, but I still feel confusion from you," he said.

"I'm not sure the confusion is going away anytime

soon." I stared out the window. My gaze searched for the source of uneasiness building inside me. "Brandon, I feel strange."

"Me too." He put a hand up to his head.

A flash of nausea hit my stomach like one of Brandon's kicks when we sparred.

"Pull over." We both jumped out of the car, breathing in deep gulps of air. Brandon looked over my shoulder. I followed his shocked gaze. A cemetery. We both were drawn to the old cemetery. Most witches communed with the dead peacefully, but it'd never been like this... at least not for me. The pain in my gut wasn't peaceful. It was raw power and a lot of it. "I don't think what is drawing us here is a good thing. We need to go."

"Agreed," Brandon said.

I rushed back to the car with Brandon on my heels. We both dropped in our seats. He tapped the gas and sped away.

"Could it be vampires?" He stared out at the road.

"Yes, but I'm not sure. I couldn't get a sense of how many before we left. Did you?" I rubbed my upset stomach.

"No, but I'm positive there were quite a few. Why would they be hiding in a cemetery? It doesn't make sense."

"My gut says they were looking for something, and that cemetery is one of the oldest." I debated whether or not to call Sorin, and I opted to text the number he'd put in my phone. He immediately called us.

"Which cemetery was it?" Sorin's voice came through the speaker.

"Oakland Cemetery." My stomach gurgled.

"Damn it," Sorin said under his breath. "The vampires are arriving. It wasn't the vampires you were sensing. Our ancestors were warning you of the danger."

"Our ancestors? You mean, who are dead?" I almost didn't want the answer, and Brandon's confusion was equal to my own. If our dead ancestors were using this kind of power to warn us, something big was coming.

"Yes, you need to learn more about our history," Sorin said. Brandon laughed, and I threw a playful punch into his arm.

"Keep your eyes open. The vampires may try a random attack to see how strong you are. They will not be out to kill you, but remember, they want to control you," he said. "I'll send some guards to your place."

"Got it, and tell them to keep their distance. I don't want them inside my apartment.". Brandon and I exchanged looks with furrowed brows, knowing the other's concern without saying a word.

"They will be discreet, Brie. Stay safe. Both of you." The line went dead.

Brandon dropped me off at my apartment after we argued about him coming up to check out my place. I hadn't told Sorin and Cecily about Nick yet, and I didn't want there to be any question about Brandon's knowledge of the relationship if I had to answer for it. My fierce argument turned out to be unneeded since Nick was not there.

I took a quick shower to wash away the yuck feeling

from earlier. My hair dried and fresh clothes on, I walked to the living room for some quiet meditation in front of the large window.

A light knock at the door startled me. I glanced through the peephole. Nick stood there with a huge smile on his face. I opened the door, and he lunged for me, practically tackling me on his way inside.

I returned his smile. "Thanks for using the front door. Happy to see me?"

He leaned me back and kissed me. When he righted me, I laughed.

"What do you think?" He smiled. "Hungry?"

"Starving." My stomach growled its confirmation.

"Good. I ordered us a pizza. It should be here shortly," he said, planting a kiss on the tip of my nose. I giggled and thought how lucky I was to have found him, despite what we still had to face. We would make this work.

"How did you get past the guards?" I asked. Surely Sorin had them here by now.

"You're not the only one with gifts," he said with a shrug. Uneasiness gnawed at my stomach. If he got past them, would it be easy for others?

"What did you do today?" I asked.

"Vampire stuff." He shrugged.

Two shrugs in the span of a few minutes. I had the sense he was hiding something from me. He probably hunted for blood, but Sorin's words about Nick's betrayal passed through my head, making me skeptical. *This is stupid. I'm being silly. I can trust Nick.*

The doorbell rang, jarring me from my thoughts. Nick

took the pizza into the kitchen, but when I didn't follow, he came back to the living room where I stood in place, like a tree with deep roots.

"Hey, you've got some vicious dark circles under your eyes," he said, "and those pretty blues are looking red. Have you been crying?" He tilted my chin up with his finger and planted a tender kiss on my lips.

"Oh. Yes. Well, I dealt with some family issues earlier." I turned my head. He matched my steps and stayed right on my heels as I walked into the kitchen. It wasn't a lie. I didn't tell him what the family issues were, but I didn't lie, convincing myself it was the right thing not to tell him. I grabbed a slice of pizza and took a huge bite of it to keep myself from saying anything else. I planned to tell him until he avoided the question about how he had spent the day. Coupled with what my father said, the timing was off.

"Are you sure there isn't something else bothering you?" He raised an eyebrow at me and gave me his cute, quirky grin.

I relaxed a little, but I wasn't comfortable enough to divulge my family history yet.

"Let's talk about it later. Right now I want to enjoy this pizza, which is fantastic, by the way. Where did you get it?" I flipped the lid over to see who made it. Luigi's. *Oh, my God.* Right down the street from the cemetery. It cannot be a coincidence. A wave of nausea swept over me. The room spun. I dropped my pizza and took a couple of steps back. My knees buckled. I reached for and missed the edge of the counter, but Nick caught me before I hit the floor. I closed my eyes as a tremendous surge of power ran through me like an internal earthquake. Nick set me down gently on the floor and let go. My eyes were closed, but I could smell something burnt in the air.

"Brie, can you speak?" Nick's voice hovered over me, but his touch was absent.

"Yes," I said, my voice a whisper.

"How do you feel?" The alarm in his voice caused me to open my eyes. Nothing hurt, but a touch of fatigue settled like a veil over me.

"I feel fine." I'd said that phrase a dozen times the last few days. "Your hands!" The sight of his charred hands caused a fresh wave of nausea. "What happened?" I struggled to stand against the weariness. I turned the water on cool, grabbed his arms just above the wrist, and thrust them under the tap.

"I'm not sure," he said, his voice calm. "But my hands lit up like dry wood when I caught you. I'll heal you know. It's a vampire thing." He pulled his hands back.

He was right, but the guilt for having caused him pain ate at me.

"Faster if you feed, right?" I moved my hair to one side to offer my neck.

"Yes, of course." He draped my hair back over my neck. "This shouldn't take long, though. It's only my hands." They were already looking better. Witches heal fast, but vampires heal much faster. I was astonished as the wounds turned from blisters to barely pink skin.

"Were you near Oakland Cemetery today?" I asked the hard question before it festered.

SUSAN PERSON

He looked confused when he met my eyes.

"Why would you ask about a cemetery? You know we don't sleep in the ground or in a coffin. You've been to my apartment," he said. My built-in lie detector couldn't get a read on his statement, but he had said way too much without saying anything. I learned a long time ago people telling the truth gave much simpler answers of yes or no to that type of question.

"This pizza place is right by it," I said, holding eye contact with him.

"Oh. Well, I asked the concierge at my building for a good pizza place, and he recommended this one." He looked back at his hands, which had healed. *I'm overreacting.* Sorin had made me so skeptical. "Are we going to talk about what happened to you?" he asked.

"I'm not sure what it was. Sometimes my emotions make my magic go all hinky, and it has been a tough day. I am sorry about it." I pulled his palms to my mouth and kissed them. He ran his fingers across my cheek. Guilt hung in my chest for not telling him it was a new power. Cecily had warned me this would happen. Transference of power from the dying Queen to the new Queen couldn't have come at a worse time.

"Let's do something normal people do, like watch TV. You can choose the movie." He draped his arm around my shoulder, guiding me into the living room.

I leaned into him, lost in our normal moment. He handed me the remote and tugged me down on the couch next to him.

We made it about halfway through the movie before

114

we couldn't keep our hands off of each other. Nick trailed a series of light kisses along my neck, and my eyes fluttered open when he stopped.

"I want to tell you something," he whispered in my ear. I wasn't sure I could take more bad news. *Please don't be a secret or a lie.*

"Ok," I whispered back. He propped his elbow up on the back of the couch and looked me directly in the eye. His eyes were warm and invited me to dive into the emerald sea of them.

"I love you, Brie Danforth." Not a lie and not a secret, but his declaration was unexpected.

I'd searched for love and missed the mark so many times I'd given up. All the time, my heart belonged to him. I just couldn't remember it. I knew I was in love with him even before I remembered the moments with him eight years ago, but I didn't expect to hear him say it so early.

"Did I say it too soon?" He took my hand.

"No." I smiled at him and debated whether I was ready to say it. Those three important words couldn't be taken back once I said them. I squeezed his hand.

"Take all the time you need. I will be here." He kissed the tip of my nose.

"I love you too, Nick." My cheeks burned as the blood rushed to them. He looked at me with a huge smile. "There is something I want to do." I paused. "And you might be familiar with it. Do you trust me?"

"Yes, implicitly."

"Good." I took off to my bedroom to find the ceremonial knife my mother had given to me as my birthright. It was from generations long since gone. The handle, beautifully carved ivory with old symbols of our ancestry, made before ivory was illegal. When I came back into the living room, Nick narrowed his eyes at me.

"I'm not sure what you're planning to do with a knife, but I assure you it is unnecessary."

"Just trust me," I said, my voice wavered with nerves. "If you don't trust me, then we shouldn't do this." I descended deep into his eyes, absorbed by the growing connection between us.

"I do. I would follow you through fire."

"Let's hope it doesn't come to that." I looked into his eyes and our connection blossomed. I let it fill me before I began the ritual. "Pure love is declared. This first union be blessed. Bless our bond and blessed be." I sliced the knife across my palm. The sharp sting wouldn't last long, but hopefully, we would.

"I'm not sure this is a good idea, Brie." Nick looked from the thin line of blood on my palm to the knife in my hand.

"It's a new lovers' prayer to bless their union." My cheeks burned what I was sure was a deep crimson.

"I see." He held his hand out. My stomach fluttered. At that moment, I believed everything would work out.

I sliced quickly across the flesh of his hand. He never made a sound nor flinched. I brought our palms together, but I was not prepared for the surge as we connected. The memories from his life flooded through me so quickly, leaving me in tears and gasping for air. I looked up at him, knowing it was the same for him. Our past, present, and future laid at our feet, and it wasn't good.

"That's not supposed to happen," I said, my breath coming in short pants. "That's not what the prayer is about."

"I don't think it was the prayer." Nick paused. "I think it is us." He kissed my cheek. The gentleness gave way to our need and desire, knowing this might be our only moment together, and Nick carried me to the bedroom without breaking our connection.

CHAPTER

EIGHT

Nick set me on the edge of the bed. I reached up, touching my necklace before removing it. It seemed wrong to leave a vial of Vampire Death around my neck. I set it on the nightstand but reconsidered and opened the drawer. It exposed a small arsenal of stakes, and the scent of sage drifted into the air. I placed the necklace beside them before I looked up at Nick. Without the necklace, I felt naked even with my clothes on. He brushed his fingertips across my cheek before sliding them into my hair and cupping the side of my head. With his other hand, he pushed the drawer closed, his eyes locked on mine.

My hands trembled as I reached for the hem of his grey V-neck t-shirt. I wanted to be perfect for him, and it had been years since I had been with a man. I stood, pulling the shirt over his head and arms, and he clasped me to his chest. His lips captured mine as I sank into him. Sweet vanilla whiskey had become my favorite scent, and I welcomed it as it enveloped me. He took a half step back and rested his hands on my waist.

"Are you sure?" His voice trembled like my hands.

I nodded.

"I need to hear you say it, Brie."

"Yes, I am sure." My voice came out in a ragged mess, softer than usual. His hands skimmed up my sides and around my shoulder blades as I raised my hands above my head. He dropped my shirt beside us, and I looked at the pool of light blue on the floor. His hand covered my heart.

"Your heart's beating out of your chest," he said.

I crossed my arms and uncrossed them.

"Brie, you have done this before, right? I mean..." His voice trailed off.

I dropped my head, and the blood rushed to my cheeks. I'd done it, but I was far from proud of it. If anything, I was ashamed of the things I'd done to conceal the pain from my past. To fill the void inside me that craved love.

His finger crooked under my chin and tilted it upward. "I will not judge you."

"Never with someone I loved." Tears welled up in my eyes as I released a piece of my past. Nick gave me strength and acceptance. I didn't need to hide with him.

"Don't cry. Just let me love you," he said, kissing my cheeks and burning a trail down my neck to my shoulder.

"We can wait." He kissed my forehead. "Until you are ready."

I raked my teeth over my bottom lip. With him so close, my thoughts jumbled, but I never felt more wanted.

"I'm ready, Nick," I said. "This is what I want. You are what I want. I've waited for you for years. I just didn't know it until today."

My shaky hands reached for the button on his jeans. "Damn." I fiddled with the button, trying to steady myself. Nick took my hands in his, kissing each one.

"Why don't I do it?" He set my hands on his chest. In one swift motion, he had the fly open, and the jeans fell to the ground. I ran my hands across his broad chest to his biceps, where I wrapped them as far around as they would go. They didn't make it halfway around the firm muscles. There had been even fewer articles of clothing between us than I thought. Nick stood before me completely free. The sight of his manhood quickened my ragged breaths. *Ok. My turn. I can do this.* I reached my hand around to unhook my bra, and Nick looped his finger under the strap on my shoulder.

"I've got this too." He gave me a wicked grin. He tugged the strap down while his lips brushed my shoulder, setting it on fire. Heat built in my body with every touch. He repeated on the other shoulder, and I couldn't contain the gasp. A growl escaped his lips as my bra fell away. It was a softer sound than the one he gave the parking attendant on our date. He trailed another blaze with his lips, searching out the newly exposed skin while sliding the last piece of material off me. I stepped out of my thong, still shivering from the touch of his hands on my legs. He ran a finger from my ankle up to my thigh, where he circled.

Scooping me up, he knelt on the bed, leaning me back

to rest against the pillows. I inhaled a deep breath at his neck, taking in the musky scent. His lips found mine with urgency as his hand explored. He ran his thumb down my neck as the journey took him to my breast. I drew in a sharp breath when he caressed it. My hands traveled across his back, trying to pull him closer, but he held strong. He devoured my mouth while his hand slid down my belly to intimately touch me.

My body arched when his hand found the mark, and a moan slipped from my lips. His touch was like an ignited fire between my legs, similar to the magical surges, but better. My head tilted back. Nick nipped my ear as his finger slid in, and my body arched again. My entire body was ablaze. It intensified as he added a second finger to the motion. No man had ever taken so much time exploring my body, but this was Nick. He'd saved me before, and here he revived a part of me I had let die in other arms.

He hovered over me. His lips were rough on mine, and I could feel him hold back. His vampire instincts were no doubt telling him to draw blood and satiate himself. I briefly thought of a condom, but vampires couldn't reproduce and our bodies healed too fast for either of us to have an STD. He teased me with his manhood. The sensation drove me mad with the promise of pleasure. I pushed my hips toward him, and he stilled. My eyes fluttered open to meet his. When our connection filled us, he lingered, each movement slow and deliberate. I thought I would explode as I spiraled up. I moved my hips in rhythm with him. His lips were everywhere at once, raging fires where they landed. We met at the pinnacle as both our bodies arched together. Through gritted teeth, he growled as I quivered and let out a moan in a voice I wasn't sure was mine. Warmth spilled into me.

"Are you ok?" Nick asked once we had a moment to recover.

"I am." I smiled, still panting. For a witch, I couldn't imagine it got any better. I opened up and let go completely with him. I'd never done that with anyone, or wanted to, for that matter. "How was it for you? I know I'm not a vampire—" My ragged voice trailed off.

"Vampire or witch doesn't matter. Didn't you feel the connection we shared? I've never felt the way I feel with you." He brought my bruised lips to his before leaning back on the pillows and pulling me to his chest. The connection we shared hummed around me, and I knew this was right.

"I felt it," I said, kissing his cheek before I drifted off to sleep.

)) ● ((

I WANTED to stay in bed enjoying Nick forever, but it was not an option for us. The heaviness of our future weighed on us like a lead saddle. We didn't know if we would be forced apart, but I would fight like hell to keep us together.

"We're going to have to talk about what happened earlier," Nick said, whispering to the top of my forehead while he stroked my hair. I kept my eyes closed and sighed in defense of our solitude.

"Yes, we are." I refused to lift my head from his chest, afraid of spoiling the moment.

"You do realize we'll have to change our futures to avoid the destiny we saw." He pressed on to the topic I wanted to avoid. Of course, I realized it. I didn't want to acknowledge the hard path we would be undertaking. I preferred being in bed with this gorgeous man wrapped only in a bedsheet.

"It can be done. We'll do it." I paused, tracing the length of his sternum before resting my hand on his stomach. "Nick, I don't want to turn dark," I blurted out, voicing my deep fears through the knot forming in my throat.

"I will not let it happen. I'll leave before I let that happen."

My stomach tightened with dread. The thought of him leaving was worse to me than the thought of going dark. My entire body shook. It caused full-on panic mode in my body and brain.

"Don't you ever say that again. It's not an option," I said, my voice betraying my frustration. The wind howled and swirled outside the window.

"Alright. We'll take it off the table for now." He pressed his lips to my forehead. My reaction surprised even me. Until this last birthday, I had become pretty good at hiding my emotions from everyone except Brandon and Grandmother. Nick had found his way through in a way no other man had, but I'd never had the feelings for another man like I did Nick.

"You knew Sorin was my father, but you didn't say

anything?" I broached the subject, uncertain I cared if he did anymore.

"I suspected, yes," he said. "When I heard he was back in town, I knew there had to be a big reason. And Cecily chose you as her successor, so it made sense. If I figured it out, Stefan has to." He pulled me up on his chest so we were facing each other. It made sense, and Sorin already thought I was a target. "Make no mistake. Your life is in danger, but I will protect you." He kissed me hard on the mouth as if he was a vampire claiming a human. It wasn't that way with us, though. It was like we could look inside each other.

"I'm a hunter. I'm not afraid to die, Nick, and I don't need protection," I said, looking into his eyes to enforce the truth. "I just need you to love me, and the only thing I really fear is a future without you." The truth spilled out of me, and there was no going back from what I said. To not hold my past back from someone gave me a different type of empowerment. The vulnerability built strength in me.

"I know you don't need protection, but you have it and my love, as long as you let me."

Clarity came and slipped away as I drifted to sleep.

When I woke in the morning, I found the bed empty. The lights flickered as the disappointment oozed from me. I moved to get out of bed, my thoughts on the kitchen. A blue swirl gathered around me, and I stood in front of the refrigerator. I gasped for air. *How in the hell?* The new trick. I gagged at the rapid movement, but it gave me a greater understanding of what Sorin meant about being in control. A power like this could land me in some embarrassing situations, or worse. *Goddess, what if I had thought of the club or Nick's bedroom?* I groaned. Control needed to be at the top of my list. If I remembered my history correctly, there had not been a witch with teleportation powers in a century or more. I needed to get to Grandmother's quick to figure it out.

The bluish-tinted swirl encroached on my vision. I slammed into the floor and rolled over on my side, feeling sick to my stomach. Crumpled up in the fetal position on the cold linoleum floor in the kitchen of my grandmother's house wearing only my robe and dry heaving wasn't exactly how I envisioned my arrival at her house. *What the fuck? This sucks.* A gentle hand rubbed my back until I stopped. *How does anyone physically survive this?* I shook so hard my teeth chattered while Grandmother continued rubbing my back. My head pounded, and I wondered if I would die right there and not have to worry about fulfilling any prophecies.

"Brie? Are you ok?" she asked in a soft, concerned voice.

"I—Yes, I'm fine," I said, taking in a gulp of air and standing upright, rubbing my head. *Calm.* I willed the shaking into submission. "What about my new trick?" I asked, cocking my head and giving her a half smile, trying to reassure her I was fine.

"Did you? No, it can't be possible." She looked at me and grinned. "Did you teleport here?"

"Well, yes," I said. "I know it wasn't a seven birthday, but something gifted me last night." I wiped my sweaty palms on my nightshirt. *Goddess. I'm glad I got up and put that on in the middle of the night.* "Cecily said some of her powers would transfer to me. Can she teleport?"

"No, she can't. It has been hundreds of years since a witch could teleport. This is truly a blessing. A gift was bestowed on you by our ancestors," she said, hugging me. "Blessed be!"

"Except for the fact I have no idea how to control it, and it doesn't make me feel very blessed when it happens." I paused, considering what she said. The ancestors were blessing me. Sorin had said the ancestors were warning us at the cemetery. I didn't even know it was possible. "I hate to admit it. Sorin is right. Emotion rules me, and I need better control." I stumbled a little, light-headed. "Why would an ancestor gift me?"

"The royal family can gift beyond the grave with source magic. They haven't done it in so long. I and I'm sure others, thought it was folklore and legends." She took me by the shoulders and steered me to the table. "Sit. It takes a lot out of you to use that kind of life force. I'll make you some breakfast."

I watched the way she bustled around the kitchen to make French toast and bacon. She remembered how much I loved them and couldn't turn down a carb-loaded breakfast. She was much more of a mother to me than my own. Mother kept me at a distance even before my seventh birthday, before she tried to bind our powers. Grandmother picked me up and held me when I was afraid of Mother that night, and her love made me feel safe.

)⟩●⟨(

AFTER BREAKFAST, my energy returned, and I took Grandmother up on a change of clothes from some I'd left there and time in the meditation room. If it helped me center my emotions, it would be good. She lit sage to clear the room, and the magic of our ancestors pulled me to my quiet place in a different way today. They called to me. I sat in the center of the meditation circle with a clear head, looking for the key to control.

I gasped and my eyes flew open, looking into the surprised eyes of my grandmother. She had created a joined circle in front of me to share in my journey. It was one of her gifts, and it allowed her passage with whoever meditated. We stared at each other for a long moment. I tried to sort through the details of what the vision showed us. It seemed like a discombobulated path going forward and backward at the same time.

"Was that the future, or was it the past? I'm confused." I reached up and grabbed my throbbing head. The pain got worse the more I tried to make sense of it all.

"I saw it through your eyes," she said, her voice encouraging. "It was the past and the future in one, dear granddaughter." She took my hand and clasped both of hers around it. "There once were many dark witches who worshiped their dark queen. They were defeated in a terrible battle where light witches and vampires fought against them. Both sides lost many lives. For those dark witches that survived the battle, the elders condemned them to death. The deaths were as brutal as the battles. Then they were all but wiped from history except in the books the council keeps locked away. They thought by destroying the dark witches and all traces of them, they could prevent it from happening again. Afterward, they found out that the Vampire King wanted to control the Dark Queen, but she refused. It was the reason the vampires turned against the dark witches and signed a truce with those practicing light. Though several challenged the truce since then, they ultimately perished in the end, and the truce held for many years."

"So, I will either be the light queen who keeps the peace or the dark queen who brings about the demise of life as we know it," I said. "Great. No pressure there." The words came out a little sharper than I meant.

"It's not as simple as a single choice. The path you walk will likely lead you to the choice, which means every step must be weighed. Darkness lurks for our most vulnerable moments." She squeezed my hand gently. "I saw your vampire boyfriend by your side," she said. Her voice was a mix of worry and agitation.

"He's not —" I protested, but I couldn't find the words. I didn't want to deny him in front of her, but I didn't want to disrespect her beliefs, either. "I don't know what he is." I pulled my hands away from her.

"He's a vampire, Brie. He will always be a vampire. You need to let him go. He was by your side as the dark queen," she said. "It endangers you both to be together. The path of the dark leaves you empty and alone. You will not have happiness there."

"No," I whispered. A lump formed in my throat. I refused to accept that being with him equated to becoming the dark queen. Determined my path would be light and Nick would be there, I set intentions in my mind.

"I saw it too," I said, my voice almost a whimper. "It's not that easy." Nothing was ever easy for me, but I'd made it work so far. I looked at my watch. "I need to get back to the apartment before—" My words hung in the air as I teleported back to my place. At least it didn't feel like my lungs were coming out through my mouth this time. The dry heaves didn't last as long, and I didn't shake, which was an improvement. I took a deep breath to clear my lungs and my mind. *Brie, you can do this. Sorin will not take it easy on you today, so suck it up and get it together.*

NINE

)) ● ((

I could not pay attention as Sorin tried to teach me focus. We stood in the ancestral library, which was my favorite room in the Great House. The smell of the old books and history did little for me today. My heart weighed heavy on the decision I had to make about Nick. To stay together could mean one or both of our lives and the lifestyle we knew, but spending a hundred years in a medieval torture chamber sounded better than being apart. What about us being together would turn a witch dark? Was it the love? I looked up at Sorin, his eyes boring into me.

"Do you have something you need to say? You certainly have not been listening to anything I have said." Agitation rang in his voice.

"I was wondering—" I stopped, not sure if I wanted to know the answer. Sorin nodded patiently, waiting for me to formulate my thoughts. "Is love the risk? Is it what turned you dark, and those who went dark before us?"

Sorin's head dropped until he stared at the floor. When he looked up, I regretted asking once I saw the pain on his face.

"Love makes you vulnerable, yes," he said. "It's more the willingness to do anything in the wake of love making it dangerous. The desperation can consume you and let the dark into your soul. It's almost impossible to remove once it is there." He sighed, wrinkling his forehead more. His voice was full of regret. I didn't want to cause him pain, but I needed to understand the cost if I chose Nick.

"But you could beat it," I said. He put his hands on my shoulders and squeezed. It did little to reassure me he had indeed beaten it. It bothered me I couldn't see his aura. I could tell he concealed it, and there was only one reason anyone would use that much magic to hide their aura. His aura must be dark.

"Yes, but it cost me much. I could easily slip back into it if I were to ever lose control. It is always on the precipice of showing itself if I give into it. It's a constant battle for me, and I don't wish that battle on you."

I sighed as his emotions passed over me. He cared. My throat ached.

"Is there a possibility love can help overcome the darkness?" I asked, desperate for some hope.

"I suppose, but it is unprecedented. It's the sacrifice for those we love which guides us on our path of leadership." He struggled through the explanation. I let his words float through my head. I realized a key piece of the witch history with complete clarification. All those who turned dark chose love before the leadership of their people. In some cases, their family, and in others their true love. *Were our roles so cruel as to deny us the thing we desired most?*

"So choosing to protect those we love over our role as a leader means the dark consumes us? It sounds like a pretty shitty choice, in my opinion. Leave those you love to their demise so you can guide your race and keep the peace. Oh, and you must be alone forever." I unintentionally got louder, swinging my arm in the air.

He put a hand on each of my shoulders, his tone apologetic. "It sounds harsh, especially to someone as young as you. You don't have to be alone, though. There are options, and your family can still be a part of your life."

"It makes me feel like I have no choice in my own life. I never asked for this." It dawned on me what he meant by options, and I tried to hide my reaction. I gagged at the thought of any other man touching me other than Nick. The door opened, interrupting us, and I turned to see Brandon entering the room. I rushed in his direction and accidentally teleported to him from the far side of the room. "Oops. Well, I guess the cat is out of the bag on that new trick," I said. A nervous giggle rolled out of me in contrast to the wide-eyed open-mouthed look on his face.

"What? How? Did you just teleport over here? I didn't think any witches could do that anymore." Brandon hugged me. "Lucky girl."

"So I heard. It's something I picked up last night. Did anything happen for you?" I hoped he would say yes, not wanting to be the only one carrying this burden. But I knew the answer before he said it, and he had the weight of serving as my Protector.

"On a day that's not a seventh birthday? No, nothing happened to me. Well, I can't feel your emotions anymore. Maybe the two are connected." He sounded even more confused than me. My chest tightened. Was our bond being severed as part of this process?

"Really? I can still feel yours." I pulled back and looked up at him. Something was happening. We didn't feel as in tune with each other as we normally did. The twin sense had only grown over the years, and the backward step was like I lost a piece of myself.

"You know what is happening. Don't you, Sorin?" I turned on my heels to face him.

"Yes," he said, keeping his voice low and in control.

"So, tell us." Brandon and I walked toward him.

"Twin guardians often carry part of the power of those they protect until a certain age. In your case, the succession rite was the catalyst. The power is finding its way to you, Brie, which is all the more reason we need to get you focused and your emotions in check. If it is moving this quickly, there is a reason." Sorin looked between Brandon and me. "I suspect Brandon probably knew something about this, too." I turned my attention to him.

"Did you?" I asked, hoping my brother wouldn't keep secrets.

"I felt something, but I wasn't sure what it was. It felt natural, and I could sense it wasn't evil," Brandon said. "Grandmother was on my list to talk to about it, but I hadn't had a chance." I sighed, at least knowing he hadn't betrayed our trust.

"Now, let's talk about the teleportation. The knowledge of this doesn't leave this room—"

"Well, Grandmother knows. I teleported to her this morning just from thinking about her." I shrugged. "It's not like I did it on purpose." Sorin rolled his eyes. *He actually rolled his eyes.* I stifled a giggle.

"No one else can know about this as your life is already in danger, and you will become more of a commodity not only among the vampires but among the witches too. Not everyone or every coven is in support of this change. Agreed?" My brother and I both nodded. For once, we all agreed.

Brandon was particularly focused during our rare joint training session. I sensed him channeling his focus to me. He gave me one of his big smiles and a wink. He put me over himself, and it had nothing to do with being my guardian. It had everything to do with Brandon's integrity.

)) ● ((

AFTER WORKING all day and into the evening to get control of my teleportation skill, my new driver dropped me off at the building. My favorite vampire waited in the driveway in his pretentious black Lamborghini. I shook my head. My driver would run to my father and tattle, of that I was sure, but I didn't care.

"Nick!" I ran to him. His broad smile melted me. He pulled me into his arms for a kiss.

"I guess you missed me," he said, still smiling.

"Actually, I'm kind of mad at you for leaving and not saying goodbye." I swatted his arm playfully. He frowned at me.

"I left a note on the pillow and kissed your forehead like this." His lips brushed the skin above one of my eyebrows, sending a shiver of delight through me. "I was summoned and had to go." He moved his lips to my cheek and pulled me closer to him. "Do you honestly believe I could leave without saying anything?" he whispered into my hair.

"I guess I did until now. Not sure how I missed the note." I said. *Oh. Because I teleported out of bed to Grand-mothers.* "We should go upstairs." I should tell Nick, but I didn't want to break my trust with Sorin, either.

"There is something I want to show you first." Nick helped me into the car. His wicked little grin didn't get past me.

"Shouldn't I get cleaned up first? You know I have been training all day," I said, my protest weak. I would have gone anywhere with him.

"There is a bag for you in the car." He winked at me and closed my door. The control freak in me hated surprises, but Nick made me want them more.

꒰꒱ ● ꒰꒱

"It's gorgeous." I admired the sun setting on Lake Grapevine as we pulled up to a lake house. The beautiful log cabin style looked rustic but modern.

He opened my door and held out his hand. "I thought we could have dinner here to celebrate your birthday. There is an outdoor fireplace to keep you warm," Nick said. *So sweet.* I hadn't wanted to celebrate my birthday since my seventh, but I did with him. He couldn't feel the cold, but he thought of how chilly it would be for me, even with the mild winter we were having. He reached in for the tote. "Your bag has a sweater, jeans, and flats for you to change into."

"You are awesome," I said. "You deserve a reward!" I kissed him.

He held my hand up the steps and let go to open the door.

Inside, I wrapped my arms around his neck. Vanilla mixed with musk filled the space. He pressed his lips to mine. My mouth parted, welcoming him. He leaned back.

"If you want to see what a magnificent cook I am, you need to go change clothes and let me get started in the kitchen." He patted me on the bottom as I took the bag from him and followed his directions to the bedroom to get cleaned up.

I showered and pinned my wet hair up in a bun while I got dressed.

Nick was fully immersed in cooking when I found him in the kitchen a few minutes later. He crooned. I leaned on the door frame to watch him. He knew I was there, of course, just like he had the first night. His vampire instincts were keen even for their kind, but he let me have the moment before acknowledging me.

"Want to help?" he said, throwing a kitchen towel over his shoulder without even looking.

"Sure." I caught the small towel as I walked toward him. The kitchen was fit for a gourmet cook and would have seemed out of place if it wasn't for all the modern amenities in the cabin despite its rustic exterior appearance.

"Then you must wear this." He wrapped an apron around me and tied it expertly at my waist while leaving a kiss on my neck. "Ok. Not really, but I wanted to see you in it." He chuckled in my ear and made me giggle. "I thought we would have a real southern meal." The smell of frying chicken hit me.

"It smells wonderful. What do you need me to do?" I asked. My mouth watered as I inhaled the mixture of spices in the batter cooking.

"Can you mash the potatoes when they are ready?" He tilted his head toward the pan with boiling water.

"Absolutely. This dinner is carb loaded. I hope you have plans on how we are going to work them off later." I waited for him to look at me before shooting him a smile and a wink. He laughed so hard I turned away, but I was sure my cheeks had already betrayed my embarrassment.

)) ● ((

"I AM SO full I feel like I am going to blow up." I snuggled up against Nick's chest on the love seat in front of the fire pit. I gazed at the crackling fire, lost in thought, and relaxed from the warmth. "I'm surprised by how much you ate."

"Vampires can and do eat human food, Brie. I thought we discussed this?" he said softly as he played with my hair. I might have annoyed him a bit by saying it. "We still crave blood, regardless of how much human food we consume."

"I know. As much as I want to do unspeakable things to you and not ruin the great evening, I know we need to talk." I said, without raising my head from his chest.

"What's on your mind?" He placed a finger under my chin and lifted my head so I looked into his emerald green eyes. He touched our lips together ever so gently, and I forgot for a moment what I wanted to say. He needed to know what I saw today, and the reality of it brought me back.

"I visited my grandmother this morning, and we saw more of the vision you and I had. Also, I learned something about the sacrifices the leaders of the witches must make." I locked eyes with him. I thought we would have a discussion, but it turned into more of me trying to convince him of what I didn't want to face.

"It doesn't have to be like the past, Brie. We can make our own destiny," he said, when I finished telling him everything, except about the teleporting. Not that I needed permission, but I wanted to show respect for the agreement with Sorin and Brandon.

"I don't think it's so simple. It would seem my destiny is already written based on whether I choose love over sacrifice." The hot sting of a tear blazed its way down my cheek. I reached up to wipe it away, but Nick gently took my wrist, returning my hand to his chest. He wiped away the tear with his thumb and brought our lips gently together. I wanted him to kiss away the prophecy and our destiny, but we only had an escape for a short time.

"I love you. No matter what happens. I love you, and you need to always remember how much." He picked me up in one quick movement, heading to the bedroom. I closed my eyes and let his love flow through me. The safety of his arms pulled my guard down with ease. A whoosh of air swirled around me, and we were in the bedroom when I opened my eyes. Nick chuckled, setting me down in front of him. "Is there something else you want to tell me?" I let out a breath, thankful he was amused and not mad. I'd have to tell my father and brother... but not tonight.

"Um... apparently, I can teleport. Who knew?" I shrugged my shoulders. I was grateful I didn't dry heave this time around. Teleporting another person hadn't even occurred to me as an option. I struggled to stay composed, but Sorin's words echoed through my thoughts. I trusted Nick, but the queasiness in my stomach said there was something wrong. It must've been my guilt for keeping secrets. "Please don't tell anyone, Nick. I'm not ready to share this," I said, pleading from my eyes to his.

"It is yours to share." He kissed the tip of my nose, and then my lips to begin his slow, sensual assault.

CHAPTER
TEN

Thursday morning greeted me with a vengeance. It was early. The sun hadn't even risen yet. My head pounded like a jackhammer tried to break its way in, and the queasiness in my stomach was a thousand times worse than last night. Witches were not prone to illness. Only a few things caused a witch to feel this way, and I started ticking them off in my throbbing head. *Poison. Pregnancy. Death.* I mentally checked off symptoms for poison and pregnancy, and I was certain it was not either of them. Nick couldn't reproduce, and poison seemed unlikely. *Death? Cecily?* My heart sped up. *Goddess, don't let that be it.*

I reached for my phone, and Nick propped himself up on one elbow, studying me as I scanned it. "I forgot vampires don't sleep much. Guess it's pretty boring watching me sleep." No messages. My heart slowed with my relief. *Thank goodness.* I set the phone down and looked at him.

"I enjoy watching you sleep. The tension you carry during your wake falls away when you sleep, and it reminds me of my human life." He ran a finger along my arm and sent chills through me. Every so often, he would say something that reminded me of how many years he had seen.

"I'm not human. Witches aren't even the same species. I never have been human, and I don't know what it means to have a human life," I said, my voice low. Humans led normal lives. Witches didn't. Nick knew what a normal life was.

"You're closer to being human than I am. You have the fragility of mortality." He trailed kisses up my arm. "Which is why you crying out in pain during your sleep worries me. You made some terrible noises like you were drowning at one point. You also glowed for most of the night. Do you remember what you dreamed?"

I sat straight up in bed. If I was glowing, then I had a new trick. Another gift.

"I don't remember any of it, but I have a terrible headache and am nauseous. Maybe it was a premonition or something happened. And you're ok?" I gasped for air. Panic struck me. Witches seldom dreamed as humans do. Dreams for witches were, more than often, foretelling and it was unusual to not remember them.

"I'm fine. Calm down. We'll figure it out." Nick smoothed the hair away from my face.

"Nick, I need to go. I have to talk to Sorin," I said, my voice shaking. I swayed with weakness as I stood, not caring I was naked. My mind drifted to several places. I thought of the bathroom and my clothes at the same time, which turned out to be a mistake. I ended up teleporting to the bathroom and then right back to the bedroom in front of the walk-in closet. My legs shook as if I had done a weightlifting routine, and I fell toward the floor with pitch black closing in on me. Something softened my fall, preventing me from crashing into the cold hardwood floor.

)) ● ((

SUNSHINE BLINDED me as I blinked my eyes open to familiar surroundings. My legs were heavy as I moved to swing them over the side of my bed. *My bed. Oh shit. Did I dream yesterday?* I tried to stand and fell back down on the bed.

"Easy," Nick said, sitting beside me on the bed. "Take your time." He brushed his lips across my forehead. "How are you feeling?"

I looked around, wondering how we got here. "Honestly? Like I was in a brawl with vampires. No offense." I gave him a weary laugh.

"I can give you some of my blood. It will help your body recover quicker."

Vampires didn't offer their blood often. *I must look pretty bad.* The reaction could be a little unpredictable, from euphoria to boosted energy. I looked up at him, and there was no denying something was wrong. His forehead wrinkled, and his face was drawn with tension.

"Hey, I'm going to be fine. Stop worrying." I said, rubbing his forehead. This had to be confusing for him.

"I am worried about you, Brie. Especially now." He squeezed my hand. *My gentle giant.* "Sorin called." I raised my eyebrows.

"You?" I asked.

"No, he called your phone, and I answered."

"Oh? I'm sure that went over like elephant poop," I said, earning a small chuckle from him.

"It did. You're right, but we need to get dressed. He needs you right away. He said to tell you as soon as you woke up." His voice was cautious, and I could tell there was something he wasn't saying.

"What's going on, Nick? And how did we get here?" I realized we were both naked.

"You teleported us here. Let's get dressed, and then we can talk about it," he said.

"You don't have any clothes here."

"My clothes are on the way, and we need to go as soon as possible," he said, almost growling words. He pressed a kiss to my cheek. When I stood up, he caught my hand in his. "It's going to be ok."

The fog in my head cleared, and I understood this was serious. My hands twitched as I dressed.

⟩⟩●⟨⟨

AT THE GREAT HOUSE, he hurried around to my side to open the door and help me out.

"Thank you. I'll call you when I'm done," I said, reaching up to kiss him. He gave me a light peck on the cheek instead.

"I'm going with you," he whispered in my ear.

My shoulders tensed. "You can't, Nick. Vampires aren't allowed."

"Sorin knows. I told him I wasn't leaving your side. He's not happy about it, but he conceded, given the circumstances." He took my hand again and led the way up the walk.

"What circumstances? I don't understand." I leaned against him as we walked through the threshold.

"I know. Our compromise was Sorin would give you the details," he said. I squeezed his hand nervous enough for both of us.

Sorin hugged me to him. It caught me by surprise. I saw my mother over his shoulder, sitting on a bench with red eyes and a tear-stained face. She looked the opposite of how she looked at the council meeting. Her clothes were disheveled, and I wondered if she had pulled another drunken bender. It was weird seeing both parents in the same place.

"What is going on?" I glanced back and forth between Sorin and my mother.

"You didn't tell her?" Sorin looked at Nick.

"It was our agreement," Nick said, stone-faced.

"I didn't think vampires honored their agreements." Sorin's rudeness to Nick caused anger to rise inside of me.

"Don't talk--"

"You dirty, filthy vampires! You should have all been destroyed years ago!" Mother stood right in front of Nick. He didn't flinch, not even when she formed an energy ball to throw at him. I threw my hand up and the energy ball froze halfway between them. I pulled it to me and crushed it in my hand. "You're going to defend him when they've taken your brother!" She stared at me with tears streaming and eyes wide.

"What?" I stumbled back. There wasn't enough air in the room. Nick caught me with his arm around my waist. *He should have told me. I should have felt it. Oh, Goddess. Were they kidnapping him while we were at the lake house?* "Is it true?" I looked up at Nick.

"Apparently so. I had nothing to do with it, though. You must believe me," Nick said. His furrowed brows made him look older.

"I do. I just need to sit down." He took one arm and Sorin the other. They led me to the bench where my mother had been sitting. She turned her back on us and headed down the hall. I must have been so overwhelmed with my own emotions last night I couldn't tell the pain and distress were Brandon's. Tears spilled down my cheeks for my brother, who suffered while I slept.

"Why would they take Brandon?" I asked. "He's your guardian, your brother, and an easy way to get to you. They have offered to trade him for you," Sorin said in a bitter tone.

Was it a coincidence that it happened the same night Nick took me to the lake house? One of the worst things they could do to me was taking Brandon, and they knew it. I wouldn't let him suffer because of me.

"Done. Where do I go?" I asked through the knot in my throat.

"You can't, Brielle. You are the future Queen of the

Witches, and you're too powerful to hand over to them." Tears glistened in Sorin's eyes.

"I will teleport in and out with him," I said under my breath, knowing I'd do it regardless of what anyone else said.

"You can't teleport with someone else. It doesn't work like that." Sorin put his head in his hands.

"Actually, it does." I looked at Nick, but I spoke to Sorin.

"I knew you wouldn't keep it from the vampire." Sorin raised his head and said in an annoyed tone.

"It wasn't a conscious choice to tell him. I teleported us unknowingly, and we both traveled." I paused, letting Sorin soak in the information. "So, I can go rescue Brandon and not surrender myself." I knew what it was like to be a prisoner in that lair, and I refused to leave my brother in that situation.

"Brie, I don't think it's a good idea. They will be waiting for a rescue attempt," Nick said, taking my hand.

"They won't be expecting me to teleport. There are only five people who know, including me, so there is no way they will expect it," I said, knowing this was the only way to get in and out of there unnoticed.

"You can't. The council will never allow it with Queen Cecily so close to her death, especially with you being the vampire's target. They know you're powerful," Sorin said, looking me in the eyes. "And then vampires could find out you can teleport, which is another issue entirely."

"You're talking about the life of your son. Brandon has always put me first, and it's my turn to repay him." Nick squeezed my hand tightly, and I took a deep breath to calm down.

"It's his destiny to be your Protector, even if it means laying down his own life. It's what he was born to do, just as you were born to lead," Sorin said. His voice was thick with the tears he held back. He cleared his throat. "Remember our discussion yesterday? Your decision is important, and you need to follow the council's advisement."

"You think saving my brother will turn me dark?"

Nick squeezed my hand again. I needed the reassurance more than I could admit. My brother was in danger because of me, and I wouldn't stop until he was back home.

"Choosing love over your destiny at any point could tip the scales." Sorin placed a hand on my shoulder. I made my mind up, but I didn't want Sorin to know my plan. He'd try to stop me.

"But rescuing him doesn't mean it for sure. I need some quiet time to think. Nick, would you mind escorting me to the garden?" I exchanged a knowing glance with him.

"You have five minutes. I'm going to see what the latest intel is. Meet me back here."

"Of course," Nick said.

I waited until we got to the end of the hall where the doors to the garden were before I said anything. A choice for love could take me to the dark, but reason stood that it would be more the love like Nick and I had versus my brother.

"Nick, you need to distance yourself from me. You'll be an outcast among your people if you're associated with me and what I am about to do." I held tears at bay and choked out the words. This was my sacrifice, not leaving my brother to die at the hands of vampires when they would probably send him back piece by piece to me to draw out the suffering. Sorin said I would have to sacrifice love for leadership, and I would willingly give up my happiness, the piece that filled the emptiness inside me, to save my brother.

"You don't know for sure where they are holding him, and you can't go in there much less alone." Nick grimaced. "If you think I am letting you go without me, you are mistaken."

"We both know there is only one place they would hold him. They want me to come to the Vampire King's palace." Bile rose in my throat. I swallowed it back down with renewed determination. My brother will not suffer weeks like I did.

"It's a maze, Brie. You'll need a guide."

"It's not like I haven't been in his mansion before." I remembered every twist and turn there.

"But not without me." He took a step in my direction. I expected his move and was already taking a step back.

"Nick, go. You must leave. Without me here to protect you, there is no telling what they will do to you." I thought of my destination and my brother. The rush of air turned into a blue swirl and carried me to the room of mixed-up memories.

ELEVEN

The smell of death filled the air of the Vampire King's palace. *Same smell. Different year.* That odor clung to me for a week after my captivity. Luckily, the room I remembered and traveled to was vacant. By the thickness of the dust on the furniture, it could have been vacant since I was last here. *Cloak.* If I stuck to the shadows, I'd be able to search without being seen, given how dimly lit the hallways were. My twin sense told me Brandon was nearby. The quicker in and out, the better. I peeked around the corner of the stone wall. Two vampires guarded a room. I wasn't sure if staying cloaked would work while I teleported, but I was going to find out. My concentration went to the room. The draftiness of the corridor covered the movement.

I put my hand over my mouth to keep from crying out at the sight of my brother. Purplish-blue bruises covered Brandon's body in various stages of healing. And bite marks. Anger built inside of me. *This place will burn.* A clap of thunder rattled the windows. *Calm*. I checked the room for cameras before I uncloaked. I whimpered and touched Brandon's face as gently as I could.

He winced. His nose sat off center, broken with a busted lip. Both fresh wounds. Dried blood smeared like paint across his face. I couldn't risk a healing spell on him until we were back at the Great House. It would leave us both vulnerable, and I needed the strength to teleport us back.

"Sis, you shouldn't have come." Brandon struggled to speak with one eye barely opened and the other swollen shut. His voice was hardly a whisper.

"There is no way I would leave you to these leaches," I whispered beside his ear.

"It's a trap, Sis. Get out of here." He said in an urgent tone.

"We're going together." I took his hand. "Then I'm coming back to destroy them all," I whispered, teleporting us back to the Great House. I glimpsed the bench in the hallway. Sorin ran towards us. Tears of relief rolled down my cheeks. My vision closed in. Everything faded to black.

I woke up in a dark room I didn't recognize by the minimal light but I did by smell. It was too dark to see the books, but the dust and old leather scent meant I was in the library.

"Hey there, slumbering beauty," Nick said. Through the darkness, I could just make him out on the other side of the couch. The warmth of his smile filled the space between us. My energy was drained as if I had run a marathon and fought a pack of wolves the whole way.

"How's Brandon?" My weariness betrayed me as my voice cracked.

"Your Grandmother's healing spell is working, but he has a lot of injuries. His arm is broken, his ribs bruised, and he has many contusions."

"Did they try to turn him?" I remembered the bite marks. *Bastards.*

"They fed on him, but they didn't release any venom. They were trying to keep him weak, not make him a vampire. It would have been a painful death," he said in a consoling tone. He rubbed my leg.

"I'm going to send them all to Hell," I said. "Sorry. I know they're your people, but I will not let this go." I sat up, raising my hand to the light, and the room illuminated at my command. I blinked, adjusting to the brightness.

"You should try to relax and regain your strength. Using your energy for such trivial tasks in this state will keep you from healing." Nick studied me.

"I wasn't hurt." Even knowing it wasn't Nick's fault didn't stop the bitterness.

"No, but you used a lot of energy rescuing Brandon. It takes time for your body to recover," Nick said, tucking a stray hair behind my ear.

"How do you know so much about witches?" I asked, shrugging his hand away. It wasn't his fault, but I couldn't take a vampire touch without thinking about Brandon's beaten body.

"I'm old, Brie, and vampires know more than you think." His answer was short enough to make me question what he meant, but I was too tired to do it now. He reached for me, and I didn't resist this time. None of this was his fault. It was mine. I leaned over into his lap, and he stroked my hair as I drifted off to sleep.

Heat and pain coursing through my body jarred me awake. I rolled to the floor, acutely aware of everything but not in control of my body. Nick stood over me as I convulsed. It was like someone stabbed me with hot pokers over and over. The room was lit up like firelight from the glow emanating from me. A powerful electrical surge passed through me like a lightning strike. A silvery-white light emanated. I screamed.

"Sorin! Sorin! Get in here!" Nick stayed by my side. I focused on him.

Steps pounded toward me, and Sorin came into view.

"I couldn't touch her without getting burned," Nick said, panic in his voice.

My senses recovered, and I wiped my hands over my face.

"If you breathe a word of her powers to the vampires, I will kill you myself," Sorin said.

"Stop," I said, my voice hoarse. "Help me up." I maneuvered into a seated position.

They each grabbed an arm to help me stand. The odor of flesh burning on Nick's hands saturated the air, but he steadied me anyway. It riddled me with guilt. He would endure pain for me, and I had terrible thoughts earlier.

"Nick, drink some of my blood. This is twice I have been responsible for burning you," I said, holding my wrist to him. I hoped he would take my offer this time. My arm trembled. I took my other hand and held it, but that did little to steady it. Sorin jumped in between us, pushing us apart.

"No! It is forbidden! He can never drink from you." Sorin's eyes looked almost black. He was being way too protective. I had blood to spare.

"He's right. I'm not drinking from you. Besides, you need to regain your strength," Nick said in a candid tone.

"What happened? I felt electric, but it was like I was cooking from the inside out." I looked at them, bewildered by the strange sensation I had. Strength, freedom, and hope mixed with relief from pain.

"Cecily passed and her power transferred to you." Sorin wiped tears from his cheek.

I stared off across the room. Grief permeated me, and my vision unfocused. I choked back a sob. *She's gone.*

Sorin guided me to the couch. I sat down, and he took a seat next to me. Nick perched on the arm of the couch over my shoulder.

Sorin's eyes were red. "This is how it has happened for centuries, but we have always kept it in secret amongst the elders until now. She passed so quickly. It didn't give us enough time to bring you to her." He looked at Nick as if he was burning him where he stood. His eyes softened as he looked back at me. "Traditionally, you would have been by her side to help ease her pain during the transition. The focus on the dying lessens your awareness of your own pain." I wept for the passing of my aunt.

"I need to be alone." I stepped away from both of them. I wanted to escape the resentment and guilt inside me. "Please go."

"I'm not going anywhere," Nick said, taking a gigantic step toward me. I tricked him once and teleported. He kept the distance close between us.

"I'm not leaving you—especially with a vampire," Sorin said, stepping up beside me. I shook my head at him. He didn't know Nick had saved me years ago, but he knew Nick had been there through several surges now. And Sorin couldn't see Nick as anything other than a vampire. The intensity of his hatred drained my life force like I was being asphyxiated.

I needed space. *Why can't they see that?* I silently called the elements to me and put a barrier between us. I took a deep breath. Both of them step toward me and hit the invisible wall. I gave them a sad smile of apology as I thought of my balcony.

The night air cleansed me. I inhaled deep breaths of it in through my nose and out through my mouth. My arms out, I stretched my chest to allow as much air into my lungs as possible. Even in my escape, visions of those I had hurt consumed me. I was responsible for so much pain to my mother, my brother, my aunt, my boyfriend, and countless others. I was not fit for the position of queen. The queen should bring peace, but how would the vampires ever want peace with someone who had hunted and killed their kind most of her life? Alone time was my way of rejuvenating, but it didn't fill the hole inside me. The hair on the back of my neck stood up, and I spun around.

"I thought I would find you here." Nick leaned against

the door. His presence brought relief to my exhausted soul.

"Yeah. I needed a little space." I covered my mouth. Tears poured down my face. He wrapped his arms around me, pulling me to him. He let me cry until I couldn't cry anymore.

"Ready to talk about it?" He placed both hands on either side of my face and wiped the tears from my cheeks with his thumbs. He found my forehead with one of the gentlest of kisses.

"I'm not ready." I shook my head. "I'm not ready to be queen. I don't know if I'll ever be ready for it. Who is going to follow someone who has never willingly followed the rules? And who is going to want peace with someone who's hunted and killed their kind? I don't even know why you would want to date someone who is known for her vampire-killing skill," I said, my voice trembled. "I'm no queen." Nick cradled me in his arms as he carried me to the couch. I nestled into his shoulder as he settled me in his lap and held me to his chest.

"Brie, your character is strong. You're honest and make no excuses for who you are. You're decisive but compassionate. You risked your life to save your brother. These are all traits of a good leader." He kissed the top of my head. "If you want to know why I would want to date you, it's because I love you. My love for you isn't something I can put into words. I don't believe there are words to do it justice, but I will try. For the first time since I became a vampire, I don't feel it is all I am. I feel alive again when

I'm with you. When I look at you, I don't see my girlfriend."

I looked down. My heart ached. I raised my head and looked into his eyes, waiting for the breakup talk.

"I see my future wife." He finished with a smile.

Wife? Warmth radiated through my entire body, and it wasn't from a surge of magical power. Words refused to form. I'd never considered being a wife. Joy sang in my heart at a future with Nick.

"I had planned to do this in a more romantic setting." He slid me off his lap into a standing position as he dropped to one knee. My heart flipped around my chest in an uneven cadence. I stared into his hypnotic green eyes. My legs were weak with nerves and my whole body trembled.

"Nick, we've only been reacquainted with each other a short time." My raspy tear laden voice was barely a whisper.

"For eight years, I wanted to find you again. There has never been another who has spoken directly to my soul before you. You've seen my past and are still by my side." The corners of his mouth turned up in a small smile without showing his teeth or fangs.

"Stand up, Nick," I said, fighting back the tears threatening the corners of my eyes. "The timing is not right for us." I paused at the hurt look on his face. Tears cascaded down my cheeks like slow-motion soldiers. Still holding his hand, I proceeded knowing I would never love another in this way. "I love you. I love you so much. I would give up everything for you, and we both know the danger in doing so. We've received several warnings about what the future will hold if we are together now. We can't ignore our destinies. This is the time for us to lead our people into a new era, and the signs say we must make the journey on our own."

My throat tightened as the magnitude of my words sank into my heart. I sacrificed my true love for the sake of peace for all races. It was my decision. My heart broke into a thousand pieces. Nick was crestfallen and jerked his hands away, turning his back to me. When I stepped in front of him, the killer of humans stood before me with his fangs bared. I didn't fear him, but I gave him distance.

"I need a minute, Brie." He said, putting his hand up between us like the invisible barrier I had earlier. I honored his request for a little time.

"Alright." I walked into the kitchen to grab the vodka from the freezer. I downed a shot. The clink of the shot glass on the counter parroted by the door, shutting quietly. He didn't want to hear anymore. Emptiness returned and took over inside me. I had no choice but to fight it. Losing him was not something I wanted to deal with ever, so I pushed it down deep inside. I closed my eyes, finding a dark place in my mind to hide it until I was ready.

Too much time had passed. I needed to return to the Great House. My new reality waited for me whether or not I was ready. I closed my eyes and thought of the library.

TWELVE

U nrest waited for me as I returned to the mansion. Sorin paced in the library with skin flushed, and the anger rolled off of him like an inferno. My exhaustion drew me to the couch, but my pride forced me to stand tall and face him as the queen I now was.

"What the hell were you thinking, Brie? I've had to make excuses for your absence. Do you have any idea how disrespectful it is to Cecily to disappear as you did?" Sorin whispered, gritting his teeth.

"I'm sorry for that. I did not intend to disrespect her. I needed a private moment before there were no more. I had to end it with Nick for his safety and for the future of our kind and the humans." The magic of my ancestors coursed through my veins and drew me to the right of succession ritual, but I had one last thing for Sorin. "You'll not question me after this. I'm your queen now."

It was an arrogant thing to say. I couldn't really say if it was because he was right about everything or because I didn't truly trust him. Either way, I wanted to shut the door on all my feelings, including those for my father.

"We must get to your ceremony. Then you will be expected to preside over Cecily's service in the coming days," he said, not making eye contact with me.

"Very good," I said, not wanting to continue the conversation.

Brandon waited in the hall for our entrance. The physical signs of his torture were gone, but I knew all too well the toll it took inside. I hugged him. He held on tight to me.

"I should kneel to you, My Queen," he whispered.

"Don't you dare," I whispered back. "I'll kick your ass if you do."

"I love you," he said.

"I love you too." Guilt laid in my gut. "I'm so sorry."

He released me and shook his head. "Let's get you crowned."

"You know there's no actual crown, right?"

He chuckled and took my arm.

I walked into the old Grand Ballroom with Brandon on my right and Sorin on my left. The pomp and circumstance surrounding the ceremony fit the regal like Cecily. The only light was from candles placed methodically around the room and ceremonial candles placed around a sphere-shaped perimeter. Power flowed as I stepped into the center. The circle was cast for the succession confirmation. It reached out to our ancestors by design for their blessing in the choice, but I already had their blessing.

Their life force flowed through me. I glowed as I stood in the middle of the circle. The shadows made me look like a sparkler that had just been lit. Wondering if anyone else could see it or if it was only for me, I looked around at wide-open mouths as if they had never seen the succession happen. Only the council and those they invited could attend, but this happened so fast that it was the council and my family, with few other witnesses. I looked for my grandmother, and she took in the sight with the same expression as the others. I would've thought she attended Cecily's, but maybe she wasn't as involved with the council then.

When the circle had been closed, two elders whisked me away to a private chamber with Sorin and my grandmother. They muttered in hushed tones among themselves for a few moments.

"Someone needs to tell me why you are whispering. I know I received the blessing. I can feel the magic of my ancestors flowing through me." They looked at each other, and the elders nodded to my grandmother. She took my hands in hers.

"Dear granddaughter, our new queen, you have been blessed unlike any queen in hundreds of years. Normally, the passing queen surrenders certain powers enhancing and complementing the new queen. For you, not only Cecily, but your ancestors, have empowered you." She paused, smiling at me but she had conflict in her eyes. "This confirms the signs we've seen building since your birth. Our ancestors have placed much at your feet, and the burden will be heavy. The vision we saw will come to pass, and your choices will be the deciding factor in the fate of all."

My lungs burned as all the air left them at the ultimate confirmation. I wanted to go to sleep for days and forget about it all, but as the new queen, I had to assure the council I would not fail.

"Thank you, Grandmother." I kissed her cheek before turning to face the small group. "Most of my life, I thought my purpose was to hunt vampires who prayed on humans. This week I have learned my purpose is much greater. It is my destiny to find a lasting peace between witches and vampires, transcending our races. I give you my word as Queen of the Witches to fight for peace while protecting humankind. We will not spill unnecessary blood, nor will any blood we spill be in vain." I looked each one of them in the eye. There I saw fear, but I saw faith too. "Do I have your loyalty?" There was no pause in the confirmations of loyalty, and I hoped they all spoke the truth.

"Blessed be." The council members exited the chamber, leaving Sorin and my grandmother with me.

"Sorin, if you don't mind, I would like to speak to Grandmother alone." I dismissed him, but he didn't move. He challenged me. *I see where I got my spirit.*

"I do mind, and you need me here," he said.

"He's right. His wisdom is valuable to you, especially now," Grandmother said, taking my arm and leading me to the couch. I practically fell into it from exhaustion, and I had little doubt it looked less than queenly. My body wanted to rest, and I suspected this was how it would be in the near future.

Sorin dutifully went through the expectations for the next week with regard to the ceremonies for Cecily's funeral. Once her funeral ceremonies were completed, there would be another ceremony for me which would lead to a formal party to celebrate my ascension to the throne. I had to declare my guardian officially, which Sorin wanted to claim for himself, but I needed to talk to Brandon about it first. Brandon made it clear he wanted it, and we had our twin bond. Even though I didn't want Brandon to take the position, I wouldn't deny him his right. Only if he could no longer fulfill his duties as guardian would I choose someone else, not sure Sorin would be the choice then either.

It was late by the time we finished, and the heaviness of fatigue labored my thoughts. I had every intention of teleporting home.

I stepped back to set my intention, but Sorin stopped me.

"Every time you travel, you are at risk. Now so more than ever. Teleporting into an area before your guards or guardian have checked for danger puts you at risk and is selfish and immature. You must envisage like a queen, Brie." His lecture made sense, and I looked at Grandmother, who nodded to me.

"I understand what you are saying," I said, too tired to argue anyway.

"We will send four guards home with you. Or do you feel the need for more?" His voice softened when I didn't argue the point. "The sooner your quarters are ready here, the better."

"Four will be fine." I touched his arm in gratitude as I answered, but I thought one would have been sufficient. I would never travel without guards again for the rest of my life. *Goodbye privacy.* The thought of living out the rest of my days in the Great House was pushed aside. That conversation would wait until after Cecily's funeral.

My small caravan arrived at the apartment building and took their places. I wanted sleep.

After trying to rest for several hours, I shuffled into my robe, needing some fresh air from the balcony to clear my head. I nodded to the two guards standing on the inside of the door. There was also one on the outside and one stationed in the lobby. Guards were master cloaking experts, so the untrained eye would never see them unless they wanted to be seen.

The night air was a source of cleansing and strength for me, and the cool air tonight was no exception. I gazed at the moon, willing it to fill the vacant space inside me. It infused me with the crispness of the night. I sank into the chase lounge and my mind played through the events of the day, eventually moving through the entire week.

A sigh escaped as my thoughts turned to Nick. This week had felt more like a year. I allowed myself to feel the love I had for him. I tried to process what my life would be like without him there. Weariness took over, and my mind was consumed with thoughts of making love with him.

Moments later, I was in dreamland with Nick, and my happiness was restored. Free from the burdens of my new life, the dream had taken me to his bedroom to lie beside him. He covered my face in gentle kisses before need gave way to our lips meeting, and the exploration began. We stayed entwined for what seemed like hours, and I was thankful to feel such paradise with him, even if I would only know it like this. As I lay in his arms afterward, I wished this was how it could be for us.

The warmth of morning sunlight relaxed me as lips brushed my neck, sending chills through my body. *Am I still dreaming?* "Hmm." Too well rested to still be asleep. I rolled on my back, stretching and wrapping my arms around Nick's neck. If dreams could feel this real, it might be my only escape in this lonely future.

"Good morning," he said, brushing our lips together. "I enjoyed the surprise last night. I was lost thinking I would never see you again." He smiled at me. "Can I make you some breakfast?"

"Breakfast? Oh shit! This isn't a dream! What time is it?" I rolled Nick over to look at the clock, and he positioned me on top of him. I let out a moan as I struggled to read the clock. *8:15! Shit!* My obligations were pulling at me, but I couldn't fight what was happening between us. I succumbed to the pleasure and enjoyed every inch of him.

)) ● ((

"YOU REALLY SHOULD LET me cook some breakfast for you before you go," he said while I secured my robe. Even after yesterday, he still wanted to take care of me. I kissed his cheek. He smiled at me, and I couldn't help but smile back.

I wasn't sure what would happen from here, but I had duties as the queen I couldn't devalue. The risks were so great, but I wouldn't stop looking for a way, even if it meant keeping my distance until I found it.

"I'm late already, Nick. You know the responsibility I have now. This will not look good," I said, giving him one more quick kiss before teleporting to my bedroom. I glimpsed a look on Nick's face I didn't recognize before I swirled away.

I thought for a moment my absence had gone unnoticed until I heard the frenzy going on in my living room. *Double shit!* Thankful I thought of my bedroom, I grabbed the first clothes I could find before joining Sorin and the rest.

"I'm here. You can calm down now." I walked in, staring straight at Sorin.

"Brie, did we not just discuss this last night? In your bedroom now. We need to speak in private." He commanded me to my face. My grandmother stood behind him with her forehead wrinkled and no sign of a smile. I straightened my back, making myself as tall as I could.

"No, you do not order me around like I am a child. The time for those sentiments has long been gone." I looked him directly in the eyes, lowering my voice to an authoritarian tone. "Everyone, please wait outside. My father, my grandmother, and I need privacy." I dismissed the guards and whoever else he had brought into my home.

By the time the room was clear, I was already calmer.

"Before you start, last night wasn't planned. I was exhausted, but I couldn't sleep, so I stepped out on the balcony to take in some night air. It's one of my techniques for relaxing. I laid down on one of the chaise lounges, and I teleported as I drifted off to sleep," I said, returning my voice to normal and remaining in complete control.

"The guards reported you gone hours ago. Why didn't you immediately teleport back?" Sorin asked.

"I thought I was dreaming." I glanced at my grand-mother. She tilted her head ever so slightly, letting me know she understood what I tried to avoid saying.

"Sorin, this is all new to Brie. Her world was thrown into a typhoon this week, and she has been left to sort through the debris. She's not the first queen to ascend the throne in such a short time, and it takes time to adjust," she said, stepping between me and Sorin. I sent a silent prayer of thanks to the higher power for giving me such a powerful force as my grandmother.

"Only a few have faced a task like hers, and no other had the destiny she has," he said, softening his voice for her. "Brie, please go shower and dress. You wreak of vampire. We have much to do today. Hopefully, the council will understand and not take this as an additional sign of disrespect for Cecily." His voice cracked on the name of my dead aunt.

"I'm sorry," I said, dropping onto the couch with a sigh. I didn't know what I was doing or why I was chosen. "How am I supposed to do this? How am I supposed to lead?" I looked at Sorin and Grandmother.

"It will not be easy, but you will be a great leader." Grandmother took my hand as she sat down beside me.

"Will I? I'm honestly not so sure. If I can't control my powers, then how can I lead my people?"

"Brie, you have always been so confident in who you are. What was the source of your confidence until now?" Grandmother asked.

"I'm good at hunting," I said without hesitation. "It's natural for me."

"Beyond that," she said. I thought about what she meant for a moment.

"It's within me. I've always been different, and I accepted it. I embraced it, knowing I was doing what I was meant to do." I relaxed, letting some of the tension go. Grandmother smiled. "I've been resisting my destiny and my new role. I need to embrace it." She squeezed my hand and her smile broadened to the special smile that can warm the heart of anyone.

"I can't apologize for putting so much pressure on you because I want you to succeed. I am sorry for not being here to prepare you for your tasks. I failed as a father, and I don't want to see you follow the same path I did. I want you to not only lead us to victory but to have love, happiness, and achievement." Sorin dropped to his knees, looking up at me, clasping my hand. "You're the hope for life. You must succeed."

Sorin had his own scars from his choices, but he cared.

"I'm going to need you by my side. Both of you," I said, not recognizing my voice. It wasn't the first time I sounded strong and confident, but it was the first time I believed it this week. "Brandon will remain as my Protector until he chooses not to be, but I want you two as my consiglieres. Can we make it work?" I paused for a moment. "Dad?" He jumped to his feet, wrapping his arms around me.

"Yes," he said. "Yes, we can."

"I am so proud of you." Grandmother hugged me.

THIRTEEN

Nick and I waited outside by the lake house for the eclipse to start. After a few months of sneaking around to see him, it should have been easier, but I hated lying to everyone about us. There wasn't a pull to the dark, and the more time passed, it convinced me this could work. I would not trade the time with Nick for any other. We were right together, regardless of what a prophecy said or what anyone else thought. This choice was ours, and I was still on the side of light.

"Let me show you something." I placed my hand on top of Nick's. I traced hearts in the sky, using our hands with the iridescent energy burning between us. It was one of my happy accidental discoveries of the bond between us. His eternal energy and my fiery energy made a beautiful glow in the air while we waited for the eclipse to start. There was power in it, too. We had both sensed it, but neither of us had broached the subject. He couldn't wield energy on his own, but I could for him using mine. It was a gift like no other.

The moon moved into position. Such a rare phenomenon was breathtaking. The total lunar eclipse turned the moon an orangish red.

A spasm of pain quivered out from my chest. I doubled over, racked with agony. Every bone in my body ached as if it broke and every muscle constricted. I stumbled away from Nick, but he caught me and righted me. His forehead wrinkled as he brushed my hair out of my face and looked over my body for wounds.

But there weren't any... at least on the outside. I didn't know what the pain meant, but I knew it wasn't good.

"What's wrong, Brie?" he asked.

"I need to get back to the Great House," I said. He moved to pick me up. "I should teleport." I tried to concentrate through the spasms and sharp cramps.

"You're not going without me." He swept me up in his arms while the air rushed around us.

Nick deposited me on the couch in the library, but the misery was almost unbearable. I writhed, unable to be still. Everything was muffled except the thunder rumbling and lightning striking on what was a clear night. I looked at Nick, understanding what the suffering was, but unable to speak. I could only see the horror and torment of my coven. Tears flowed down my face as I touched his. The pain eased. I closed my eyes and absorbed the gravity of what it meant.

When I reopened them, Nick held my gaze. Difficulty would constantly hamper our life from here on out. Our secret was no more, and I would have to step back from it to lead my people.

"I'm going to find Sorin," he said. I grabbed his hand.

"He'll be here shortly. He already knows we're here," I said, my voice rough and weak. My attention was drawn to the door. Brandon and Sorin entered together, almost on cue. Even through the residual pain, their bond still surprised me.

"What is he doing here, Brie? You know he shouldn't be here," Sorin said. I was glad Brandon was with him when he slid onto the couch next to me. My twin, my protector, buffered the strain between Sorin and me.

"For the first time in months, I can feel your pain, Sis. What is it?" he said, seeing my tear-stained face and narrowing his eyes at Nick. "Are you hurt?"

I looked from him to Sorin, then to Nick, taking his hand.

"It has begun. One hundred witches slaughtered tonight." The affliction eased as they crossed over one by one. Terrible and magical all at once, they appeared in an ethereal state. It was the most lucid vision I had experienced. Nick squeezed my hand tightly.

"Nick, you need to go. The council will not be tolerant of you being here, especially when they learn of this." Sorin said, without looking at him.

"I will stay. Brie is my soul, and I'll not leave her like this," Nick said, his deep melodic voice distracting me for a moment as he inched closer to me.

"We'll be here for her," Brandon said, placing a hand

on Nick's shoulder in a brotherly manner. I tilted my head, watching him.

"Nick, they are right. I should have teleported in here alone. I put you in danger, bringing you with me," I said. The coven would not be kind to him. In fact, my gut said they would be as brutal as what I witnessed in the vision. *He needs to go, and he needs to go now.*

"I didn't give you a choice. Did I?" He gave a soft smile. "And I'm staying by your side," he said, holding my hand as I stood. I had to get him out of here.

"Brie, we need to know what you know. What happened?" Sorin said, his voice as weary as mine.

"It was quick but felt endless. They were executed, and then their souls passed on almost like it was through me. The pain was excruciating. It was like someone turned me inside out and set me on fire over and over again. Their torment was mine." An image of the slaughter came to me. I gasped. Hot tears poured down my face, and I collapsed to the floor. No one could catch me this time, and my legs folded under me. In the puddle of tears on the hardwood floor, I saw the faces of those murdered. I saw the brutality of their deaths as the vampires dismembered them and set them on fire. My skin glowed as I absorbed the enormous loss to our coven. "Children. Some of them were only children." I cried out in horror, and a deafening clap of thunder shook the room.

"You need to relax and get control of the elements." Sorin paused, touching my hair. "And so we face your destiny, Brie. There will be many more until you lead us all to peace. These were brutal but quick deaths to get your attention. The next will be long tortured, and it will grow in a diabolical nature until they rule or there is peace," Sorin said.

"You could see the images?" I asked.

"Yes, we all could. You were projecting to us." He squeezed my shoulder. For a brief moment, he could be fatherly. Projecting was another rare gift given to me, as the ancestors put their faith in me. These gifts were substantial, but a peek into how to prevent this war would be better.

"Oh." I worked to regain my composure and considered it as a queen would. I cleared my throat and wiped away my tears, standing up on my own. "I don't want to fight death with death, especially since the vampires are technically already dead." I paused. "Sorry, Nick." He gave a single nod. "I need to meet with the Vampire King alone."

"Stefan would never take an audience with a witch," Sorin said.

"He's right" Nick paced back and forth. "I'll go with you."

An appearance in his father's court with me was a death sentence for him at worst and punishment in the form of years of torture at best. My heart pounded.

"Nick, then he will know you and I are together. Your life will be in danger," I said. "I need to go alone. It's me they want. He will take an audience with the Queen of the Witches." I considered entrance options, but only one would do. "Besides, if I teleport into his mansion, he will not have a choice."

"That's not a good idea," Brandon said. "Teleporting puts you at risk every time you do it, and it drains some of your energy, making you vulnerable. As your protector, I should go with you."

Teleportation got easier each time. It didn't weaken me much at all.

"You do all realize I could teleport out of here right now and end this argument, right? It is out of respect I am not." The door opened and distracted me. I sighed with relief when I saw Grandmother standing at the door. My relief was short-lived when I saw how white she was. I ran to her and hugged her. "You know?" I asked by her ear.

She nodded, and it was the first time I could remember her being speechless.

"Let's go sit down." I took her by the arm and led her to the couch.

"The time has come for you to lead, granddaughter," she said for only me. "This is not just any prophecy. This is the Blood Moon Prophecy. This lunar eclipse is the first in a series of four known as the Blood Moon Tetrad."

"I am ready now, Grandmother," I said, keeping my voice low. Nick's vampire hearing probably picked up the conversation, but the others wouldn't. Not that I cared if they heard, but this was for Grandmother. She squeezed my hand, and I saw the tears in her eyes. These were people she had known all of her life, and children she had watched grow. Her face looked older today, with wrinkles from the pain. I stood to draw everyone's attention. "I am going to see Stefan, and we can discuss how it will happen. You all need to accept right now that I'm the queen, and this is my job. I'll not sit back and let others die in my name."

"Then we need to talk about the prophecy and will need a strategy," Sorin said.

"Nick, I can't ask you to raise a hand to your people. Leave us so you will not have to lie." I took his hands and met his eyes for our special connection. I needed him to know I wasn't sending him away, but I was giving him a way out if he needed it.

He narrowed his eyes like he tried to bore through me.

"Brie, you're my people now. For the last time, I am staying by your side." *How could I deny him when he'd already risked so much to be by my side? How could I tell him no when I knew I'd do the same?* There wasn't any going back for me or for him.

"Let's get to it." Sorin pulled maps and books out onto the large table. "The Blood Moon Prophecy can only end in two ways. Peace or the End Times." I nearly gagged on the words as they left Sorin's mouth. A brief gust of wind caused branches to brush against the window. It was the only outward sign of my emotion.

Everyone pitched their own strategies over the course of a couple of hours. None of us could agree on the next steps. The frustration built in me to the point I wanted to explode. A lightning strike outside the window warned me to reign in my emotions. I closed my eyes and counted silently from twenty until I was composed again. When I reopened them, everyone stared at me.

"We need surprise on our side, and the longer we wait, the less likely we are to surprise them. I appreciate all your input, but I have made my decision." I paused. "I will tele-port into the mansion on my own." Everyone belabored their version of safe options, but that kind of option wasn't reality.

"You can't, Brie," Sorin said. "If you die, there is no succession plan, and the End Times will be upon us. The vampires knew we were in transition, and this was the time to attack us. You need guardians with you at all times."

"Your father is right," Grandmother said.

"I agree," Brandon said. His aura reached out to mine. He tried to read my emotions, but mine pushed back. I'd never not let him in, and I didn't consciously do it this time.

"I must agree as well," Nick said.

"Are you all wanting to go? You think we should all go together?" I dropped my head and pinched the top of my nose. When I looked up again, everyone looked at me as if the decision was made. "I don't for one second think it's a good idea."

A strange sensation came over me, as if I was light-headed and about to pass out, but I was coherent and aware. Drawn to the window, I walked over and observed the massive blood-red moon in full glory staring back at me. It looked as though it paid homage to those we lost tonight. The power it exuded drew me in. It appeared to pulsate with the blood of our coven. Entranced, I reached my hand in the air to touch the enormous moon, and I glimpsed it ripple. Someone pulled my hand down. *Sorin.* With my fist firmly in his grasp, he turned me around. I saw a peculiar look on each of their faces, and I looked from my wrist to Sorin's face to see the same look on his.

"Did you not hear us calling your name?" he asked in a forceful tone.

"No," I said. A weak voice was all I could muster.

"Brandon, there is a mirror in the middle drawer of the desk. Can you bring it here?" Sorin said, without looking away from me or letting go of my wrist. "Look at your shoulder," he said. Brandon put the mirror in my free hand. I first looked at my right shoulder and saw nothing. When I looked at my left shoulder, I gasped. There was a symbol I had never seen before tattooed on my arm. An open heart with the Celtic Triquetra symbol in the center marked my skin with four blood-red moons almost dripping from it. An old Celtic sword pierced them all with ornate feathery scrollwork winding through the entire thing. Overcome with the beauty of it, I also sensed the pain it foretold.

FOURTEEN

"Even more than you realize, you have been chosen for this destiny." Grandmother ran her hand over the fresh tattoo. I shivered. "Does it hurt?" She looked confused.

Everything else disappeared for a moment. "Hurt? No, but it is sensitive. Vibrations waved through my body when you touched it. It's like reverberation from loud music or sounds," I said.

"No witch has been marked like this in centuries," Sorin said. "The Queens of old were the best of the vampire huntresses, and they were the only ones known to have carried this mark." Sorin turned to my boyfriend. "I'm not sure it's safe for you here, Nick. The vampire huntresses who wore the mark took a blood oath to protect their people against all vampires."

Nick walked to me without hesitation and took my hand.

"For the final time, I am not leaving Brie's side," he

said, followed by a low feral growl. As far as I could tell, no one heard it but me. I squeezed his hand and drew his attention.

"It is your choice, Nick, but I know it will not be easy for you. The consequences will be great, and you will face them a lot longer than our lives will last. We are all concerned about what it means for you. Your own people will ostracize you, and you'll be hunted to the end of your days." And my path required me to be careful with my choices. I'd have to walk a narrow line until death claims me to keep from going dark.

His eyes softened into a smile. The special smile he had for me melted the tough exterior I tried to display. Anything I said to dissuade him would be wasted.

"How wise you have become in such a short time." He caressed my cheek. "I will not fight against you. I would trade my immortality to spend one day with you. I am in love with you, and I would not exist away from you," he said. "When your life ends, then so shall mine." He brushed his lips across my cheek in a feathery kiss.

Love. He took all the broken pieces of my heart and put them back together like decoupage, making them beautiful and new again. For the first time, I understood how deep his commitment was to me.

"If you're going to meet with Stefan, we need to cover your new beauty mark. He knows witch history and will likely recognize it," Nick said. "Do you have some makeup in your purse?"

"Who needs makeup?" I skimmed my hand over my

arm without touching the tattoo. The tattoo disappeared, only to reappear moments later. "What the--"

"Brie, the mark of the huntress can't be hidden by magic. It is a mark of honor," Grandmother said.

"You should leave it uncovered as a show of power," Brandon said. "They will know you are strong and blessed by a power they cannot imagine."

"I agree with Brandon. If you are going in without an army, you need to show you're not weak." Sorin said.

"I don't think it's a good idea to go in basically baring your soul," Nick squeezed my hand so hard it was painful. "Stefan does not like to be challenged, and I've watched him end those who dared to. If you teleport in with an ancient huntress mark on your arm, he could take it as a declaration of war before you even get the chance to speak."

"Nick, you make a good point," Grandmother nodded her head. "I think he is right."

I looked around the room at each one of them with their voices swimming in my head. Overwhelmed by their emotions, I took a step back, with my head spinning. They all rushed to me.

"Stop!" I spread my arms out wide and silence washed over the room. For a quick second, I thought I had teleported to a peaceful place, but I was still in the library. No one was moving. I touch Nick's cheek and nothing. I grabbed Grandmother's hand, and it was warm and soft. "Grandmother?" I said. There was no response. Desperation and panic churned around me. *What have I done?* I'd frozen them in time. *But how?*

And how was I to undo it? Maybe I didn't do it. Was it a sign that I should go it alone to the castle? Thoughts flowed randomly through my head. Maybe the opposite word would free them.

"Go," I shouted. Nothing. It echoed back to me, like someone or something compelling me to carry on. "I'm sorry. I hope doing this will release you."

Not knowing how long I had, I ran to the rooms being remodeled for me and put on a jacket that concealed my new tattoo. The guards placed along the way were preserved in time. Time stopped for the entire Great House. Maybe it had frozen for the entire city, including the Vampire King. I went over the map of the castle and planned my strategy. Teleporting to the room Brandon was kept in seemed like the best option. I figured it wouldn't be used that often. My mind was made up, and I made sure I had a few tricks up my sleeves for the Vampire King. I would show him just how powerful this witch was if he wanted a fight.

A sickening taste of dread washed over me, and I regretted teleporting into the castle alone. Not one vampire was frozen in time, and I had to take pains to avoid them. I could've popped back over to the Great House, but I wanted Stefano to know what was coming for him. This was the moment. He would meet a sinner, not a saint, today. The bile rose in my throat and only got worse as I made my way through the mansion. It reminded me of what the hunt was like in the beginning. A terrifying thrill and nothing else could touch the adrenaline rush until today.

The main room was empty when I reach it. The location would have been a throne room originally in castles, but they had redecorated this one more like an office. A large office. There were no less than three sitting areas and a desk larger than the President's. When I was certain there was no one in the room, I walked toward the desk. A rodent scratching noise came from behind me and stopped me halfway. I spun on my heels. Older vampires were known to disguise their sneak attacks to sound like animals. The tingling sensation on my neck gave him away, and I turned back toward the desk to face him.

"Are you Stefan?" I regarded him and touched my heirloom necklace, confirming the vial of Vampire Death was concealed in its place. The killer in front of me had the foul rotten smell of a vampire, unlike the sweet vanilla of rich whiskey scent Nick had.

This vampire was head and shoulders taller than me. His blue eyes twinkled. He laughed in response. A sharp pain shot through my head, and I fell to the ground. His laughter cut off.

My head throbbed. I tried to force my heavy eyelids open. I found myself in an uncomfortable position, and the more I struggled, the worse it felt. My eyes fought against me, but they eventually opened. The contraption binding me was chosen deliberately. I saw red with anger, causing the wind to howl outside. *A damn medieval stockade.* He had me placed in the device to add insult to my capture. Vampires compelled humans to torture witches during the Salem Witch Trials, and they took great pleasure in seeing the witches humiliated. It was one of the few times in our history the vampires were able to gain the upper hand.

"Oh, she is awake, sire." I heard a vampire speak, and I immediately tensed up. *Sire? That's as medieval as this stockade. What a pompous freaking ass.*

"Miss Danforth, please excuse these crude accommodations, but we cannot risk you casting spells or attacking us." The tall blond vampire with Nordic good looks spoke. He looked me up and down with his arms crossed over his chest.

"Something tells me you knew exactly what you were doing, locking me up in these, and you better be thankful you did," I said. I didn't technically need my hands to control the elements, but better if he thought I did. "Just who are you?"

"My name has no doubt crossed your lips many times. I am Stefan, the King of the Vampires," he said. "I have been looking for you for a long time." He softened his words.

"Why would you be interested in me?" I asked to see what he divulged.

"Because you will lead us to victory," Stefan said in an animated tone.

"I'm a witch. How would I lead vampires to victory?" I tried to distract him while I worked on unlocking the mechanism unnoticed. There were some huntress skills I would consider priceless, and lock picking was one of them. He wasn't close enough to use the Vampire Death on, but I'd call every element at once to end him if needed.

"I'm going to turn you and make you my bride, of course."

Mother fucker.

He revealed his goal in a confident tone as if I should have known his damn plan. I hadn't seen this sick twist, and I gasped at his honesty and my stupidity. I walked right into his trap.

"Fuck you." The rebel in me seized that moment to surface, and I would do it again regardless of the outcome to see the look on his face. It was pure rage.

The back of his hand collided with my cheek, and blood trickled from my mouth. Teleporting to safety was an option once my hands were free, but it could be my only chance to get information from him. I tasted the salty blood in my mouth and felt a small drip from the corner. When he came closer, I didn't feel the same sense of warmth I felt when Nick was near me. My stomach rolled as he licked blood from my face.

"Cecily would never have spoken to me with such insolence," he said, with our faces too close for comfort. His eyes twinkled and danced with the wicked evil inside him. The mention of my aunt's name pissed me off, but I decided this must be part of his game.

"As if you know my aunt." My cheek swelled. The skin stretched tight.

"Oh, I knew her well, Brielle. I was not only her confidant but her lover, which is how I know all about you." He clutched my chin. His wicked grin sent chills down my spine. *What the fuck!* I refused to believe Cecily would've ever betrayed her people with him. If she screwed him, there was a higher purpose. My emotions were too high to get a read from my internal lie detector, so I had no choice but to trust my gut that he made it up. "And what do you think of my son, Prince Nicholas?" I assumed he was trying to shock me again, but I already had the information he tried to offer. I played along.

"What do you mean, your son?" I feigned my surprise.

"He hasn't told you? You must be quite the morsel, because he was expected to deliver you to me and instead has kept you to himself. I'll have to break you properly to the ways of the vampire world. Before long, your huntress ways will be forgotten." He laughed, a wicked, malicious sound.

What a bastard this evil shell of a former human was. I didn't believe Nick was supposed to deliver me to him, and even if he was, he had chosen not to do it. I regretted not accepting Nick's proposal earlier. I would have married him on the spot. More than anything, I wanted to get back to the haven of his arms, so I pushed all the thoughts from my head save the means to kill Stefan. I ran through several scenarios quickly, but I felt something pierce my neck before I could execute any of them. I twisted to see what it could be. At first, I thought it was a vampire bite, but there was only one stick and darkness followed.

When I came to, I found myself alone and bound to a bed by heavy chains. *Son of a bitch*. Memories flood back from eight years ago, and it wasn't the good ones. The room was pitch black, and I couldn't get my hands together to make an energy ball. The chains were so heavy

I could barely lift an arm. Sharp razor-like pain radiated from my wrist as I tried to raise my hand. I couldn't teleport without my hands. Blood trickled down my arm, and I winced as the teeth on the inside of the cuff dug deeper. A tear ran down my cheek. I whispered. "Light." I didn't even hide my surprise to see Stefan seated in the chair next to the table, holding the only small light in the room.

"Your power is even more impressive than I expected." He nodded in my direction and in the blink of an eye was on the bed in front of me. He held my bleeding wrist in his large vampire hand. He was taller than Nick, and the menacing look on his face didn't resemble any form of humanity. Darkness filled his eyes in a way I had never seen. He searched for something in me. Fear perhaps, but I wouldn't let him see it. I buried it deep within me. He pulled my wrist towards his mouth, never taking his eyes off of me. The cuff dug deeper, spilling more of my blood. Sorin said it was forbidden for Nick to drink from me, but I didn't know the exact reason. Stefan surprised me when he cast my wrist away and leapt from the bed instead of lapping up the blood running steadily down my arm.

"What will happen if I drink your blood, witch? I know what will happen if you drink mine." He laughed and walked casually to the bed. His finger ran through the blood and up my arm, past my neck. He stopped on my lower lip. At unnatural speed, he grabbed my jaw and squeezed. "I could turn you right now." The pain brought me back to my senses even as another tear rolled down my face. I pushed my current status of queen out of my mind and thought of my huntress tactics. This wasn't the first time I had to face a vampire, and I let my training take over.

My clothes had been changed and all of my weapons taken. I looked around for anything to use, but this room had been prepared for me. There was little that could be used and nothing within reach. Stefan's hand went up my other arm. It froze as soon as he touched my new tattoo. He pushed me backward on the bed and pounced on top of me, pinning me down with such force I lost my breath. The razor cuffs dug in, and I winced.

"I killed many who wore this mark. I didn't know the coven still used it," he said, his words a hiss. He put us face to face before licking my neck. He raised my arm off the bed, letting the blood run down. I grimaced against the pain, refusing to cry out or use my powers to take it away. He started with his tongue on my shoulder and tasted the blood up to my elbow. When he stopped there, he studied me. "Your blood tastes different, Brielle. It's quite exceptional and almost familiar."

I found the comment strange and unnerving.

"I want more, but I am afraid I will drain you dry. You're much too important for me to ruin you before I claim you."

Hell's Fire flashed in his eyes. "They'll be in to prepare you shortly." He left before I could ask questions. My wrists were in enough pain I wanted to cast to numb them, but I wanted to feel every moment when I killed the Vampire King.

FIFTEEN

Five young women who could not be older than eighteen or nineteen entered the room to dress me. It shocked me and made me nauseous. They were not vampires, but they were shells of humans. There was no spark in their eyes. None at all. Wearing black wrap dresses hitting just above the knee, they moved like robots, obviously under Stefan's control. Although not identical, they bore a striking resemblance to each other, with long, dark hair and pale skin.

They brought in a wedding dress, and it was not unlike one I would have chosen for myself. It was a simple lace fit and flare with an open back and buttons all the way down. I daydreamed for a moment about wearing a dress like this to meet Nick at the end of the aisle and becoming his wife. One of my hands was freed.

A vial of blood being held in front of my face by one of the girls was a harsh reminder of the reality. This is how he was controlling them, and he wanted me easily controlled for the wedding. Vampire blood didn't always have the same effect on witches as humans. Looking at his blood confirmed for me I had to kill Stefan right away.

"You can take the vial back to your master and tell him I said he can stick it up his-" I stopped when I saw the fear in her eyes and the way she trembled. He controlled them, but they were alert and not as robotic as they appeared at first. He had struck fear deep in them. "Will he punish you if I don't drink it?" She nodded, too afraid to verbally confirm he would.

"He wants you healed for the ceremony," the young girl whispered. Healed and controlled. My first thought was to pour it out. I didn't need his blood to heal, but I would heal faster with vampire blood. I touched the young woman's cheek and saw a glimpse of an innocent girl in her. I had no desire to drink vampire blood, but I couldn't let this innocent suffer at my hands.

The vial in my hand, my lips curled up as I held it close to my mouth. Repulsed and afraid I would gag, I pinched my nose, drinking it like a shot. I handed the vial back and looked for a way to spit it out, but they were watching me.

Goddess, damn it.

They waited.

Some of it slid down my throat. It had no resemblance to the vodka I was accustomed to drinking. I could feel the thick blood everywhere it touched. It coated my tongue and my throat and warmed each spot it passed over, which was odd given how cold the creatures were. His blood snaked through my body. Nausea clenched my stomach. It wasn't normal. Their blood should induce euphoria.

Dizziness forced me to lean on the bed for support. I coughed, splattering blood in a fan pattern out across the white cover. The girls drew in sharp breaths, and I could feel how nervous they all became instantly. They all took giant steps, backing away from me. Did he poison me? It didn't make sense for him to poison me, given his plans. If he put his venom in the blood, then I likely wouldn't survive the change with this reaction. My body writhed, and I couldn't hold myself up any longer. I hit the floor with a thud. The arm still cuffed stretched across the bed. My body convulsed, and I struck my head on the nightstand. I saw stars all around me.

It seemed like only seconds had passed, and I was at the lake house with Nick. The full moon was straight up, nearly blocking out the starry night sky. We were seated out by the firepit and could feel the warmth. I looked into his eyes and watched the smile on his face broaden as the corner of his eyes turned up to match. "I love you, Brie." I smiled back at him. Something pinched my arm where my tattoo was. When I touched it, my hand blood covered my hand. I looked up to see the faces of those lost in the red moon, and their blood dripped onto us. It came down heavier. I screamed and wanted to take cover, but my body wouldn't move. Nick refused to leave me, even though the blood drove him crazy. His eyes were wide and his body jerked.

"Nick?" I said, focused on the form I saw through blurred vision and a throbbing head. I tried to sit up, but the pain in my head pushed me back down. I tried to locate the source, but I couldn't quite figure it out. There were no longer chains on my wrists. I was still alive and not a vampire, and I was still in the vampire castle. I could tell by the darkness and the stench of death always in the air. The dream with Nick was just a dream, and I had to free myself.

"No, but Stefan will need him here before the wedding." The vampire's voice was full of hatred. "You are a beauty. I can see why father and Nick are so taken with you. There is something unique about you. It would be fun taming you to my needs." I shuddered. As he leaned in closer, the words registered with me. The hateful vampire was Nick's elder brother, Gaius. Stories of his torment were as regular as the sun rises, but they didn't do justice to experiencing it. He enjoyed feeding on and killing witches for sport much more than he enjoyed humans, and I suffered my share of beatings in his captivity. *Thank the Goddess Nick got me out of here.* The coven spoke of his ways of control, which were, from all accounts, stronger than even Stefan's. He didn't seem to remember me or Nick setting me free.

I was in dangerous territory with him. Stefan had plans, but Gaius was about inflicting pain, and cowering to his father's wishes wasn't his style. With my hands free, I thought about teleporting, but I wanted a shot at Stefan first. If I left now, I might never get this close again. I wasn't anywhere near strong enough for a fight, but I had to at least try if it could prevent the war.

Nick, please forgive me, and know I love you. I didn't come here to die, but I am prepared to do so. I wish I had married you the day you asked, but in my heart, I am already married to you. I finished my inner discourse knowing Nick would never hear it, but I needed to put it out in the universe for hope. I slid my hands behind my back as I prepared for battle with myself as the only weapon.

"I must go prepare for your wedding," Gaius said and walked out the door. I sat in shock. He didn't touch me. I guessed he must have really feared Stefan to not even lay a finger on me. As soon as he left, I jumped into action. *Cloak.* It took a lot of concentration to maintain the simple act in my weakened state.

No guards? This wreaked of a trap, but I was blessed for a reason. Even with my energy down, I was stronger than most.

I made my way through the castle once again and more than anything I wanted out of there and back in Nick's arms. If I ended Stefan tonight, we could have a lifetime together. I stopped to sense where Stefan was. His trail led me to the throne room. He was alone with his back to the door. I uncloaked as I walked into the room. I wanted him to know the huntress who had come for him.

"Brielle, you found me." He turned to face me with a smile on his face and gestured to the chair across from him. "I'm glad you have recovered. We have much to discuss before the wedding. I have summoned Nick to join us." Nick's name from Stefan's mouth made me want to vomit. I couldn't stop a sire's summons. Nick wouldn't have a choice.

"Stefan, we need to find peace for our people." He

wasn't the kind of person you reasoned with, but I hoped I was buying time and not giving away my ultimate goal. I sent up a prayer for the gifts I had to reach through into his evil mind. Not all prayers are answered.

"And so we shall once you have been turned," he said, smiling again.

I tried to gauge an opportunity to end him. I decided we were alone enough that I could take the chance. I took a step toward the sword hanging on the wall when I heard a scuffle come from the other side of the door. The door flung open, and I nearly erupted into tears at the sight of Nick. Sorin and Brandon took a place on either side of him. The three men in my life unified for a cause. It would have made me happy in another situation, but here, I only wanted to get them out in one piece.

"Brie, has he harmed you?" Nick's eyes were the pure fire and rage of a killer as he looked me over from where he stood. My body ached for him being so close, yet unable to touch him for comfort. I wanted to run to him and wrap my arms around his neck, but Stefan stood between us, facing Nick. I took a deep breath and went for the sword, praying it was sharp enough to sever Stefan's head from his miserable body. I forced myself into a run and leap move. Stefan beat me to it, standing in front of the sword. I cursed his vampire speed. He gracefully reached his arm up and back to grasp it. I dove as he swung it at me. Stefan was skilled in handling the sword and moved like he had fought many battles with it. He wouldn't risk killing me before he got what he wanted, but I feared for those here to save me.

"Let's go!" I ran towards my family with my arms outstretched, having every intention of teleporting out of there.

"You can't take us all. You are too weak." Sorin kept his voice low as I got closer. I tried anyway and failed.

"We will fight," I said.

Stefan's Royal Guard arrived almost on cue. Brandon went for a foot sweep. Stefan jumped it like a rope and landed a kick in Brandon's chest, sending him into the guard. Nick landed a blow in Stefan's chest. Sorin ran at him, but Stefan ducked out of the way. The guards circled us.

"Let them take us. I have another way out," Nick said, in a voice low enough only we could hear. They backed us into a corner, and in no position to argue, surrender was our only option.

"Take them to the cells," Stefan said.

The guards shackled each of us to the wall, and relief washed over me seeing these didn't have the teeth piercing the wrist. It was a minor comfort to know they didn't plan on draining us. These were designed to hold the worthiest of opponents. I guess it should have been flattering he thought so highly of us, but it pissed me off how he anticipated every move we could make. As a huntress, I was nimble, patient, and strong, but as a queen, I felt weak and impetuous.

"Cast a healing spell on yourself, Brie," Sorin said through gritted teeth as soon as we were alone.

"I'm not sure I can yet." The pain of a bruised rib and my head still throbbing. "Is anyone badly injured?" I asked, looking them all over. The guys all shook their heads no. Nick didn't meet my eyes.

"How are you, Brie?" he asked. "What did he do to you?" I couldn't tell if he was angrier at me or at Stefan.

"I'm fine, Nick." I wanted so badly to grab him by the chin and force him to look at me, and I wanted to caress his face more. Tears at the corners of my eyes threatened to fall, and I swallowed hard.

"Tell me what he did," Nick said in a deep, commanding voice.

I recounted my experience to him, and his jaw tighten when I told him about Stefan licking the blood from my arm and the impossible situation leading me to drink his blood. He wore all the rage on his face. His jaw was tight, and he ground his teeth.

"You couldn't drink his blood?" Sorin studied me.

"Well, technically, I drank it. It just wouldn't stay down. It was like food poisoning." I wondered why he cared so much about this one little detail. He didn't turn me. I'm not even sure if he could after the reaction I had.

"You have another vampire's blood coursing through your veins," he said. His eyes focused on Nick like a laser, and Brandon followed suit.

"It's not his fault, Sorin. I performed a new lovers' prayer and mingled our blood." They both finally looked at me, and Brandon raised his eyebrow. I was about to roll my eyes at them when Nick made a grunting noise. He pulled his shackles out of the wall like they were paper mâché, leaving dust and debris in the air. It covered all of us in a layer as it settled. He broke the shackles from his arms. I gaped at his strength.

"We'll not have much time before they realize what is happening," he said, breaking my bonds before moving to Brandon and Sorin. Sorin punched him in the face as soon as he was free.

"How dare you touch Brie!" Sorin said. His actions set me into a rage and Nick only hung his head. I moved between them, pushing them apart with my hands.

"Newsflash, Sorin. I wasn't exactly a virgin."

His eyes flashed.

"Let's just teleport out of here. Screw Stefan and screw if he knows about my powers. My gut says he knows more than we're giving him credit for, anyway. Take my hands." I glanced at everyone.

"I'm not going," Nick said. His voice was so quiet. It meant trouble. I only saw him then. "I can't let Stefan get away with what he has done to you. Having tasted your blood, he will be able to sense you and will chase you to the ends of the earth."

"Hey, I'm a witch. Remember? Spells and stuff?" I put my hands on either side of his face. He put his hands on my wrists and leaned down, placing one of his feather-light kisses on my lips. He gently pulled my hands away. I could see the conviction in his eyes.

"I love you," he said, squeezing my hands.

"I love you." I squeezed his back. I'd tried my way and failed. It was his turn, and I didn't have a valid argument to stop him.

"Get them to safety. I'll find you when I am done."

I nodded to him, knowing full well I had no intention of letting him do this alone. As soon as he crossed the doorway, I grabbed a hold of Sorin and Brandon, and I teleported us back to the library at the mansion. The surprised look on their faces when I jumped away from them to teleport would have been funny in any other circumstance.

When I teleported back, Nick scooted to the front of my mind, which put me directly between him and Stefan in the throne room. *Stefan must really like this damn room.*

Exhaustion pained my body, but I still had a monumental task ahead of me. It took only seconds to realize they hadn't touched each other yet, but it was immanent by the low feral growls coming from both of them.

"My own son would dare betray me!" Stefan said, growling at Nick. The evil dripping from his words made my skin crawl. He eyed me with even more interest now, with the knowledge I could teleport. *So he didn't know.*

"I could say the same about you, father," Nick said, his voice low and not melodic. Chills ran up my spine. He tucked me behind him with one hand, and I squeezed it to let him know I was fine.

"I am a powerful witch." I reminded him in a whisper. He didn't acknowledge me except to squeeze back.

"You would choose this witch over your family?" Stefan took one small step toward us. "You were always weak, Nick. I should have known you would not fulfill your chosen path."

What path? Is he talking about the vision?

"Make no mistake. Brie is my destiny. I will marry her

one day, and I will always choose her first. She will never be yours."

"You are a fool" Stefan lunged at Nick.

The scuffle shoved me aside and knocked the wind out of me. I gasped for air.

Stefan had a wooden stake in one hand. He stabbed at Nick, but Nick was quick enough Stefan only grazed his shoulder. I dove at Stefan, but he leaned out of the way. Nick slammed into Stefan's chest with both hands, sending him hard into the wall and the stake flying. The stone wall cracked at the impact. Nick caught the stake and pinned Stefan with the wood weapon positioned over his heart.

I could see the anguish on Nick's face. Despite the horrible being Stefan was, he'd been Nick's father for the last two hundred and fifty years.

"I can't do it," Nick said, not taking his eyes away from Stefan. Stefan only laughed.

I squeezed Nick's shoulder, and we teleported back to the mansion.

SIXTEEN

W hen we arrived safely in the library, I started trembling uncontrollably. Nick wrapped his arms around me, holding me against him. He kissed the top of my head as we sank to the floor. I let out a single sob, releasing some of the tension.

"Sshhh. You are safe now," he said.

"You scared me, Nick." He tensed. "I thought I was going to lose you. I'm not sure I could face a world without you."

He relaxed then and pulled back a little. His lips pressed hard against mine. He was full of passion, and my lips swelled when he broke away. I stared up into his eyes. Our special connection consumed me for a moment.

"You, Brie. It is only you. You are my life forever."

My tears fell with abandon. What is our forever? A vampire and a witch? Can there be a forever?

"It is only you for me, too. My heart is full of the love I have for you, and it would shatter me to be without you." I touched his face and relished the look in his eyes of complete adoration. Our declaration could have been marriage vows. Any reservations or walls I had up were gone after facing the possibility he could die.

Sorin cleared his throat as if he had done it a few times, and I was acutely aware of everyone in the room with us. I looked at the faces of my father, mother, brother, and grandmother. *This is going to be a shit show.*

"Sorin, I know you want to go through the events and strategy now, but right now I need to heal Nick and clean up. I'm sorry, everyone, but we need a few minutes to ourselves." I grabbed Nick's hand. I led him to my newly remodeled quarters at the mansion. I refused to move in like the elders. They tried to reason with me that no queen had taken residence outside of the mansion during their reign. I didn't care. I wanted some sense of normalcy, so my compromise was to have quarters at the mansion and retain my condo. I could not deny the convenience of the new quarters as we rushed to it, holding hands.

Nick slammed the door shut and pushed me against the wall. He claimed my mouth. We were both on a high from the events of the day, and I wanted him with every part of my body. My mind, though, wandered back to the altercation between Stefan and Nick.

"What's wrong?" Nick asked, his voice concerned.

"How were you able to best Stefan today? Younger vampires don't usually overpower their makers?"

He led me to the bedroom and sat down on the bed, pulling me into his lap.

"I'm not the average vampire."

Um..no kidding.

"I have always been stronger than the other vampires. Stefan knows this, and he doesn't have a death wish no matter how consumed he is with power. Are you disappointed you are not the only special one in this room?" He smiled at me.

I shook my head. He looked down at my hand and idly played with my fingers. I waited for him to continue.

"It comes at a cost. My bloodlust is worse than others, and the memories you saw of mine were only a few of the innocents who died at my hands." The sadness in his voice wrenched deep in me. "Your blood is calling me right now. The scent is a sweet mixture luring me to you."

I swallowed hard at his revelation. "Has it always been like this?"

"Yes."

I wasn't sure how to react to his confession, but he had certainly had many opportunities to drink my blood had he chosen not to.

"How do you control it?"

"I am a vampire, Brie. I drink animal blood and bags from blood banks when I can, but there are times when I must have human blood." The disgust in his voice made me regret asking the question. He didn't savor the power like most vampires, which might be why he was given the strength he had. The night in the alley, he drank from a human. I saw him wipe it away.

"Is this about my blood, or do you care about me?" I voiced my fears, making myself vulnerable in a new way.

He closed his eyes for a moment. When he opened them, I saw hurt in his eyes. Hurt I put there with my question.

"Brie, I was thirty years old when Stefan turned me. I lived a human life until then. My family was murdered for our kingdom, but I was away on peace talks. Being the only surviving heir, I should have been focused on restoring my family to the throne, but Stefan offered me a way to avenge their deaths. My family lives only with me now because of my choice." He looked away.

"I lost my humanity for so long, giving into vengeance readily. Stefan used my strength to gain control and eventually become the vampire king. When I realized he had exploited me, I felt guilt for my actions, and I started finding pieces of my humanity that had long been buried. When I saw you the first time, I felt human again. Desire. Love. Compassion. Hope. I wanted something again. They were strong and carried a power all their own. My humanity had finally returned in full, so you saved me. When I say you are my soul, it is the truth." He searched my eyes. "In answer to your question, I love you. I want to marry you." He kissed my forehead.

"I love you." I raised my lips to his.

"Marry me, Brie." It was a statement in his breath as it caressed my lips. Not a question, but it still needed an answer.

The pain of my silence was on his face as he waited for me to say something. No one who would ever reach through my walls to my heart the way he had. The love I had for him pulsed through my body as sure as my own blood. I remembered his words when he said his time would end when mine would. Tears pooled in my eyes at his total commitment to me, but he looked away, tears gathering in his own eyes. It had to be worry. Worry I would reject him again.

"Yes," I whispered. His eyes closed, and he let out a soft breath before looking at me. The corners of his eyes moistened. "Yes," I raised my voice.

He kissed me with a feather-light brush of his lips before pushing me back on the bed to express his love another way.

As we lay entwined and exposed, I smiled at the thought of being his wife. I daydreamed about the lake house, and what our life would be like there.

"Hey, beautiful," he said, tilting my head towards him and kissing my forehead.

"We're going to be in trouble. Sorin already treats me like a petulant teenager." I ran my hand across his chest. "We better get cleaned up and back to the others. We are going to need to get our strategy down. I'm sure Stefan will not delay long with his next attack."

Nick nodded. "Shower?"

"Together? Absolutely."

We were both silent, absorbed in thought, as we left my room and walked down the hall. I pondered our future as I walked, but I wanted to ask Nick where his thoughts were. He slowed his pace, placing a finger over his lips.

"There are others in the library besides your family," Nick said, being cautious as we approached the door. "Maybe I should go? I want to stay, but not if your loyalty will be questioned."

My loyalty would be questioned, regardless. I laced my fingers through his and gripped his hand. I had not only accepted my destiny, but I figured out what needed to happen to fulfill it. I smiled at him. He returned it with a hint of confusion at the corner of his eyes.

"We do this together," I said. We passed through the doorway hand-in-hand. Silence fell over the room, and looks of horror and shock focused on us. The elders studied us without saying a word, passing judgment with their condescending looks. Thunder rumbled from anger, and I took a deep breath to calm myself down.

I laid out my plans for my family and the elders. Nick remained silent through all their objections. Even when one said he should be staked through the heart with the rest of the vampires, he barely raised an eyebrow. He focused on me, and let me fulfill my role, which was more than could be said of Sorin. I was so frustrated with him at one point I was about to ask him to leave when I looked at Nick, and he shook his head in an almost imperceptible way.

We got nowhere on our strategy, and I could not help but blame Sorin. It almost felt like he was trying to undermine me. He supported none of my ideas. Brandon hung back and said little. He was mostly watching Nick. Grandmother was supportive, but I heard the buzz around the room asking why a vampire was in a witch High Council meeting, especially given his position in the vampire order.

When we finally called it a night in the early morning hours, I was beyond exhausted. I thought about staying in my new quarters at the mansion, but I longed for my bed and alone time with my new fiancé. It caused a stir leaving with him in his Lamborghini, but no one tried to stop us. Of course, the guards were in pursuit with their black SUVs.

The ride was silent other than stolen smiles and glances. When we parked, Nick insisted on coming around to help me out. I felt something on my left hand as we strode through the lobby. I missed a step at the sight of the beautiful antique cushion cut ring on my hand. Nick caught me and straightened me. I looked from the ring to him and back several times before I could speak.

"How?" I smiled at him. "When?" Love overwhelmed me.

"I've carried it with me waiting for the moment you'd say yes, and when we were getting out of the car, I slipped it on your finger." He stood a little taller, with a pleased look on his face. He held my hand in his. "It was my mother's ring, Brie." His face softened.

I melted to him and wrapped my arms around his neck, kissing him with a healthy dose of passion.

"I love it almost as much as I love you, and I am honored you would want me to have your mother's ring." I looked at it on my hand with a smile.

"I would have never given it to anyone before I met you," he said, kissing me. After forcing ourselves apart, we hurried across the lobby to avoid stares.

"This is going to make for an interesting conversation in a few hours." I broke the silence we had resumed in the elevator on the way up to my apartment. I gave a weak chuckle. "We don't have the elders' support."

"Let's deal with your family and the elders later. I only want to focus on my fiancé at the moment." He pulled me close, kissing the top of my head.

Something felt strange in the apartment the minute I walked through the door. Nick obliged me and walked the full length of it, checking for anything that might be amiss. We found nothing, but I was on edge the rest of the night. Nick held me tight and made light strokes along my bare back as we drifted off to sleep. I could not shake the sense there was something off.

CHAPTER
SEVENTEEN

H ands shook me hard, but I couldn't focus through the fog to respond. Everything seemed gray and moved in slow motion around me. I knew they had moved me, but I only saw blurry glimpses when I tried to open my eyes. My chest felt constricted, and I struggled with every breath I took. I wanted to fight back when someone picked me up, but my arms and legs didn't respond. I listened, as best I could, to see who was near me. Nick's voice came through in bursts, and the worry in it sent chills through me. Panic set in, as I could tell I was in a large vehicle.

A siren sounded. *Ambulance.*

Bright lights bared down on me. *Hospital.*

The haze cleared. Nick and my family crowded around me. My head pounded like a hangover times ten, but I could see the worry on everyone's faces. The morning sun was bright to my sensitive eyes, and my body ached. My throat was raw, barely allowing me to swallow.

"What happened?" I asked, forcing myself to sit up. They all exchanged looks.

"They are calling it a gas leak, but we can call it Stefan," Sorin said. Nick squeezed my left hand, his covering the engagement ring. Brandon was on the other side, holding my right hand. I looked up at him and saw worry. It seemed strange a vampire would try to kill with a gas leak. They are lethal predators in their own right and wouldn't need such dramatics to kill someone.

"Brandon, you are my Protector. What does your gut say?"

His grip tightened on the hand he held.

"I don't believe it was vampires, but someone wants us to think it was." He looked right at Sorin, who watched Nick like a hawk.

"I'm not convinced it was vampires, either. They would want it known. Someone tried to frame Nick," Grandmother said, focusing on Sorin.

"Who gains anything by framing me? Unless they wanted to anger me into unleashing my wrath," Nick said, looking at Brandon and Grandmother before following their gazes to Sorin.

Did they all really think my father would do this? He did care for us, but was it in him to do this?

"You are mistaken if you're implying it was me," Sorin said with conviction. "I would never try to murder my child." He looked at me and tears welled in his eyes. I knew he spoke the truth.

"Sorin didn't do this." I mustered the strongest tone of command I could. "I doubt Stefan did either, but it could have been a rogue vampire, I suppose." It still didn't seem like vampire style, but we weren't exactly in the normal zone anymore. "I need to get out of here and back to the mansion. The longer I'm gone, the greater risk someone in our coven will try to retaliate."

"You're not going anywhere," Nick said, placing a firm hand on my shoulder. I looked at his hand and raised an eyebrow at him. He removed it quickly, but not before Brandon got a good chuckle.

"Was anyone else harmed?" I asked, needing to know no one else was injured because of this war. No one said anything and stared at each other. "Tell me."

"There were several humans exposed to the gas, and they are being treated. One is in critical condition," Grand-mother said.

"We need to heal them," I said, moving to get up from the bed.

"You are in a weakened state and in no position to heal anyone." Sorin shook his head. "There are capable doctors here to take care of them. You need to heal yourself. No one here can cast a spell strong enough for you."

"They are injured because of me. I will heal them, and I will be fine."

I swayed as I stood up and Nick steadied me. Grand-mother helped me dress, and I visited the room of each person. We saved the critical but stable patient for last since it required passing through so many cameras. Grandmother distorted the images as we passed by so I could save my strength to heal this last injured human. Revenge was my first thought when I saw a young girl no more than seven in the hospital bed. The irony did not escape me. She was around the age I was when my life changed.

"This is the price of this war. An innocent human child." I felt the pain stir deep in my belly, vowing silently I would make the person responsible atone for injuring this beautiful little girl. I touched her red hair, and she opened her bright green eyes. A smile crossed her face, lighting up the room.

"Are you my fairy godmother?" she asked. Her voice was soft and sweet.

"I am." Although, I'm not aware of any fairy godmothers who have tattoos. Everyone would be sure she had a dream. I placed a hand on her forehead and healed her. Her labored breathing returned to normal. I relaxed. My knees gave way, but Nick scooped me up in his arms.

"Someone is coming. We need to go," Nick said.

"Cloak," I said, my voice weak. I could hear Nick and Sorin arguing over who would drive me, but my thoughts were on the little redheaded girl. She represented what we would lose if we didn't stop this war. Nick must have won the argument because he put me in the passenger's seat of his car.

"Do you think she will be all right?" I asked, the car roaring down the road.

He took my hand in his, running his thumb over my knuckles.

"She will be just fine. She has a fairy godmother," he said.

"Let's find out who she is and make sure she is taken care of." I stared out the window.

"Whatever you want." He brought my hand to his lips. "Brie?" His voice broke on my name.

I turned my head to look at him.

"I was afraid you wouldn't make it. I resolved to challenge Stefan and allow him to stake me."

He'd said before he didn't want to live without me, but the resolve in his voice crushed my heart. I turned in the seat where I could look at him directly.

"Don't you ever say those words again. I will live longer than a human, but I am mortal. I will die, but you will go on."

His pain written in lines and creases on his face.

"I will not. I can't walk this earth if you are not here, so make sure you are here for a long time." He tried to lighten the mood with a smile that didn't reach his eyes.

"I have no intention of leaving this world anytime soon." I knew there was a chance I wouldn't be able to keep that promise, but I needed to reassure him.

The elders assembled in the library at my request as soon as we got to the mansion and wasted no time trying to figure out who tried to assassinate me. The scent of the old books bound in leather helped calm me. I found strength in this room from the connection to our ancestors. Their healing powers coursed through me.

The surveillance footage from the building had been obtained and was being reviewed. The elders had suggestions on what we should do to the person who did this, and their strong recommendations involved some medieval punishments too close to Stefan's tactics. I knew becoming queen would mean people challenging me, among other things. I hadn't anticipated facing multiple adversaries at the same time, but a team confirmed Stefan's whereabouts at his castle. Of course, that didn't mean he couldn't have arranged it.

By mid-afternoon, my strength had returned, and I no longer felt the effects of the gas. My focus returned, and we were making headway. I jumped at a knock at the door. Sorin looked surprised at the man entering the room and moved to greet him.

"Alastair! My old friend!" Sorin embraced the man in an expensive black tailored suit with a warm hug. In the short time I'd he'd been here, I had never seen Sorin respond to anyone with such affection. My senses went on alert. He was a warlock, not a vampire, but I wasn't sure if he was friend or foe.

"Sorin, I didn't expect to see you here, but I guess you returned to support your daughter." He turned to face me. "My Queen." He took a knee in front of me, placing his arm over his heart and bowing his head. It was an old-world gesture I'd never seen anyone actually do, but everyone except Nick followed suit. It was the ultimate sign of respect for the queen. Their adoration touched me.

"Please rise." I hid my surprise in my authoritarian response.

"Your Highness." Alastair reached for my hand for what I thought would be a shake, but he held mine in his, covering it with his other in a too familiar way. "I'm Alastair Kingston, and I am pleased to meet your majesty." His accent was pure British, and I knew right away who he was.

"Alastair is the leader of the European coven," Sorin said.

"Yes, I recognize his name." I turned to Alastair. "Your name precedes you. It's a pleasure to meet you, but please do not stand on formality. Brie will be fine when we speak." I forced myself to sound like a queen and ignored the pit in my stomach.

Alastair's family lived in London for hundreds of years through many generations. Not only were they royal among witches, but they came from English aristocracy. He and Sorin stood about the same height, and his dark hair reminded me of a boy I used to play with in the mansion.

"Our allegiance is to you as always," he said.

I was sure I saw a smirk on his face. My already raw emotions built, and I had to let out a calm breath to gain control.

"May I present my brother, Brandon Danforth." They shook hands, but Brandon's vibes matched my leeriness.

It's not just me.

"Alastair and I have met many times." My grandmother didn't extend her hand.

He kissed both of her cheeks, but she didn't seem as pleased to see him as Sorin was. I noted he ignored Nick, and I forced an introduction.

"Alastair, this is Nick." I kept the nature of our relationship private at the moment until I knew Alastair better, assuming Sorin hadn't told him. He nodded to Nick and shook his hand, but he didn't speak to him. Nick returned the nod and remained silent.

He and Sorin walked to the other side of the large room. Their conversation was hushed, but their laughter drifted over to us.

"What's the deal with him? And since when do coven leaders travel without security?" I whispered to Grandmother.

"They don't," she said.

"His security is here, Brie," Nick whispered. "They are waiting in the hall."

"How well do you know him, Grandmother?" Brandon asked.

"Well enough to know it is no accident he is here now," she said in a worried tone.

"I feel strange around him. Not bad, but definitely not good," I said, keeping my voice low.

"It's not good. I feel it too," Brandon said.

"He has a son, Brie. It was the plan you two were to be married, but it seems that has changed," she said, looking from Nick to me and fiddling with my engagement ring.

Shit. The ring. We hadn't had a chance to tell anyone.

"An arranged marriage? Since when do witches take part in such an archaic practice?" I fought against raising my voice. Brandon chuckled, and I shot him a look full of daggers. Nick closed the space between us, lacing his fingers through my free hand.

"Brie, we are built on our traditions and rituals. We've always arranged marriages for our royalty. Your parents were arranged, but they fell in love before they knew," she said, looking off.

"And look how great that turned out," I mumbled. "What about you and grandfather?"

"Yes, we were arranged, but we also fell in love before we were told. Typically, the children of the arrangement spend a lot of time together growing up. It just seems natural when they are together. With you and Callum living on different continents, you only met a few times."

I remembered Callum as soon as she said his name. A dark headed sweet little boy who always liked to tie my hair in knots. It was the only mischievous thing he did in the time we played as kids. Looking at Alastair, I saw Callum in him. The same dark hair, the same dark eyes, and the same sweet smile. However, my instincts told me Alastair's wasn't as sweet as Callum's was many years ago.

"I haven't seen Callum since I was about twelve or thirteen. Why don't I remember Alastair?"

"He only came once at the same time as Callum, and you were quite young," she said. "Alastair was in love with your mother, but she was wholly in love with your father." I surmised she was still wholly his, too. She was so broken without him.

Arranged marriages may have worked for my ancestors, but my destiny told a different story from theirs. The thought of marrying anyone other than Nick made me feel physically ill, and there was no way I would go through with an arranged marriage. First Stefan tried to marry me, and then an arranged marriage? I seriously might lose my mind. Nick was the only one I was marrying, and that was final.

"I am queen, and I will choose who I will marry," I said, keeping my voice low. Nick squeezed my hand, but he said nothing. I looked up at his face. His eyes darkened and his forehead creased. He was not only angry but angrier than I had seen him. I was about to ask Brandon, Grandmother, and Nick to adjourn to my quarters where we could continue the discussion in private when a small bit of the conversation between Sorin and Alastair drifted to me.

"A vampire? It's not allowed. He will need to be executed for the knowledge he has," Alastair said. I heard it, which meant Nick most certainly heard it. I grabbed his hand tight.

"No one will be executed without the order coming from me," I said, surprising myself at how strong it was. "Anyone who touches another vampire will answer to me, and forgiveness is not in my nature. Just ask my father." I took a step closer. "Nick is my future husband, and we will together bring peace to our people. By people, I mean human, witch, and vampire."

A clap of thunder rumbled the mansion. I closed my eyes, pursing my lips together and inhaling deeply. I had done so well controlling my emotions until that point. An uncomfortable silence fell over the room, and I felt like my arm was on fire. My tattoo was glowing. The dual vision hit me fiercely. Two possible outcomes. One light. One dark. Bloodshed would happen in both.

CHAPTER
EIGHTEEN

☽ ☽ ● ☾ ☾

Grandmother knew I had a vision, and she made an excuse. I could hear her voice in snippets, and she ushered me to my quarters. I was wrapped in the vision most of the walk. She seated me on the bed and took both my hands in hers. "I know. You must keep this to yourself. The knowledge will not change the outcome." I looked at her and nodded. Nick and Brandon entered the suite. Some of my family would live and some would die before this was over, and I pushed it down deep inside me to hide in the dark.

"You are to meet Callum in the sitting room before dinner." Nick's voice strained. "His father and your father will make the introductions."

"Sis, I'm no expert on love, but it sounds like they are trying to force you into this." He looked bewildered by the events. I wondered if he had a future wife waiting in the wings.

"Thanks, Brandon." I squeezed his hand a little tighter

than usual. "Can you and Grandmother give Nick and me some privacy?"

He winked at me. "Sure, Sis. Come on, Granny. Let's see what chocolates they have out today." He knew full well she hated it when he called her Granny, but she loved her chocolates. She playfully pursed her lips at him and took his arm, strolling out of the room.

I waited for the door to shut. "Nick, this changes nothing for us," I said, my voice full of conviction.

He paced the floor. His face contorted similar to the painful expression vampires have when they want to feed.

"Maybe it would be better if you married one of your own kind," he said, his voice broken.

"Seriously? After all, we have been through together, and you are going to say that now? Give up that easy?" I threw a little energy ball at him. He swatted it away, but not before it reinforced my anger with a little zap.

"Ouch," he said, chuckling. He leaned over, planting his hands on the bed on either side of me. Our faces were close. "I was just thinking out loud. Seeing how it sounded. I guess you must love me." I shook my head and giggled at him.

"Well, I kind of like you." I smiled at him.

He kissed me hard, claiming my mouth, but broke away after seconds.

"Just like me?" he asked, his voice filled with passion. My body tingled as he slid his hand under my shirt around my waist to caress my back.

"I agreed to marry you, so I must like you a lot," I said, raggedly drawing breaths.

"So you like me a lot?" he asked, his voice rough. His lips traced over my neck, placing soft kisses.

My breath and speech fought against each other as I whispered, "I love you, Nick."

He smiled against my neck as if he had won a battle all by himself. He looked me in the eyes as if searching for something.

"Brie, I love you," he said, staring into my eyes like he was trying to burn it into my brain, but it was already there. His fervent assault erupted on my mouth.

"Get him out of here," Sorin said to the guards. Nick and I both jumped, startled by the interruption. Fixated on Nick, I didn't hear the door open. Few people had access to the inner part of my suite and I had guards at the door, so I didn't even consider locking it.

"No. You will leave him where he is." I said, my voice still breathless. The guards stood in the doorway, not crossing the threshold, and looked at me. It honored me they accepted me as their queen. Sorin slammed the door in their faces hard enough the fixtures on the walls rattled like a minor earthquake.

"Are you trying to break our alliance with the European coven?" He said his face red.

"Aren't all covens under the rule of ours?" I asked, my voice almost normal. "And just when did you plan on telling me about this arranged marriage?

"Yes, they are under our rule because of peace treaties and alliances. Don't be a naïve fool, Brie." He looked at Nick, who wasn't bothering to button the two buttons I had just undone. "You should choose better bedfellows, my dear daughter."

I couldn't help but laugh. Who is he to give me advice on who I sleep with? He wasn't around while I was learning the ways of the world.

"Please, Sorin. It's not like I was ever going to be a virginal bride, my dear father," I said, throwing the words back at him. I saw Nick wince out of the corner of my eye. I regretted the words as soon as they left my mouth. No, I wasn't a virgin, but I could count on both hands the number of men I had been with through the years. Witches and warlocks don't bind themselves to the same ritual of virginal brides the humans once did.

"You need to figure out where your loyalties and priorities are. Again." His words stung, but I heard the truth, too. I would have to pacify Alastair and Callum to maintain the alliance without losing Nick. "I'm not your mother, Brie. I'll not let you get away with latent rebellion. The cost is too high."

"Do you even know what she put me through? Put us through? Your son and I?" I asked. He surprised me when I saw his face soften. His hand rested on my cheek. It was a father's touch. I had wanted this my whole life, but it came too late with the anger coursing through me.

"Yes, I do. I asked your grandmother to keep you and protect you. When I heard what happened to you and you had walked to your grandmother's house, it was a sign. It is what brought me back from the dark. My decision was made than to find my way back, but the dark had a deep hold on me. It took years to break free." He knelt in the way Alastair had in the library. Tears fell on his knee. I choked back a sob and pulled on his arm.

He hugged me to him. My father's embrace was what I needed today. He centered me, and I experienced his love for me for the first time. He embraced me for a long time before pulling back.

"You need to get ready, and Nick is welcome to join us." His tone had changed. It was resigned. He was giving me the freedom he never could when I was younger. The freedom to make a choice.

I wanted to ask Nick to sit this meeting out, knowing it would be easier without the tension, but I couldn't. He had made so many sacrifices for me, and I needed to make a few for him.

Nick and I walked into the sitting room, looking every bit the power couple we were. I always hated this room. It was so formal and stood for so much of what I did not agree with about the witch society. Contempt was written boldly on Alastair's face, but Callum's was different. His face showed the kindness I had always associated with him. He had grown into a tall, dashing English gentleman, and I smiled at my longtime friend. He returned to me the same warm smile he had when we were kids.

Callum went to bow as his father had when we met, but I grabbed his arm. I wrapped my arms around him, hugging him as the long-lost friend he was. "Callum, it has been years."

"It has, Your Highness," he said.

"Brie will work fine. It's what you have always called

me," I said, smiling at him. He'd matured, but he was still my friend. His aura open, welcoming, and free to read.

"Then please call me Cal." He returned the smile, facing Nick, who looked uncomfortable and angry all at once. My strikingly handsome man was jealous.

I almost giggled. His confidence wavered. I'd have to make sure he understood what I saw in Cal, which was a friend.

"Cal Kingston. Please to meet you." Cal offered his hand.

"Nick Domenico. It is always nice to meet Brie's friends." He stressed the word friends but shaking Cal's hand, he visibly relaxed as if he sensed the goodness in him, too. Cal had a way with people even when we were kids. He could reach the good in them and bring out the best. People gravitated toward his kindness and charm, and after seeing his aura now, I understood it even more.

"Would you mind if I borrow your fiancé for a few moments?" Cal asked. Nick begrudgingly and wordlessly motioned his approval with the wave of a hand. Cal and I walked out of the sitting room to a side parlor, where we could speak candidly away from everyone. I was nervous about leaving Nick alone with them, but I trusted him to keep his anger in check. Cal and I needed to talk, and I hoped he perceived the situation similarly to how I did.

"Did you know about this arranged marriage?" His voice jumped a few octaves. The shock matched my own, and I let out a breath.

"I had no clue until earlier today." Not sure how much information I should give away. My suspicion crawled up my spine, and my eyes narrowed at him. "Did you know about it?"

"No! I had no inkling until my father told me as we were in the car coming from the airport!"

"Cal, what are we going to do?" I asked, my voice thick with desperation. I could refuse and so could Cal, but what would it mean for the alliance if we did? My body trembled at the magnitude.

"There are a lot worse things than being married to you, Brie, but I have no desire to fight your fiancé for you. I, too, love another."

I sighed with relief.

"I agree with you. You are a fine choice for a royal marriage, but I am certainly not the average royal. Nick and I belong together, and I have every intention of marrying him."

"It will be hard for you, Brie. You are revered first as the best vampire huntress in two hundred years and now as the most gifted queen in more. Being married to a vampire will make them question your loyalty to the covens, as well as their loyalty to you. They want their amazing queen to lead them into a new age, but I'm not sure they are going to understand their vampire huntress hero being with a vampire." He said, his voice soft and kind. *Hero? They talk about me?*

"The Blood Moon Prophecy says I am the one who will bring peace between witches and vampires. My relation-ship with Nick could serve as an example," I said. The prophecy wasn't a secret anymore, so telling him didn't give away any power.

"There is a difference between peace and acceptance. Your subjects may not be as accepting of the huntress who holds the record for number of vampire kills marrying a vampire.

He gave me a weak smile. I listened intently to what Cal had to say. He had been raised as a royal and groomed to rule in the future. He seemed to know more than I did about what the people wanted in their rulers.

"How would they even know the number of kills I've had? It's not like we publish it in a monthly newsletter." I was no longer proud of my triple-digit total as a huntress. It was once the most important thing in my life, but my priorities had changed.

"They have kept you sheltered from so much of the world surrounding our covens." He shook his head. "There isn't a witch alive who doesn't know the princess who graduated from the training academy in one year versus the required four years. The princess immune to the tricks of the vampires. The princess who has now become their queen." He gave me a genuine smile.

"I never knew this. How did I not know?" The shock of hearing the interest people had in my life made my voice sound like someone else. I never wanted the spotlight, and yet when I became queen, I would be in that very spot. Everything would change. It already had. I lamented the anonymity I thought I once had.

"I suspect they intentionally kept it from you to keep you grounded, and it looks like it worked." He nudged his shoulder into mine as he sat down beside me on the large overstuffed couch. I absorbed his words for a moment.

Royalty had never seemed important to me growing up, and I considered the notion Brandon and I might have been kept at a distance from it to prepare us for the battles we face today. An odd awareness came to me at the realization we didn't really know who we were. At least I didn't.

"We are here to support you and will not be taking our leave until our duty is done. Why don't we go along with it for now?" He said, rubbing his chin with his thumb and forefinger.

"What? The arranged marriage?" I narrowed my eyes at him. Nick would kill him.

"Yes. We could pretend like we are going through with it." He acted pleased with his idea.

"I'm not liking that idea. Besides, Sorin will never believe I would give in so easily." Nick wouldn't believe it either.

"If Nick's not around, he would, right? Ask Nick to stay away until we figure it out." Cal laid out his plan, but my gut clenched. My heart constricted. I had a powerful response telling me to beware. Nick would not like this, and it felt like a betrayal to me.

Sorin and Alastair had left by the time we rejoined Nick. My heart broke as soon as I saw him. His forehead wrinkled with mistrust as we went through the plan. Cal explained he would need to stage a fight with me and disappear for a while. Nick looked like he would spontaneously combust. Anger showed on his face and in his eyes.

"No! We will not do this." He looked me square in the

eyes. "Brie, you can't think this is a good idea. No!" Nick shook his head. His voice was deep and menacing, not the melodic sound I was used to hearing.

"I don't like it either, but it would take the focus off of us if they thought we weren't together anymore. This will help us keep the alliance secure between the covens." I was sure Nick was about to strangle me, but I reached up, touching his face to let him know I was still his.

He closed his eyes and leaned his cheek into my hand. His sigh scented the air with vanilla, and he opened his eyes. He grasped my hand, pulling it down from his face and holding it. I recognized the menacing look of a killer when he turned to face Cal. He was giving in for me, but it cost him.

"Fine," Nick spoke in one syllable, which was never good. "If you touch her, I will drain every drop of blood from your body." The growl Nick let out was familiar now.

I turned his face back to me and looked him in the eyes for a moment. I didn't need to use magic to calm him down. Our bond could do it. I kissed his cheek, and we planned the faux fight for after dinner. We kept it from Grandmother and Brandon, so they would have genuine surprise when it broke out.

)) ● ((

EVERYONE HAD a great time at dinner telling stories and laughing. Everyone except Nick, that is. He was miserable and brooding, and I honestly wasn't sure if it was part of the act for the fight or if he suffered in silence. The fight started as planned by us excusing ourselves to step out into the hallway, but when it came time to slap him, I couldn't do it. The others were eavesdropping, and it wouldn't be as convincing if I didn't do it. I couldn't raise a hand in anger, even fake anger, to him, though. He looked at me with pleading eyes. He knew this was important, and he took matters into his own hands as the others started filtering into the hallway.

"I should have let Stefan have you. You're not worth the fight," he said, just as we had planned. I didn't count on how it would affect me. The air left my body and my face dropped. It was the culmination of my fears. I strove to be the best at everything because I never felt worthy of love. I had shoved the notion of love deep inside me until I met Nick. Hearing those words come from his mouth crushed me. I tried to convince myself it wasn't true, but I swam in the sadness it made me feel. The thunder and wind roared, and lightning struck outside the mansion. I turned away from Nick. Sorin and Brandon ran to me. Brandon looked at Nick with the look he got when we hunted.

"Get out, Nick. You are not welcome here. Ever." Brandon was too calm. The only time his voice was devoid of emotion was when he turned everything off but anger.

I sucked in air but couldn't get any. It was like all the oxygen was gone.

Grandmother put her hands on either side of my face. "Rest."

)) ● ((

I DIDN'T SEE him leave, but I woke up on the couch knowing Nick was gone. It felt real. It didn't seem like a fake fight. I fought back the tears and the lump in my throat. I was thankful for the alone time. A knock echoed through the suite. I closed my eyes and sighed. I willed whoever knocked away.

The door opened, revealing Cal. It surprised me the guards let him back without checking with me. He pulled the chair from the corner up to the couch and straddled it.

"That was pretty harsh," he said. I looked away, still fighting the tears. "You know he didn't mean it. I could feel the love between you two. But what happened to the plan?"

"I couldn't slap him. I couldn't bring myself to do it, so he tried to pull it out of me." My broken voice wasn't much more than a whisper. Cal placed a hand on my forearm.

"You almost lost it. The weather was out of control," he said, keeping his voice soft. "Remember when we were kids, and I said you were different?" I gave him a feeble smile, nodding. "You punched me in the arm and threatened to stake me like a vampire if I told anyone."

I laughed, remembering it well. I never would have done it, of course, but he bought my threat way back then.

"I know what you are saying. It wasn't real, and everything is going to be alright." I smiled at him, rolling my eyes.

"Yes. Exactly. Now, get up and get dressed. You owe

me a tour of your city. I'll meet you in the foyer in 20 minutes." He gave my arm a little squeeze as he left me alone. The last thing I wanted to do was go out on the town. I wanted to dwell in my self-pity, but duty called. I took a deep breath, sending a silent prayer telling Nick I loved him and got up to make this farce look real.

NINETEEN

Cal and I roamed the city, but Nick was never far from my thoughts. It got late when we ended up in front of Club Red. I froze in place despite Ian motioning us to the front of the line. Vampires intermingled with humans, and I wanted to touch my vampire. I felt Cal's gaze on me and tears brimmed in my eyes as I turned to face him. I blinked them back, determined not to cry.

"Nick and I met here. I wasn't thinking about coming here." I paused. "This is also the best spot to hunt vampires." The sadness in my voice betrayed me. I no longer had the desire to kill vampires.

"Well, let's see what all the fuss is about, then. Shall we?" He waited at my hesitation. "We have both of our security teams trailing at a safe distance. We will be fine." He took my hand, and I flinched away. I wasn't afraid of vampires in the club, but I was afraid of memories of one vampire stirring the longing in my heart at his absence.

"Let's head back to the mansion. It's getting late, and I am tired," I said, taking his elbow and waving to Ian while we walked toward the guards.

"Do you think it is possible?" Cal asked, interrupting the silence.

"What?"

"Do you think you could bring peace for all? The witches, vampires, and humans?" he asked.

"It's prophesied as my destiny, so I don't think I have a choice in the matter." I paused for a moment, wondering if it really was possible. "My heart has changed. I perceive vampires completely different now from when I hunted them. The desire to shed their blood disappeared. I think, if it can impact me this way, it is possible."

"Oh, I think witches are more than capable of peace. The vampires are such violent creatures. There might be a few who still have a touch of their humanity, but I don't see it in the masses." Cal let his thoughts roll off his tongue. I thought about what he said, and his words pricked me as I thought of Nick. "How will you do it, Brie?" He gazed in my direction with genuine curiosity.

"Honestly, I'm not sure what I am supposed to do, but I feel Nick and Stefan are key to it. I haven't figured out how yet. My visions are glimpses of the future, but it always changes. With pieces to work with, it's hard to define them. They are ever-changing like a riddle. My grandmother gets it more than I do, but she leaves the puzzle for me to solve. She and father have both said it needs to be my decision," I said, finishing as we arrived at the car to take us back to the mansion.

During the ride back to the mansion, we chatted about our lives since we last saw each other. It surprised me how much training he had given his status. My status had been kept a secret, but his wasn't. The royalty didn't train as much as the others, but his father prepared him well for this battle, it seemed. If I didn't know better, I'd think Alastair anticipated the prophecy.

We said goodnight with a warm hug, and I couldn't wait to get to my room to check my phone. I didn't take it with me, afraid I would stare at it all night. No messages.

Nick must be pissed. I tried to sense him, but I could not pick up his location. He could be anywhere. I couldn't teleport to him, but I wasn't sure I wanted to see where he was. I couldn't remember the last time he fed, and he needed to hunt. I sent him a text with three simple words.

> I love you.

My mind and body ached with exhaustion from the day's events, but I couldn't rest. The four blood moons appeared each time I closed my eyes, and I saw the choice again and again I would have to make at some point. My vision was clear, and I wasn't lying when I told Cal they change. The one saving grace from the visions I had was Nick's constant presence in all of them.

I checked my phone again. Nothing. I checked it a dozen or more times during the night, hoping for a text from him, and my heart sank a little when there wasn't one. I eventually drifted off to sleep for a short time, contemplating our wedding. I hadn't had an opportunity to even think about it since we got engaged, much less the engagement. A loud banging at my door jarred me awake. It seemed like I only slept for minutes. *What the...* Everyone should be asleep. *Are we under attack?* I grabbed my robe and hurried to the door.

Nick. Relief and happiness flooded over me, after seeing Nick's face at my door. I threw my arms around his neck and held him close. He returned my embrace, kissing my cheek. I could smell fresh blood on his breath. He had fed and fed a lot from the pungent fragrance.

"How did you get past the guards?" I asked. "Where are my guards?" I looked around the hall.

His only answer was to pick me up and carry me into my suite, kicking the door closed. He walked straight to my bedroom, closing the door the same way, but he stopped to lock it without putting me down. There wouldn't be a repeat of the incident with Sorin. When he made it to the bed, he laid me down, positioning himself beside me. He pushed stray strands of hair out of my face, kissing my forehead, then my cheek, and finally my mouth with his feather-light kisses. My body tingled with energy. Being with Nick reminded me how alive I was.

"I'm sorry," he said, whispering in my ear, our cheeks touching. "I shouldn't have said it. Anger made me crazy, and I wanted the stupid fight done and over. I wanted to run."

Even now, he's willing to take the blame. *Goddess, I feel guilty.*

"You have nothing to be sorry for, Nick. I shouldn't have asked you to do it. It was a stupid plan, and we were stupid to go through with it," I said. He closed his eyes, and they were wet with tears when he reopened them. "It's really fine. I still love you."

"I need to tell you something, Brie." He looked away for a moment. I saw distance and sadness in his eyes. He seemed to drift away from the present. I put my hands on either side of his face.

"You can tell me anything. You forget how strong I actually am. I know there are times you hold back because you are afraid I can't handle it. Let's move past holding back from each other. Our positions are going to require us to face unimaginable challenges soon. We need to make sure those challenges are not coming from us. I will love you no matter what you tell me." I kissed him softly. My body yearned to fill the void building between us, but this was one time I needed to let words do the work.

"It could be a game changer for us." He paused, taking a deep breath. I looked him in the eyes to connect in our special way. "Gaius is dead. Stefan planned to have me executed. Gaius and his men stood against him in my favor, and Stefan ended them." He sighed. "Gaius was ruthless, but he was fiercely loyal to me. Stefan called it treason."

Nick paused again to take a deep breath. So that's why Gaius let Nick spend time with me during my captivity.

"Stefan will be after me, so I must leave to raise an army against him. Staying here will only bring danger to you and your family." He stared at me for a long moment as I grasped what he said. With Gaius dead, Nick would be the next in line to become king when we executed our plan to overthrow Stefan.

"Nick, I don't want you to leave. We make mistakes when we are apart. I can't think straight, and I don't think you can either," I said, pleading with him.

He stood and paced the floor. "Stefan will come for me, and it will put you in direct danger. I will not have you hurt for my sake." He shook his head.

I stepped into his path. "Stefan is going to come after me no matter what because he wants to turn me into a vampire and make me his bride. I'm already in danger, and it has nothing to do with you. Stay. Please. I need you here by my side." My heart raced. Pain flashed across Nick's face as he decided.

"I can't say no to you, and I'm not sure that's a good thing," he said with a tired smile. A small laugh escaped from me, and he trapped it with a kiss. I tasted the blood from his feeding. It should have repulsed me, but it didn't. My body ached for his touch to let me know we were us again.

)) ● ((

I WATCHED NICK SLEEP. He appeared so peaceful and young. Footsteps pounded across my suite, and I grabbed my robe. The door knob on the locked door to my bedroom jiggled. A swift knock jarred Nick awake and startled me.

"Brie, are you in there?" Brandon asked through the door. I let out a breath, thankful it wasn't Sorin.

"Yes. I was about to take a shower," I said. Nick ran to

the bathroom with his clothes, and I tried to control my giggles. The sight of his bare derriere was a marvelous view.

"Your guards appear to have been under a spell, and there has been a development." Nick must have used mind control over the guards. They trained against it, and I made a mental note of it as another one of Nick's special gifts. Brandon continued as I opened the door. "We worried Stefan might have come for you while we were all asleep."

"Yes, I know. Gaius is dead, but Nick is Stefan's first concern now. He'll hunt him first before coming after me." Saying it out loud solidified it in my mind. I swallowed hard because bursting into tears did not sound queenly.

"Is Nick here?" Brandon glanced at the closed bathroom door and narrowed his eyes at me. "Seriously, Brie? After what he did yesterday?"

"It was an act, Brandon. We thought it would take some pressure off. It was Cal's idea. He is in love with someone else, too." I rolled my eyes at him as if he should have known better. It was a mistake.

"You should have told me, Brie!" He did the whisper yell thing, which meant he was pissed.

"Did you find her?" Sorin said, calling from behind Brandon. Brandon gulped air. "I looked-"

"She's fine." Brandon crossed his arms over his chest and glared at me. I crossed my arms and stared back at him.

"Thank God," Sorin said, standing beside Brandon.

"Brie, we need to meet in the library right away. An attack is imminent. Get dressed and meet us in there."

Brandon didn't tell him Nick was there, but he turned on his heels to follow Sorin to the meeting without saying another word. It was unlike him to not give me a chance to explain. It registered with a deep sadness in my stomach. We had been close our whole lives, never judging the other one, but I felt like he judged me for being with Nick. Then again, I kept the fake engagement from him. I deserved a little judgment.

Vin stepped out of the bathroom.

"Ready to face this head on?" I asked.

"Me being there is going to cause problems. They already had trust issues before last night and before-" Nick's voice trailed off, and he swallowed hard as he towel dried his hair. "Before Stefan murdered Gaius. There isn't a chance in hell they are going to trust me now."

"As the queen, they're expected to trust me and follow my decisions. We've been through this a dozen times, Nick. We do this together." I inhaled deeply. "My visions have shown we must be together regardless of the outcome." I waited for him to respond, and the long silence tortured me. I was sure he would want to run on the realization.

"I'm in your visions?" He asked, his forehead creased. "Do we have a normal life?"

All I wanted was normalcy, even when I was a feared hunter. I craved normalcy, but the visions showed anything but. Falling in love with Nick gave me hope for it, but being in love with a vampire wasn't exactly normal.

Having visions about your future wasn't normal. Being the Queen of the Witches was not normal. My life was not normal, and it never would be.

No, but it's interesting." I said.

"Tell me what you have seen." He held both of my hands against his chest and stared into my eyes. I debated whether to tell him the whole truth. It was my burden, and it didn't have to be his, too. I owed him the same candor he gave me.

"Visions are only snapshots and snippets of what could be, Nick. They are ever changing, and they are rarely definite." I paused, and he nodded for me to go on. "I've seen many things, but the one constant in all my visions is you're by my side, whether I choose light or dark. You choose the same path as I do, and honestly, it scares the hell out of me." I searched his face for a reaction. He pulled me to him and kissed the top of my head.

"I feel like I can breathe now," he said. "Knowing we will be together brings me more joy than you will ever know, Brie."

"Even if we are dark?" I asked, muttering against his chest.

"If that is what you choose, then yes," he said against the top of my head. It frightened me he would follow me there, especially given how he fought so hard to find his humanity. I wanted him to say he wouldn't let me go dark. "Let's go face your family and the elders."

)) ● ((

Nick and I walked into the library together. The tension in the room weighed on me. I explained what the plan was to Brandon, Sorin, and Grandmother, with Nick interjecting with the information he had from the vampire world.

"I'm going to ask the elders to join us," Sorin said.

I sat with my hands in my lap and twirled my thumbs. Nick laid his hand over mine.

"It's going to be ok," he said.

I nodded.

Sorin returned in a few minutes. "The elders are right behind me. I suggest you two are not touching."

Nick stood and held out his hand for me. We positioned ourselves on the opposite side of the table just in time. The elders entered the room. The tensions swelled to a suffocating level.

Sorin had me walk the elders through the plan.

"There are many vampires still loyal to Nick. He'll be able to raise a large enough army to give us an advantage over Stefan. My only concern is trying to attack his castle, where we think he will want to stay because of security. Nick knows the layout well enough, but it would be a disadvantage for the witches. If we lure them out to the field and woods on the grounds, we will have a much better chance," I said, looking up to everyone staring at me, including Nick.

"It should work." Sorin was the first to speak. "You should remain here. It is risky to have all of us there, and especially you." I couldn't believe he agreed to it in front of the elders, and I was even more shocked everyone nodded in agreement.

"I'll be there, otherwise there is less motivation to draw Stefan out, and I will entertain no discussion on my choice." I asserted my right as queen. "Besides, I'm still the best hunter in the coven."

The room fell silent, but no one challenged me. I wasn't sure if I still had the huntress in me, but I wasn't about to admit it. Secretly, I hoped the huntress in me would make an appearance on the battlefield. "The next full moon is in five days, and we must be ready since our powers are always stronger during that phase."

"Are you sure you don't want to wait until the next Blood Moon?" Sorin asked.

"It's three months away. Stefan will not wait that long to attack." It was not a guess. I had seen it in a vision. It would be a rough battle with losses on both sides.

"Then we have a lot of work to do." Sorin nodded. "Brandon, put together a training regimen for all available witches." He surprised me once again by turning to Nick. "Will three days be long enough to raise your vampire army, Nick? We'll need at least a couple of days here with the combined army."

Nick didn't seem dazed at all at the question. "Yes, many of them contacted me last night when Gaius was murdered," he said, the pensive look returned to his face. He suffered from the loss of his brother. Family was important to Nick even if they were terrible.

"Brie, will you be training?" Brandon asked.

"No, I'm going to travel with Nick to show the vampires we are unified." I'd been in a vampire lair more than once, so I could handle Nick's friends.

"Do you think it is a good idea as queen to be the only witch among a vampire army?" His concern was betrayed in his broken voice.

"I'll be fine, Brandon," I said. I felt close to him again in the moment. He hugged me, and I flashed into a vision with his touch. The battle we worked toward was the one I saw in repetitive visions. It would be my turning point and the turning point for our fight.

When I came back to reality, I had been moved to the couch. Everyone had left the room except Sorin, Brandon, and Nick. Brandon was seated on the couch beside me. I looked up at him, ready to speak, but he put his finger to his lips to tell me to keep quiet.

He leaned over to whisper in my ear. "I know." He squeezed my hand and kissed my cheek. He turned to Sorin and Nick, who were arguing about something. "She's awake." They both rushed over to me as Brandon gently backed out of the room. *He knows.*

CHAPTER
TWENTY

I convinced Nick and Sorin I was fine, even though I was curious about how Brandon knew what I saw. Sorin and Nick argued about me leaving with Nick, and he continued the argument with me. I finally told him I had a vision showing I returned safely, and he stopped protesting. It wasn't like me to lie, but I was exhausted from the conversation. More than anything, I wanted distance from the Great House. I needed fresh air to clear my thoughts.

It wasn't until Nick pulled up to the first vampire's house Nick had already been in contact with that I realized I had no idea what I was going to say to them. I suddenly became nervous, and my palms were sweating. Nick looked down at the hand he held and at me with a raised eyebrow.

"Are you sure you want to do this?" he asked, walking to the door.

"Yes, but I don't know what to say," I said.

"Be yourself, Brie. Don't throw any energy balls. They probably wouldn't be receptive to those." I looked up at him, mortified he thought I would. He laughed. I punched him in the arm with my free hand, and it made him laugh harder. He accomplished his goal of relaxing me. He was gifted in his own ways, even if he didn't fully realize it himself.

"Jerk," I said under my breath. He spun me around to face him, planting a kiss on my mouth. "Still a jerk, but I love you." When he released me, I flashed him a smile.

"I love you too." He smiled.

The door opened before we knocked, and I was shocked by how handsome the vampire was who answered it. I must have not allowed myself to really look at them when I hunted. He had strawberry blond hair just below his chin, and it was more strawberry than blond. He looked about twenty-five, standing eye-to-eye with Nick. He took me in from my feet up and then stared Nick down. I squeezed Nick's hand more for me than for him.

"This one's a little young for you, Domenico. I thought you had a thing for the blue hairs," he said, never taking his eyes off Nick.

"And I thought you would have learned some manners by now, O'Kelly." Nick chuckled as he threw his arms around the man. "It's good to see you."

"It's been a while, brother."

"Too long for my taste," Nick said, smiling. "Malachi, I want you to meet my fiancé, Brie." He gestured to me. "Brie, this is my oldest friend, Malachi O'Kelly." I held out my hand to shake, but Malachi surprised me by kissing it instead.

"It is a pleasure to meet a woman capable of getting Nicholas to commit," Malachi said, flashing a wicked grin. *Vampire charm.*

"It's wonderful to meet a friend of Nick's. I hope you have some stories to share." I smiled at him, and he winked with a nod. Nick cleared his throat and glared at Malachi.

"Come in, you two," Malachi said, motioning for us to follow. His home was a beautiful old home on the outside and completely modern on the inside, down to the security system, which included drones. The huntress in me couldn't help but observe. We sat in the plush living room with a large, oversized black leather sectional. I felt small compared to them on the enormous piece of furniture.

"Gaius is a significant loss to the cause, Nicholas. I'm sorry, my brother. Stefan was wise in taking them out. It will cause lesser vampires to cower in his favor," Malachi said, his voice heavy.

"You are right on both accounts. Will we have the numbers with those weaklings returning to Stefan?" The bitterness in Nick's voice caught me off guard. I flinched ever so slightly, but he noticed. He must have thought I was cold, because he wrapped his arm around me, drawing me to him.

"It will be close in number, but our skilled forces are greater. He will send the lesser vampires to die first," Malachi said.

Nick nodded and looked down at me. "Malachi is the general of my army."

"Oh." I couldn't think of anything to say. As they discussed their plans, I stared at the fire raging in the fireplace. My mind focused on the vampires they referred to as weaklings and lesser. They showed little regard for them, and it bothered me. My Blood Moon tattoo tingled, and it troubled me. This would lead to bloodshed, not peace. Here I sat with two powerful vampires as the Queen of the Witches, a reformed vampire huntress, and the one destined to bring peace. I didn't want to shed blood despite my past, but Stefan had already shed both witch and vampire blood, leaving us no choice.

I suddenly felt trapped and couldn't breathe. *Cool air.* My lungs needed it. I ran for the door and out into the front yard, gasping for air. The hair on my neck stood up, alerting me to the predator nearby. I dropped to my knees on the grass, letting the air fill my lungs. I didn't ignore my senses, but I couldn't fight without air and assumed it was Nick and Malachi behind me. A hand grabbed my shoulder, and someone flipped me onto my back with fangs bearing down on my neck. My training kicked in, and I reached for the stake in my boot. Before I could take aim, Nick tossed the vampire through the air like a rag doll. I watched the body fly across the yard, landing against a tree at least a century old. The growl from Nick was from the killer in him and not the jealous growl from other times. He had intended to rip the vampire to shreds. I stood between the injured vampire and Nick. Malachi slipped his arms under Nick's, locking his hands behind Nick's head.

"Brother, that is one of my guards. One of your loyal subjects. I'm sure she thought Brie was our dinner escaping," Malachi said, reasoning with Nick. I shuddered at his words.

"Nick, I don't want bloodshed. Not tonight." I said, staying as calm as I could. I glanced over my shoulder at the vampire. The lean figure made her way slowly towards us. The vampire stepped into the light, and she looked like she was maybe twenty. Her hair was a shoulder-length brown bob, and she had hazel eyes full of fear.

"Prince Nicholas, my apologies. I didn't know you were here," she said, dropping to a knee and bowing before him. It was the first time I heard anyone call him Prince Nicholas other than Stefan, but there was more here between them.

"Ella?" Nick asked. There was surprise and something else in his voice. I turned to study him.

He had recognition on his face as it softened toward her.

"Yes, my Prince." She stood, but dropped her eyes to the ground. The change in the mood was palpable. She raised her head and looked at Nick through her eyelashes. The effect on him was obvious. The woman, Ella, was a lover. Of that, I was sure. I didn't need either of them telling me.

I had enough skeletons in my closet to know. Uneasiness took over in the pit of my stomach. I wanted to turn and run away to not see the reaction. I wanted to teleport back to my balcony. Neither of those would have been the act of a queen, and the latter would expose one of my secrets. I watched back and forth between the two of them as they had their moment. The longer she held his gaze, the more I wanted to gouge her eyes out. It was only a few seconds in reality, but it was too long for me.

Nick shook his head and cleared his throat. "Ella, this is my fiancé, Brie. Brie, this is Ella," Nick said, his voice stiff and formal.

"Hello, Brie. I've heard so much about you," she said, forcing a smile.

Funny you've heard of me since I've heard nothing of you. The queen in me rose above the petty jealousy. Ella was beautiful, but Nick asked me to marry him.

"Hello. It's always a pleasure to meet Nick's friends." I said, mimicking the greeting Nick had given Cal and not missing the quick glance she gave Nick.

"Malachi, Brie and I have other stops to make tonight, so we must take our leave," Nick said, his voice returning to normal. He seemed rushed to leave, but I wondered if it was for my benefit or his. His comfort level had shifted, and it was obvious Ella was the reason. I looked at her again and found her gaze locked on Nick.

A gust of wind blew as the anger rose in me. Leaving was exactly what we needed to do before I conjured a hurricane to take her to the next continent or, better yet, a deserted island.

"I'll walk you to the car," Malachi said. The three of us walked away, leaving Ella staring at my fiancé.

)) ● ((

W<small>E MADE</small> two more stops to high-ranking vampires, and thankfully, there weren't any more lovers trying to attack me or undressing Nick with their eyes. I stared out the window of the car, debating within myself whether I should bring it up and risk looking like the jealous type or let it go. The thought of Nick and Ella together was eating me inside.

"You're quiet, Brie," Nick said. I turned my head to look at him, forcing a small smile. "You're never quiet."

"Just thinking."

"About?" Nick asked. Do I even have a right to ask about it? Why wasn't she in any of his memories of the past I saw?

"I was thinking through the events of the night."

"You agree with our choices, right?"

"Yes, I have faith in our plan. I was thinking about what happened at Malachi's." I tackled the subject, not wanting a wall to form between us.

Nick nodded understanding and reached over, taking my hand. He laced his fingers through mine with ease.

"Ella is the past. You are my future, Brie."

I felt the truth in his words. All I needed was honesty, and he gave it to me. It should be enough.

"It looked like there was still a connection between you two, and I hate I sound like a jealous girlfriend." I struggled to keep my voice even. The shakiness gave away my insecurity.

"Fiancé. You are my jealous fiancé." He smirked. "I love you, Brie. I love you in a way I could never have loved Ella."

"I love you." I paused. "So what happened with you and Ella?"

Nick sighed. "It was a long time ago before you were even born, Brie, but I'll give you the short version. She and I were betrothed in marriage, but I found her in bed with Gaius. Stefan had her banished from the castle at my request, and I have not seen her since until tonight. End of story." He gave me the shortest version possible and shifted in the seat. I decided not to push it any further tonight, but I could ascertain there was more to it. When he was ready to talk, he would tell me.

)) ● ((

WHEN WE FINALLY RETIRED TO the mansion after filling everyone in on our progress, I expected we would go straight to bed. Nick had other plans. He locked the door to the suite and wordlessly led me to the couch.

"I don't want you to doubt my love for you ever, and I believe the truth keeps us strong," he said, brushing a loose strand of hair from my face and looking deep into my soul.

Well, great. I'm an ass for being jealous.

"Nick, what happened in your life before we met is your past. Our future is not dependent upon it, and I don't want you to feel you have to tell me every detail. It doesn't change how I feel about you," I said, smiling as I touched his face. He kissed the palm of my hand.

"I want you to feel secure." He fiddled with the engagement ring he put on my hand. "There was a time when Gaius was a better man than me. It was before I found my humanity. He was jaded, but not the ruthless self he had become in recent years. Ella was a beautiful young woman in a kingdom we acquired, and Gaius and I were both enamored by her. We had a competition to see who could bed her first. I succeeded, and I wanted her all to myself, so I promised to marry her after I turned her." He cleared his throat.

"Gaius couldn't stand to lose, and he continued to pursue her before and after her change was complete. The night before our wedding, I went to her chambers, but they were empty. When I found her, she was with Gaius. I lost it and nearly ended both of them." The pain in his eyes was almost unbearable, and I squeezed his hand. "It took Stefan and six of his guards to stop me. The next night, after she healed, Ella came to me asking for forgiveness and saying Gaius had told her about the bet we had. She said she loved me and had made a mistake because she thought I didn't love her. I had my way with her, and then I told her I never loved her, which was true. Love wasn't what it was. I asked Stefan to banish her. I felt guilt over it after I started finding my humanity, but I never thought I would see her again."

I put my hands on either side of his face. He'd made himself vulnerable to me. "You're not the same person you were then. You are a good person now, Nick."

"I don't feel like a good person right now." He sighed.

"It's called remorse." I searched his eyes and saw guilt.

"It's important to me you know I love you. No matter what you hear or what happens. I love you."

"I feel how much you love me, Nick, and I love you as much, if not more," I said, kissing him.

"There is no possible way you love me more." We fell asleep on the couch snuggled together. It was one of the best sleeps I could remember having until the dreams came.

I dreamed over and over again of Brandon dying on the battlefield. No matter what I did to save him, something would happen I couldn't stop. I felt hopeless and alone in my quest to save him. The strange thing was when it was Nick, I could always find a way to save him. It frustrated me, and I wanted to find a path to save both. After about the fifteenth time waking up, I snuck out of the suite while Nick slept. I figured if I was restless, I might as well put it to good use and headed to the library.

I looked up my predecessors and their sacrifices. My determination to find the answer I wanted consumed me. A presence entered the room, and I looked up to find my brother with a cup of tea.

"Hey, Sis. Thought you might want some company," he said, sitting the tea on the table beside me.

"How did you know I was in here?" I asked.

"I have been able to feel you again lately. I think the closer we get to battle, the stronger the twin sense gets." He shrugged. "What are you reading?"

I stared at the ceiling. My attempt to keep from over-flowing the corners of my eyes.

"It's ok. I've accepted it." He hugged me and then sat at my feet.

He may have accepted it, but I refused to think it was the only way. I bit down on my already raw lip.

"I can't give up," I said. "We'll find a way to save you."

"If it doesn't happen, promise me you will always choose light," he said. It sounded like he was giving me advice as if he knew my internal struggle, and maybe he did. I wanted to promise him, but I couldn't get the words out. I squeezed his hand, looking away and fighting back tears. "Brie, you have to choose light. It's the only way you will fulfill your prophecy."

"I will try to always choose light." I couldn't, in good faith, make a promise knowing the visions I had, so I gave him the only assurance I could. We spent hours combing through the history of our ancestors, neither of us wanting to sleep and my stubbornness refusing to let me give up. It was to no avail, and I felt lost as the morning came.

TWENTY-ONE

P eople stirred around in the mansion, but we weren't ready to give up on our search. Brandon and I both looked up as the door creaked open, and I was relieved to see Grandmother. She had a knack for finding us when we didn't want to be found, even when we were kids. We always hid together in the tiniest places our kid bodies would fit.

"I thought I would find you both in here," she said, smiling. "Alastair and Cal will join us for breakfast, so you two are expected, but let's talk first."

"Is Alastair pissed?" I covered my mouth. "I mean, is he angry?" No matter how old I got, or that I was a queen, I still felt awkward swearing in front of my grandmother. I expected her to pull out a bar of soap to wash my mouth out like she did the first time I cussed in front of her.

"He will get past it," she said, brushing it away. I blew out a breath. "I want to talk about you two." She sat in one of the wingback chairs and motioned for us to sit on the couch. "What have you two been up to this morning?" She eyed us.

We exchanged looks like kids with their hands caught in the candy dish. "I couldn't sleep, and I was doing some reading. Brandon brought me some tea and joined me," I said.

"Mmm hmmm." She nodded. Neither of us ever got away with hiding anything from her.

"Grandmother, we were looking to see if anyone in the past was able to avoid the sacrifice," Brandon said. And like in our childhood, Brandon was the first to give up a secret.

"And what did you find?" she asked in a curious tone.

"We found no precedence for it," I said, looking away.

"There was one," Grandmother said, her voice compassionate.

Brandon and I both leaned in with our full attention on her. *Finally, some good news.*

"He sacrificed himself to avoid his destiny, and he ended up giving into the dark." Her eyes glazed over, and I could tell she relived a memory. Brandon and I stared at each other. We knew who she meant.

"Sorin," Brandon and I said together. Grandmother focused back on us.

I leaned back on the couch.

"Yes, he gave up his destiny for the love of his family, and he paid a high price for it. Destiny has a strange way of coming full circle when we try to avoid it." She paused. "You two should spend some time with him. He has much wisdom he could share with you. He loved you even when he chose the dark over the light." She stood up, and we followed her movement. "Now, you two need to go get ready for breakfast."

I found Nick still asleep on the couch where I left him, and I sat down next to him. It was so unusual for a vampire to sleep much at all. They usually barely napped. I touched his cheek and watched his eyes flutter open and fill with love as he gazed at me. I would never tire of seeing his special look for me.

"Hey, handsome. Are you okay? You've been asleep for hours." I brushed my lips across his cheek.

"Good morning, beautiful." He wrapped his arms around me, drawing me closer. "I'm hungry. I need to go hunt, and not at a blood bank, so I am at my strongest for the battle." The thought of him hunting humans gave me chills, and I selfishly wanted him by my side today for my strength and sanity. Being away from him was torture of a different kind.

"Why hunt when you have a perfectly good neck right here?" I asked, leaning my head over to expose my neck to him. He placed a gentle kiss there instead.

"You're quite the temptress, my lovely fiancé, but I would never drink from you, even if it wasn't forbidden for me to do so." He turned my head toward him, placing a soft kiss on my lips.

"I don't understand. I thought drinking each other's blood was done in vampire relationships. And I am the Queen, so I guess I get to decide what is forbidden now." It disappointed me he turned me down, but it reassured me in a strange way, too. It's not like he didn't drink witch blood. I'd seen it in his memories.

"In a vampire relationship, yes, they would share each other's blood, and even in a human and vampire relationship, they do sometimes. It is dangerous for a witch and vampire to share, because there are some unforeseen effects of which I believe we experienced one already." He pressed his lips to my forehead.

"True. I guess I had assumed at some point it would become part of our relationship," I said, a slight sting of rejection hanging in the air even though I understood the explanation.

"Endangering you is not something I would willingly do. I'm shocked the ultimate vampire hunter would want her blood sucked so readily." He smiled at me. I shoved him away and jumped up from the couch. He caught me and trapped me in his lap, reminding me even weak his reflexes were faster and his physical strength more. "Of course, I could make one little exception," he said, smiling against my neck and placing a kiss there. I giggled at how playful he was. These were the most normal moments we had, and I treasured every second. If we had five minutes where we were normal out of a day, then it would have to be enough.

"We have to get ready for breakfast," I said. "With Alastair and Cal." I didn't turn around, but the wind rushed around me as he blew past me to the bathroom doorway.

"Then we better make this fast." He scooped me up

and carried me to the shower, chuckling mischievously the entire way.

)) ● ((

WE WALKED to the dining room hand-in-hand, smiling and laughing as an engaged couple should do. Of course, the smile quickly left when Sorin grabbed my arm. He dragged me out for a word with me like I was an errant teenager. Nick growled a warning, and thank goodness for Grandmother, who took his arm and seated him beside her.

"Sorin, stop doing this. It makes you look crazy, and it makes me look weak." I said.

"You may have made your choice with Nick, daughter, but flaunting it in front of Alastair is not diplomatic." His jaw was set and his voice was calm. I thought he pulled me aside to scold me, but he was trying to advise me. He could approach it better, but I appreciated his guidance was sound. "He will be offended by the lack of respect. There should have been a conversation between you, Cal, Alastair, and me before you invited Nick back into the mansion. I know part of this is my fault for not being here to teach you the royal customs, but I thought your mother would have done some of this." The frustration he felt finally broke through the longer he spoke.

"Don't blame her. She tried, but I was more interested in hunting. I would skip etiquette appointments with her in favor of training with Brandon. You are right. Cal and I had a conversation already, but it was thoughtless of me. I'm in love and happy, and I forgot we're not normal people." I had to behave like a diplomat and a queen, and I had to stop letting my heart lead every step.

"Did we just agree on something?" Sorin smiled.

"I think we did, Dad." I smiled back and watched his smile grow. "Do you think we could make some time this afternoon for Brandon and me to chat with you?" Grandmother was right. My brother and I needed to spend time with him.

"Of course." He wrapped an arm around my shoulder and led me back into the dining hall. Everyone stood with formality as I entered the room. He led me to the head of the table, and I decided I would never get used to sitting there. The chair looked like a mini throne, but it was still larger than the other chairs. It was one of the many archaic practices I had discovered we still upheld since becoming queen. I would make some modern changes during my rule.

"Please be seated." I sat down. "My apologies for the disruption, but we had a private matter to discuss." I smiled at everyone. Nick's forehead was wrinkled as he looked at me. I nodded to him. I noticed my mother was holding out her glass for a refill of mimosa. It takes a lot to get a witch drunk, but she was nervous. She looked at me and smiled as she took a drink from the glass. The smile wasn't her normal smile, and it made me uneasy. I took a moment to look around the table, and everyone else seemed like they enjoyed the breakfast. Grandmother and Brandon chatted with Cal. Sorin and Alastair were engaged in a conversation. Nick stared at me.

"My Queen?" Alastair asked.

"Brie, please." Cal took advantage of my delayed response to the title and interrupted before his father could speak.

"Brie, I told Father of our discussion and mutual decision. I'm afraid he is being a rather pompous arse and blinkered about it, so please excuse him. I think we should discuss it properly in private if you please." Cal raised his voice. I had to hide the smirk at the way he handled the situation, and I heard Brandon cough to cover his chuckle. Everyone else stared at them, either with mouths open or forks in midair or both. It was unusual for children of royals to stand up to their parents for fear of being disinherited, but it appears it was something Cal and I have in common.

"Yes, agreed. Why don't we convene in the library after breakfast?" I said.

"Lovely," Cal said. He had a huge smile like he'd won a bet.

Conversation was casual for the remainder of breakfast. Nick went in search of his regular diet while I met with the others in the library. The conversation should be for the four of us as Sorin suggested. Brandon wanted to join, but I asked him to stand outside the door. Mother disappeared, and Grandmother waited with Brandon. I hoped this did not turn into a shouting match.

"Before you start, Father, I want to make sure you know this was as much, if not more, of my decision than Brie's. We are both in love with other people and want to marry them. We are adults and control our own lives." Cal said as soon as the door shut. I was proud of him for making a stand.

"Cal, this isn't about love. You and Brie have a duty to the witches and your destiny." Anger dripped from Alastair's voice, but he tried hard to mask it.

I studied him. He was complex, but there was definitely a pretense in his actions.

"I've seen my visions and hers, Father. We are not together in them. Our paths are not converged," Cal said. *What?* He was more like me than I realized. I stepped closer to him. Why hadn't he told me?

"Cal, you have visions? You've seen mine?" I asked, not hiding the shock.

"Yes. Sorry. I meant to tell you when we were touring the city, but the guards wouldn't give us enough space," he said in a remorseful tone.

"Alastair, our children are adults. They must choose their own paths just as we did when fate came for us," Sorin said, his voice casual. I felt a warmth inside from his fatherly support. I didn't miss the reference he made to fate coming for them, and I wondered what Alastair's role had been. *Surely not a Protector.*

"You can't be siding with them. You know the implications," Alastair said. He narrowed his eyes at Sorin.

"Yes, and I know what will happen if we try to force them. Support their choice. We never had the luxury of choice until it was too late. Let them dictate their own destiny in a way weren't allowed to. It will turn out better for them." Sorin was pretty convincing, and he earned my respect a thousand times over.

"Fine, but you are going to clean up the mess when it all goes to Hell. Literally," Alastair said, skulking from the room, slamming the door.

I stood with my mouth gaping open, and Cal's face looked like I felt mine did. Sorin rubbed his temples before he spoke to us.

"You two need to make sure you are making the right choice. Alastair is right in a way. It's not just your lives on a tipping scale here. It is all of ours and the humans. Take some time to talk to each other. Share what you know, and most importantly, do what you know in your heart is right." Sorin warned us as he left us alone in the library.

I expected Grandmother and Brandon to join us, but I suspected Sorin told them to leave us be as no one entered the room. My choice wouldn't change. It would always be Nick, but I wanted to know more about Cal's visions. We did as Sorin asked, and it amazed me how much Cal and I were alike. He had acquired powers through the years, and we shared many of the same. I was more powerful and had powers he didn't, but it had never happened where there was a witch and a warlock so blessed at the same time. We knew it meant something, but we didn't know what. We were searching through the books for any information or relation to the prophecy when Nick walked into the room. He was pensive and stress rolled off of him.

"I'm sorry to interrupt," he said to us both before looking into my eyes. We connected, and I forced myself back to the moment. "Stefan is summoning me, and I must go."

Fuck. Cunning bastard. He knows he can get to me through Nick. "I'll take us there then," I said.

"No, he is probably hoping and expecting for you to teleport with me. I've called Malachi to go with me." My heart constricted, but his logic was right.

"Nick, come back to me." I respected his choice and threw my arms around his neck. He held me tightly. When he pushed me back, he kissed me softly.

"I love you, Brielle Danforth. You will be my wife," he said, his voice quiet in my ear. I could feel the blush on my cheeks as I looked up at him.

"I love you too, Nicholas Domenico," I said, keeping my voice soft. He let me go and disappeared in a flash. I wanted to follow him, but I stayed despite the horribly broken harmony in my heart.

Cal and I continued to search the books for anything on our situation. We found nothing even remotely close.

"Rubbish. All of it," Call said.

The next step was to look at the prophecy, but my mind drifted to Nick, wondering if he was safe.

Our instincts were dead on. Three of the books referenced phrased it in a similar way. The prophecy stated we would be strongest together as one, which in witch speak meant devoted to each other as in marriage by these interpretations. I questioned that. Cal would always be second to me unless I died. No matter how strong he would become, I would always be stronger. The answers we found were not to my liking. It read as if we were forced to choose each other, and we had no intention of doing it. We discussed options until Brandon came to tell me Sorin was ready for us in his personal study. Cal and I hugged each other in commiseration as I left, and he stayed to look for more answers.

Brandon and I were almost at the door of Sorin's study when a vision hit me hard and fast. It was a quick snapshot of Sorin being impaled. Fear shot through me. I couldn't tell where or if he died, but I was sure I wouldn't be getting the vision if it wasn't his death. I leaned on the wall and looked at Brandon. His eyes were wide.

"Did you see it?" I asked.

"Yes, you projected to me," he said. I caught my breath before we entered the room. Sorin sat on the couch with our ancestral book waiting for us.

"Come sit beside me," he said, giving me a gentle smile. He looked happy, and I shared a look with Brandon to make sure we were on the same page to not tell him. Seeing someone's death was an awful curse, but to tell them it was coming seemed much worse. I resigned to stop it as I would stop Brandon's. We sat on either side of him as he told us our family history.

TWENTY-TWO

"Then we come to my story," Sorin said. "We knew the prophecy would be fulfilled with your generation. My role was to guide you to fulfill it. I would be King, and you would begin your journey upon my death. I thought I could spare you from the prophecy by abdicating my position to my sister. Unfortunately, the sacrifice I made couldn't stop the events already in motion. I felt the pull of it continually, and it drove me to the dark for relief as an alcoholic craves a drink. Trying to avoid it only brought it sooner rather than later," Sorin said, his voice full of regret.

He'd shared most of this before, but I was in a better place to receive it this time. His message was clear. There was no avoiding it.

"Why me? Why us?" I asked, not out of pity but wanting to understand why we were the only ones who could fulfill this prophecy.

"Because we are the direct descendants of the first

witch coven. Our bloodline is the first of our kind. By birth, we are the leaders and the protectors," Sorin said.

"What about Cal? Are they from the first family, too?"

"No, but they are pure from those the first witch coven made into witches," Sorin replied.

"Made into a witch?" Brandon asked, echoing the confusion I felt. "I thought witches were born either pure blood or halfling?"

"Today, that is true. However, the original coven commanded magic differently, and they could create witches. The spell required vampire blood mixed with their own to do it. The vampire would be drained dry and beheaded after the ritual for fear it would control the new witch." He took a deep breath.

Holy shit. Vampires were used to create witches. It turned my stomach into a mass of knots. My entire life was spun around vampires who hated us because we hunted them for hunting humans, but that wasn't the heart of the hatred between our species.

"If they created them from a vampire's blood who clung to his humanity, then they were driven to the light. If they created them from a vampire's blood who had let go of his humanity, then they were inclined to the dark. They eventually performed a ritual, releasing them from their control and giving them the ability to choose light or dark, which is where we are today. Our bloodline has always had the choice, but the others are still driven by their origins, even with their freedom."

"So Alastair and Cal have vampire blood in their veins? I'm confused," I said, reaching up to touch my necklace.

"No, not exactly. The blood used in the ritual never flowed through their veins. Alastair is from one of the darkest lines, but he chose light. Cal's mother is from a light line, and it appears Cal takes after her."

"Why did we never know this?" Brandon asked.

"It is the reason the witches and vampires went to war for the first time. The first coven wanted to eradicate the vampires so their blood couldn't be used to make any other witches once they released the ones they created. The knowledge is only told to three people in a generation to ensure it is not lost and mistakes are not repeated. Those told are bound by an oath of secrecy. The story is written in a book bound by magic only the king or queen of the coven can open or read." Sorin looked at us, waiting for it to register. We were two of the three.

"Who will be the third from our generation?" I asked.

"You should tell Nick. It's time a vampire understands the real story," Sorin said. I leaned into him, and he wrapped his arms around both of us. The truth helped me heal in ways I needed. The shock of our history hung between us, but we felt like a family, even in all chaos.

My mother was next on my list to visit. It was time we healed the open wound between us, too. It wouldn't be so quick to heal, but I had to take the step in that direction. To be a good queen, I needed to be whole, and it couldn't happen as long as I carried contempt in my heart for her. It was time to move on from my childhood scars.

With the help of the guards, I found her drunk and lounging in the formal drawing room. She must have consumed a lot of alcohol to mask the pain, leading her to the intoxicated version of herself. I saw two empty champagne bottles on the table, but I guessed there were more somewhere around the mansion.

"Mother, let's go to my room," I said, trying to pick her up. For such a small person, she was sure heavy as dead weight. I couldn't send her out like this, and she didn't have quarters at the mansion, so my suite seemed the best choice.

"My baby's getting married," she said. Her speech slurred, and the smell of alcohol on her breath was pungent. I held my breath and leaned away.

"Yes, I'm getting married," I confirmed to the drunken version of my mother. I sat her back down on the couch, seeing no way to get her out of there without being noticed.

I told the guards at the door to give us some space and meet me at my quarters in five minutes. When they followed my orders, I teleported us to my living room in the suite. While I continued to gain strength each time, it was her first time. The rush was hard on her, and she vomited the contents of her stomach all over the wood floor. I held out my hand and froze her before she fell into it. I levitated her to the couch, gently setting her down. Cleaning up vampire guts sounded immensely better than cleaning up the vomit. I gagged from the smell. As I turned to head to the hallway to find something to clean it up, I saw Nick standing in the doorway.

"Need some help?" he asked. His eyes looked dark with deep purple circles under them, and I worried about him.

"Yes, the guards will be here any minute. I didn't know

what to do with her." I shook my head. Nick rushed off without a word, returning with a mop and bucket. He had the vomit cleaned up in what seemed like a minute, thanks to his vampire speed.

"Thank you," I said, looking up at him as the guards arrived at the door. "We'll be here until dinner. My mother isn't well." I shut the door before they could see much.

"I'm going to take a shower," Nick said.

I looked at my mother, who had passed out cold.

"I'm going to join you," I said, taking his hand leading the way, stopping only to shut the door between the bedroom and the living room. I secured the lock. I wanted to ask about his meeting with Stefan, but I needed to wash the day away first.

The hot water ran over us. I held onto him with everything I had, and he folded around me. It rejuvenated me being close to Nick. I looked up into his eyes, and pain creased the corners of his eyes. The dark circles looked even worse than when I saw him at the door. "You still haven't fed, have you?"

"No." He clenched his jaw. "Stefan's summons interrupted my hunt."

"Nick, will you please drink from me? I'm worried about you," I said. "I'm not going to judge you by the memories if that's your reservation.

"I will not use you like a blood whore," he said, clenching his jaw harder.

"You're not using me like a blood whore. I'm your fiancé, and I am offering it to you freely." His expression relaxed, letting me know he acquiesced. I kissed his neck in reassurance and exposed mine to him. He kissed a trail, starting at my shoulder up to the spot he desired on my neck. His lips burned, and his hands grasped my hips, pressing me against him. My eyes fluttered with desire.

His fangs pierced my skin with a pinch, but the pain gave way to pleasure. It felt damn good. I ran my hands over his body and through his hair. I tried and failed to stifle a moan from escaping. I didn't want him to stop, but the alternative was not an option. When he finished, he stared into my eyes and pushed me against the shower wall. His powerful lips were on mine, and I reached for his hardness, running my hand over the length of it. He slammed the shower knob, turning it off. His fingers ran through my hair while I stroked him. The soap scent mixed with his vanilla aroma, and I bit down on his shoulder. He scooped me up and carried me to the bed.

"Your mother?"

"She's out for a couple of hours," I said, my voice breathless. Not wanting to think about her.

He positioned himself between my legs. I dug my nails into his back.

"I don't think I can be gentle," he growled in my ear.

"I don't want you to be," I said. Gentle wouldn't satisfy me today. "I want you inside me."

He thrust into me.

"Goddess." My nails ripped flesh down his sides.

His hips dug into my thighs with each thrust, and I climbed to a peak of colors. He captured my mouth and moan into it. I clenched around him, and he joined me in ecstasy, filling me with warmth. This feverish and wild way was new, and I couldn't complain.

Afterward, I smiled, satisfied to see the dark circles disappeared. I snuggled up to his chest. He held me tight, kissing the top of my head. We only had a few minutes before we had to get dressed for dinner, but I wanted to squeeze out every second I could with him.

"So, do you want to talk about why Stefan summoned you? Or are you keeping that to yourself?" I asked. "I was worried about you."

"He tried to convince me to rejoin him. I suspect he heard of the army we are raising and wanted to confirm if it was true," Nick said, stroking my hair. "I'm kind of surprised he let us go without torturing us if I'm being honest."

"You were gone a long time. I considered teleporting there," I said, searching his eyes to find what it was he kept from telling me.

"He offered a trade, Brie." He paused, looking away. "If I bring you to him, there will be no war. I told him to go to Hell."

"Thank the Goddess," I said, taking in a deep gulp of air. "You know he wouldn't keep his word." I would turn myself over to him if it meant peace, but Stefan had no intention of making peace. He wanted to use me as a weapon. I sat straight up in bed as I figured out why he wanted me.

"Brie, are you alright?" Nick sat up next to me.

"I know what he wants me to do. It's not entirely about the prophecy. I mean, the prophecy would put a damper on his plan, but it is about my bloodline." In my heart and out loud, I spoke the truth. My tattoo glowed in confirmation.

"I don't understand what you are saying," Nick said.

"I'll explain after dinner. I promise." I jumped out of bed to get ready. "If we're late, Sorin will be too pissed to hear what I'm saying." I needed my family present when I told them what Stefan's end game was.

Mother stirred on the couch. I helped her to the bathroom while Nick excused himself.

)) ● ((

WE TOOK our leave of Alastair and Cal after dinner and drinks. I was relieved Brandon, Grandmother, Mother, and Sorin were already in the library when Nick and I arrived. The concern on their faces was justified. I motioned for everyone to take a seat around the table and closed the door.

"Dad, I know there are only three of each generation who know the actual history, and you passed it to Brandon and me with permission for me to pass it to Nick as well." I turned to Grandmother and Mother. "Do you know what I am speaking of?"

"Yes, I do," Grandmother said. She nodded her head, confirming my suspicion she was one of the three from her generation.

"I haven't a clue what you mean, Brie," my mother said, rubbing her head. Brandon and I had seen her like this many times over the years.

"Sorin-" I paused, looking at him with a small smile. "Dad, can you explain it to her for me? It's important for what I have to tell you all," I said.

He obliged me and gave her the abbreviated version. The look on her face was a combination of hangover and shock, and I chided myself for wanting to laugh at such a serious moment. I looked at Nick, who didn't look as shocked as I expected. He locked eyes with me, and our connection was powerful. He didn't have to voice it. He had already figured out what I was about to tell the group, and he shifted uncomfortably.

"The reason I wanted to make sure everyone understood the history is because I know why Stefan wants me." I looked around the room at blank faces except for Nick's. Understanding Stefan's thirst for control and power, he grasped what the threat was. "It's more than stopping the prophecy and peace. He wants to use me to make dark witches he can control. If he turns me into a vampire, he can control me and any witches created by me." No one said a word. The shock silenced them, so I went on. "They would be more powerful than any other adversary, and there would be no winning against them."

"Brie, that is ridiculous. Why would you even think it would be possible?" Mother asked. Of course, she would be the skeptical one.

"Because she's right, Katerina." It always struck me as strange hearing someone call my mother by name since I share it as my middle name, but it was even more so hearing it from Sorin. It was like a time warp I had to fight not to step into every time they were in the same room together. Sorin looked directly at me. "You won't be able to attend the battle when we attack. It's too risky, and even more so now his true plan is exposed. If he captures you again, we might not get to you in time."

"You are right, but I can't send people to die without taking the risk myself," I said. I had made my resolution to be there. The only way to prevent the visions was to be there and change them.

"Your risk isn't dying, Brie. It's being captured to create an army of dark witches, which is, unfortunately, worse than death for our kind," Sorin said.

"I can take Mandrake root with me in case I am captured," I said. Everyone spoke at once. I tried to focus my emotions. Thunder rumbled. Lightning struck outside the window, and I took a deep breath. Brandon was in front of me, taking both of my hands.

"Remember when we hid under the stairs at Grandmother's house when we were playing hide-n-seek? We worried her sick because we forgot we were playing the game. We played under the stairs for hours, making little energy balls and trying to read each other's thoughts," he said, chuckling. I laughed at the memory, and his effort to calm me down worked. Then again, it always did. Nick was beside me with his hand on my shoulder.

"You two were always hiding from me." Grandmother laughed.

"This time was different. It was the first time Brandon tapped into his magic on his own and made an energy ball," I said, smiling. "Thanks, Brandon."

"Poison is not an option, Brie," Sorin said, moving to

stand between Brandon and me, ending our walk down memory lane.

I agree," Nick said. *They choose now to agree on something.*

"Brandon, what do you think?" I waited for my Protector, not my brother, to answer. He carefully considered what I asked before he answered.

"I know it is important for you to be at the battle. I will stay by your side the entire time. Even if it means giving my own life as your Protector, I will gladly fight for not just my queen but my sister." He was self-assured in his answer. I wished I could share his confidence. All the visions of him dying, and we couldn't stop it. Every action took us closer. I studied him for a moment and looked at Grandmother. She only nodded. One thing was evident. My choice would be made on the battlefield. I thought of the vision I had of Sorin and wondered if it was from the battlefield as well. Death knocked at the door for many of my loved ones, and the determination to prevent it grew within me.

"I'll stand at your other side," Nick said.

"I want you there, but you will need to lead the vampires who have sworn their allegiance to you," I said, touching his arm.

"We'll all be unified and shedding our blood for the same cause. We should stand together." He was firm. I grimaced at the thought of bloodshed, but there was truth in what he said.

"Then we will stand together." I smiled up at him

against the uneasiness I had. I portrayed strength and confidence that I wasn't sure went to my core.

The decisions made whether they were right or wrong, and we parted ways for the night. As Nick and I walked back to my suite, I felt drawn to the chapel. I gently guided our path to the centuries-old ornately carved doors where Nick froze. His gaze went up to the cherub at the apex and back down to the handle.

"The Great House was built around this chapel."

"I can't. It's hallowed ground," he said, staring at the chapel doors. I felt a tingle inside me, and it came to me what to do.

"Trust me?" I asked, standing between him in the door.

"Always." He looked into my eyes for our connection. I briefly relished our bond. It coursed through my body like electricity and ignited my soul.

"Take my hand." I extended my hand to him with a smile. He obliged. My pink aura became visible to him and engulfed us both.

He glanced over at me. "What is this?" His voice full of wonder.

"Safe passage," I said, taking a step forward. "Don't let go of my hand."

"Never," he said, taking every step I took into the beautiful old chapel with its old-world charm. We walked up to the front and knelt. I began my silent prayer for guidance in the days to come.

Goddess, I pray to find the path of light and for it to include the safety of my family. I thank you for allowing me the means to bring Nick into the sanctuary of the chapel.

When I was done, I looked at Nick to find him still praying. My heart filled at the sight. I stayed still for several minutes until he was finished.

He opened his eyes and was on the verge of tears. We meandered our way slowly back out the way we came wordlessly. I watched as Nick took in every feature along the way like a wide-eyed child.

"It's been two and a half centuries since I entered a chapel," Nick said, pulling me into his arms as soon as we were outside the doors. "Thank you doesn't even come close to the gratitude I have for you." I smiled up at him, and he lowered his head, letting his lips linger on mine. "Do you know what I prayed for? What I've wanted more than anything since finding my humanity?"

"What's that?" I was pretty sure of the answer, but he needed to say it out loud.

"Forgiveness." He kissed me again. I sensed a change in him. He was stronger now and more in touch with his humanity. I brought some form of peace to one vampire. It made me content for the first time in days, and I fathomed peace for all might be possible. I had hope and so did he.

TWENTY-THREE

)) • ● • ((

Alastair's soldiers had arrived during the night, and the beautiful rolling green behind the mansion was full of them all the way to the wall surrounding the property. Our coven mingled with them, and it warmed me to see old friends reuniting. During my restlessness again the night before, I had read up on Alastair's family, making my insomnia useful. The Kingston's were a long line of ruling witches in the European coven. The most famous one was known as an oppressor. His lineage consisted of dark for generations, but I found it interesting how they fought for the light. The oppressor, John, had been a particularly ruthless killing his own father and two elder brothers to gain his power. He then slaughtered his brothers' wives and children to ensure the only succession belonged to his line. He got his wish, probably sooner than he wanted, because he was then, in turn, killed by his eldest son who chose light.

I trusted Cal. He clearly chose the path of light. His

aura was pure in his choice, and it came through in his every move. I even envied how easy it seemed for him. Alastair gave the complete opposite. He made me uneasy each time we were in the same room, and I didn't trust him at all, despite his friendship with Sorin. Nick felt it too, and he was leery of bringing him into our confidence. We needed his soldiers, so we were forced to divulge much of the plan to him.

Nick and Malachi agreed to bring some vampires to the Great House to work on combat. Witches have magic on their side, but vampires have strength and speed on theirs. The two different styles of fighting exposed weaknesses on both sides. I feared for the vampires allowing themselves to be so vulnerable. The fear I felt for them contrasted strangely with the hatred I once carried as a huntress. I watched Nick and Malachi interact with the witches as if it was normal. They were at ease with them, and I found their fortitude impressive.

Nick nodded, and I followed his gaze to find Ella. He acknowledged her. She must've felt my gaze as she looked directly at me. The look on her face was unreadable to me, but I'm sure she felt caught. Nick had my trust, but I was also sure Ella was still in love with him. I nodded to her as Nick had done.

I walked up to the session Nick and Malachi were holding and observed them. Their fluid movements were a blur against the witches. I was struck most by their ability to anticipate the other's movements as if in tandem. Nick turned the session over to Malachi and walked over to me with a smile on his face. He enjoyed the training. He picked me up and swung me around, earning a laugh from me. When he set me down, he placed the softest of kisses on my lips. Everything went silent, and we looked around to see everyone staring at us. Witch and vampire alike were mystified by the relationship between the Queen of the Witches and the Prince of the Vampires.

"Let's break for lunch. We can resume this afternoon." Sorin's voice boomed out over the crowd. I was thankful when everyone obeyed him, and the attention turned away from us. It seemed everywhere we turned, there were reminders of how abnormal our relationship was. Despite what others thought should be normal, including me, we had our life and our normal, which was important to me.

The soldiers dispersed quickly, considering the sheer numbers there were. We had turned one of the ballrooms into a buffet-style serving area to accommodate them. Sorin waited for the area to clear completely before discussing progress.

"Nick, are the witches being respectful enough?" Sorin asked.

"Most of them are, but there are a lot who don't want lessons from vampires."

"That's to be expected," Brandon said, giving Nick an apologetic look.

"Is it enough is the real question," I said.

"It has to be," Sorin said, looking past us. I followed his gaze to find my mother.

"Go," I said, pushing him gently with a smile. He stilled loved her, and she him.

"Brandon, go eat. I'm fine here." He shrugged and left Nick and me standing to ourselves.

"I'll send the vampires to hunt for a while," Nick said to me. I'd arranged for blood bags to be stocked, but most of the vampires were used to warm-blooded extractions. I had to concede that the vampire hunters would not interfere.

"Why don't you go with them? I need some time to meditate. I haven't been able to do it lately," I said, smiling at him. He hadn't drunk enough from me to sustain him, and I figured it out soon afterward. He held back because he didn't want to hurt me.

"I'd rather stay with you," he said, melting me with his soothing voice and mesmerizing emerald eyes. The soft scent of vanilla whiskey drifted up to me. I inhaled.

"You need your strength as much as the rest. Do it for me." I stifled the urge I had to rip off his clothes at the moment. He gave me a playful wink before gathering up his group and leaping the wall. *Animal blood.* I found some relief to see them jump the wall towards the woods.

Finally alone in the quiet sunlight of the cool day, I meditated for guidance. With so many witches and vampires here, I could move more freely. I gave into my visions and let them take me where they may. I levitated along the meditation path to my first stop to find Nick. He looked handsome and smiled at two small children. They were our children. Even in this alternate place, I realized children wouldn't happen, and they were only a metaphor for something else. The two little boys were the choice I had to make. As soon as I made the association, the vision whisked me to the battlefield of my visions with Nick and Brandon facing their deaths. How would I decide who lives and who dies? I shook my head, and the images blurred. When it reformed, I saw only darkness and Sorin standing before me, impaled. The image confused me. Desperation in me took over. I had to figure out what it meant, but I couldn't solve the puzzle.

Leaves rustled, and branches snapped. My meditation broke. Someone walked in the woods past the wall. My eyes flew open. I looked around to find myself alone on the knoll. I walked silently to the wall to hear better. The voices were barely recognizable from this distance, but I could just make out one as Alastair's. As I strained to listen, I could only catch pieces of words. If I teleported, it would give away my location to them. I had to find out what he was up to, and my gut told me it was dishonorable.

I took a deep breath. *Cloak.* Cloaking came easy. Witches learned to do it early in their training, but some were better than others. My next move required me to levitate, but I wasn't well practiced at it. I jumped and landed hard on the ground. *Second try.* I closed my eyes and focused. When I opened them, I floated over the grass. It took a couple of tries to get to the right height and moving the right direction. I couldn't figure out how to move faster, and I rolled my eyes at myself as I moved at a turtle's pace. Alastair and his companion came into sight.

When I moved close enough to see them, recognition hit me. Alastair and Stefan's second in command, Oleksiy, were deep in conversation. I pointed myself to a branch overhead where I could duck behind the trunk of the tree. The vampire might still see me if he looked hard enough, but I had to take the chance if I wanted to know what they were planning.

"Stefan is displeased you haven't delivered her yet," Oleksiy said. *Her? Is he talking about me?*

"Stefan should have kept her there when he had her," Alastair said. "They will attack in three days on the full moon when they are strongest. Stefan should move the attack up by a day and surprise them here. They will never expect it, and it will be a sure win." *Traitorous bastard!* My gut had been right, and I wanted him to pay.

The huntress in me fought to show her strength, not against a vampire, but against the treason of a royal witch. Thunder rumbled from the anger inside me, and I tried to focus on the cloaking spell. I struggled to find inner peace, but the thunder rumbled louder and lightning struck in the distance. The wind blew hard enough that I nearly lost my footing, and I had to leave my hideout. Alastair and Oleksiy went their separate ways, and I watched with disgust as Alastair crept around the wall, headed for the entrance on the side that only a few knew existed.

When I was confident they wouldn't see me, I leapt from the branch, praying the levitation would work. I stayed cloaked just in case I was in sight of one of them. I had to focus on the levitation, and the cloaking spell wouldn't hold between that and my emotions out of control. There was still a good distance to cover before I would be over the wall. I saw Oleksiy in the distance pause and turn around. *Shit!* Get me to the other side of the wall.

As if commanded, my movements sped up, but they would have been humorous to anyone who could see them. I performed some strange movements similar to a freestyle swimmer's as I moved through the air. I let out a breath as I cleared the wall and saw Nick looking around. My cloak released, and he caught sight of me. The smirk on his face and shaking of his head told me I looked as silly as I felt. I dove for him and tackled him on the lawn.

He erupted in laughter. "What was that?" Moments were rare to see him in such an unguarded I had to take it in and commit it to memory. I memorized every line on his face, from the way the smile touched his eyes to the relaxed way of his jawline. It warmed me inside, and the love I felt for him radiated from me. It encapsulated us in a protective bubble, if only for a few seconds.

"It would be my flawless spying technique." I laughed, and he chuckled quietly in my ear. "I think levitation is best left for objects, not people."

He gave me a soul-searching look, and I felt exposed as I gazed back into his eyes. His fingers raked through my hair and gently pulled my head to his until our lips met. He kept the kiss soft and brought our lips together for another slow, tender meeting. My body relaxed as I gave into his lead. He deepened the kiss, and I tingled with excitement. He broke the connection and laid his head back on his arm, staring at me as if he too needed to memorize me.

My lightheartedness left me as I thought about the days to come. I narrowed my eyes at him. "What are you doing out here? I thought you were hunting."

"I sensed another vampire when we leapt over the wall. I sent the others on patrol, and I came back looking for you. I panicked when I couldn't find you, but I could tell you were close," he said, tracing my jawline. I kissed the tip of his finger as I rolled off of him.

"Nick, I was spying on Alastair and Oleksiy." I stood up, smoothing out my clothes.

"Oleksiy? What would they have to talk about?" he said in a shocked tone and brushed the pieces of grass from his clothes. The sight of him even covered in grass caused my breath to catch.

"They are going to attack us the night before the full moon for the element of surprise. Alastair is working with Stefan." Our timeline was screwed, and how would we move it up without Alastair telling Stefan?

"It certainly explains how Stefan knew the things he did when he summoned me," Nick said.

"What did he know?" I raised an eyebrow at him. "And why didn't you say something?"

"He knew about your visions, and he knew details." Nick was pensive. "It seemed less important than his other request."

"We need to tell the others without tipping Alastair off that we know." I wrapped my arms around his waist, needing to feel the safety only he could give me.

"We can casually walk through the house talking about wedding plans," he said, kissing the top of my head. I looked up into the sea of emerald eyes and smiled. "It would be an excellent cover while we gather up those closest to you."

"Oh, right! We are getting married," I said. He wrapped his arm around my shoulders as we set about finding the rest of my family.

"Yes. Yes, we are. Shall we have a big wedding or a small wedding?"

"Before I became queen, I would have said small. Now, we are a queen and prince getting married, so I think duty will dictate a large royal one," I said, controlling the urge to roll my eyes.

"It's our wedding, Brie. I think we can make some decisions," he said. "Where do you want to get married?"

"Here." I paused. "In the chapel," I said, knowing it would be a raw subject. I felt him stiffen at the mention of the chapel.

"I want it to be perfect for you, but I don't see how we could get married in the chapel if I have to hold your hand the entire time we are there." He sighed.

"We'll figure it out," I said.

My guards waited at the library door as I had asked them to earlier in the day. As long as Nick was here, I didn't have to be under their constant watchful eye. It gave me a moment to breathe, and I needed a few of those moments. I sent the guards in search of my family with the message to talk about wedding plans.

Behind closed doors, Nick and I started through our strategy on how to move our plan up to tomorrow night. We were in the middle of debating strength versus numbers when my family arrived.

"Brie, do we need to discuss wedding plans today? I think we have more pressing matters," Sorin said, throwing his hands in the air. It amused me when Brandon winked at me and chuckled. Grandmother followed right behind him with my mother in tow.

"I brought you some cheese and fruit because I am sure you haven't eaten lunch." Grandmother smiled at me. Mother looked at us both, and the papers on the table in front of us shaking her head. She was sharp when she was sober, and I was relieved she wasn't drinking.

"I have something to share with you all, and it's not wedding plans. This might be particularly hard for you to hear, Dad, but I assure you it is the truth." I paused, looking at Nick, who nodded his encouragement. "I was meditating when I heard voices over the wall. When I went to check it out, I found Alastair and Oleksiy, Stefan's second in command, engaged in a conversation."

"Brie! You went over the wall without your guards? What if you had been captured?" His words came in a flurry, and the anger radiated off of him. I wanted to take a step back from his fury, but I stood my ground.

"It's a good thing I did, or we wouldn't know Stefan plans to attack us the night before the full moon." I watched as Sorin processed what I said. The change on his face was obvious. The anger subsided, replaced by the creases of worry.

"We have a lot of work to do," Brandon said, moving straight to the table to look at what Nick and I had in front of us.

"We sure do, because we are going to attack tomorrow night to still have the element of surprise," I said.

"Can you have both the vampire and the witch armies be ready by then?" Grandmother asked.

"We can, but we need to figure out how to do it without Alastair having the opportunity to relay it to Stefan," Nick said.

"For Christ's sake, send him on some diplomatic errand, and then go without him." Mother chimed into the conversation.

I nodded. "It's not a bad idea. We could send him away and then call all the troops here. Moving that many people to the vampire castle unnoticed could be challenging. The expert cloakers could cover everyone or I could try to teleport us."

"That would make some of our most valuable resources too weak, including you," Sorin said.

"There is a small farm not too far from the castle. No one pays attention to it. We can make it the rendezvous point," Nick said, pointing to it on the map we had spread out on the table.

"How sure are you they wouldn't think to look there with a pending battle?" Sorin asked.

"It's my farm," Nick said, looking Sorin in the eyes. "Since it is my personal retreat, my personal guard keeps the perimeter clear. They would alert me if there was any movement." He paused. "I bought it for when I found someone to share it with" He turned to me, and I saw a twinkle in his eyes I didn't recall seeing before then. He had been keeping this for a surprise.

"One more thing. I am going to tell Cal," I said. I hadn't mentioned it to Nick. He growled when everyone else gasped. "Before any of you say anything, Cal is light. We are connected by the prophecy, and we need him as part of this. Trust me as your Queen."

I expected an argument, but I'd stand firm on my decision. Cal was part of this. They all exchanged looks before anyone spoke.

"Are you sure of this?" Sorin asked, taking my mother's hand. If they made each other happy, I hoped they had found their way back to each other.

"Yes, completely."

"Then we are behind you," Mother said. Her support jolted me with surprise.

"Do we think we're ready for this?" I nervously looked around at my family.

"Brielle, you were chosen for this long before any of us knew you would be born. If you are leading us through this journey, then we are on the right path," Grandmother said, putting her arm around my shoulders. "Maybe we should do a prayer." She motioned with her free hand for everyone to gather around. Nick stood off outside the circle, and I watched him pace. "Nick, come stand between me and Brie." I squeezed Grandmother's hand for thinking of him. She had every reason to hate vampires, but she accepted him. She swung her support our way. Her love was in her every action.

"I'm not sure I should. I am damned," he said. I inhaled a deep breath. Yes, it was common knowledge vampires were damned, but it was the first time I heard him say it out loud.

"Maybe not. Remember the chapel," I said, making

room for him in the circle. Even after his prayer for forgiveness, he still thought he was bound for Hell.

"Brie, you should send the prayer." Grandmother inclined her head to me, a knowing smile on her face. She had seen this night in a vision already.

"Blessed be our Goddess. Guide us on our journey and protect us if it be your will. We pray for the safety of those who fight for life, and we pray." I paused. My tattoo burned. I moved my arm around a little and continued. "We pray you will see fit to lead us unquestionably along the path you have set forth for us." I felt my pink aura move out around the circle, and I smiled as it seemed like an approval. "Fill us with the knowledge to lead us to peace for all. Blessed be."

When I opened my eyes, my aura still surrounded us all. I looked around at the wonder and amazement in the eyes of the group. I glanced up at Nick, who smiled down at me. I reveled in the closeness. It was the closest all of us had been in quite some time. I gently broke the circle by releasing Brandon's hand on my left. Nick wouldn't let go of my hand even as he leaned over to whisper in Brandon's ear.

CHAPTER
TWENTY-FOUR

) ·) · ● · (((

I went in search of Cal alone and found him meditating. I observed him for a moment, amazed by the power in the white light aura surrounding him. The pureness of his commitment to the light convinced me even more so I was right in looping him in.

"Cal?" I called. I didn't want to disturb his solitude. I understood how important it was better than most, but we were setting things in motion. He took in a deep breath and let it out before opening his eyes.

"Did you come to meditate with me?" he asked, his voice full of warmth. I would have been irritated if someone had disturbed me, but he welcomed me.

"No, I need to talk to you about the battle and your father."

"You look worried." He gestured to the spot in front of him. I joined him, sitting cross-legged on the floor.

"I am." I paused. I needed practice on how to break news. The regular me would just blurt it out, but the queen in me said I should be more reserved. Be more diplomatic. "Our plans to attack on the full moon have been discovered." His face tightened, and the worry passing across his face was genuine, as far as I could tell. "Stefan plans to attack us the night before to flip the element of surprise."

"We can't let him have the upper hand."

"I agree," I said. I reached over, touching his hand. He studied my face. After a few moments, he nodded.

"Our visions make more sense to me now. It's my father, isn't it?" he asked.

"Yes, he has betrayed us." I kept my voice soft. I thought Sorin had betrayed me and my family, so I knew the pain the news must cause him.

"I had hoped against hope he would not do so." He dropped his head. I let him have some time before I spoke.

"Did you see his betrayal in a vision?" I asked.

He raised his head. "I did, and I chose not to tell him. I wanted to give him the opportunity to choose the right path without my influence." The anguish in his voice and on his face accented the tears threatening to spill over from his eyes.

"I don't always share my visions. Sometimes you have to let them control their destiny just like we are ours," I said, squeezing his hand.

"He has always been drawn to the dark. I've never understood the attraction he has to it." He shook his head.

"It was his decision. There is something you should know." I told him the hidden history of our kind to help him find peace with Alastair's choice. Then I told him what Stefan's goal was and our counter plan.

"I'm with you, Brie. You are the only chance for light to win," he said. "And I trust you." Cal exhibited resilience like no other. The light in him drove his decision to stand with us, even though he would be against his father.

)) ● ((

AFTER DINNER, my family scattered to make final arrangements for tomorrow, and I planned to participate. Nick insisted on us having a private chat. When he opened the door to my suite, it was lit only by candlelight. The incandescence from more than what had to be a hundred candles stole my breath as the glow sparkled and danced on the walls.

I looked up into Nick's eyes. The flames flickered there. His love for me shone brightly in the sea of emeralds, and my heart skipped around in my chest. He stood there so perfectly in his gray t-shirt and jeans, leaning against the door frame. I blushed at my thoughts and made note of the sweet, knowing smile on his face.

He walked in, turned around to lock the door, and then slowly turned to face me. My pulse quickened as he sauntered in my direction. When he reached me, he raised one hand to my face and ever so gently caressed my cheek. I closed my eyes, giving in to his touch.

"I wanted to touch you like this outside the club the first night." Nick echoed my thoughts. He brought his free hand to my other cheek. My eyes fluttered open to his intense gaze, and we found our special connection. The energy soared between us. I let go of everything, and I watched my pink aura envelop us. Nick licked his lips before lowering his head to mine to give me a soft kiss. Even a gentle kiss from him could cause desire to burn in me. I leaned into him as he deepened the kiss. I found the hem of his shirt, but he stopped me before I could pull it up.

"There is something I want to say to you first." He suddenly got serious. My palms slicked with sweat as he took my hand and led me towards the couch. "It's not anything bad, Brie," he said, smiling. Nervousness gnawed at me, and I thought I would be ill.

"Nick?" I questioned. He put his hands on either side of my head and kissed my forehead.

"If tomorrow is the last time to lay my eyes on your beautiful face, I don't want you to have any doubts about how filled my heart is with love for you. When I say you are my soul, I want you to not just know but feel the truth in my words." His words were soft and warm, but the implications didn't escape me.

"Don't talk like that." I fought through the lump in my throat to speak. I turned my face away, closing my eyes to fight the tears. Nick crooked his finger under my chin, guiding my face back to his. He placed another soft kiss on my lips.

"Open your eyes."

I met his gaze.

"Our reality is we will be in a battle tomorrow. There will be bloodshed and death on both sides," he said.

I blinked back the tears, remembering my vision of choosing between Nick and Brandon. An impossible choice.

"I thought it was too late for me to find love, and then you cast your witchiness over me." He smiled.

A giggle erupted from me as I smiled back.

"The love I have for you took me by surprise. I don't want to lose you, but if tomorrow is the day I must leave this earth, I want you to know I love you solely and purely with the depths of my being."

A tear broke free and rolled down my face. My blood hummed to life with my internal lie detector, confirming the truth in his words. It came at a time I didn't need. I believed every sweet word as it rolled off his tongue.

"I need to know you will fulfill your prophecy even if I'm not here, which is why I am asking you to stay away from the battle tomorrow. To find peace, you have to live."

He couldn't believe I would agree to that request.

"I had a vision of the battle." My conversation with Cal earlier flashed through my thoughts. "If I don't go, both you and Brandon will die. If I go, I can save only one of you." I closed my eyes, covered my mouth with both hands, and let out a long breath, trying to maintain control. When I opened them, I saw Nick leaning back with his eyes closed.

"Brandon said he had known since he was seventeen this would be his fate." He looked at me, letting out a breath.

"He told you that? I had no idea he had known this

long." I had the urge to find Brandon and force the details out of him, but he had made peace with his path.

"You shouldn't have to watch us both die," Nick said. The resigned tone of his voice caused the nervousness in my stomach to return. It wasn't like him to give up so easily. It hurt me, but I pressed the subject.

"Did you not hear me? I can save one of you." The thought of choosing between them broke my heart.

"Brie, neither one of us could ask you to make the choice, nor would we be able to live with ourselves if you chose us over the other." The sadness in Nick's voice hit me like a punch to the stomach.

"And I could live with myself if you both died?" My jaw clenched. "This is my sacrifice. This is part of the prophecy." Heat filled my body as the anger rose in me. I wasn't mad at Nick. I was mad at the damn prophecy. I was mad at the sacrifice required by the queen fulfilling the damn prophecy. "Do you know how bad I want to say fuck it and take you and Brandon away? But there would just be another sacrifice made in my place like Cecily made for Sorin."

"You're right. I've waited two hundred and eighty years to find you and have the love we have. I will not give into this as our fate." He leaned forward, claiming my mouth. He moved slowly as he removed my clothes. His deliberate actions were in complete control, and I surrendered to him and my desire for him. He took me slow and gentle, loving me.

We laid on the couch for a long time, enjoying the bond and being close to each other. Without warning,

Nick scooped me up into his arms and carried me to the bedroom. I let out a small scream, earning a huge smile and a chuckle from him. If only this had been our fate instead of the prophecy. There had been so much I didn't know about vampires when we met and, most importantly, the onus for the feud belonged more to the witches than the vampires. If I had known this from the beginning, I would have never fought a relationship with Nick at all. Of course, it could be said it is part of what made us realize our importance to each other. Nick left a trail of sweet kisses up my arm towards my neck.

"Nick, there is something I want us to do." I grabbed his head between my hands, forcing him to look at me. The huge grin on his face told me his mind was on something entirely different.

"What's that?" he asked. His wicked smile broadened with amusement.

"I want to commit to you through the blood-bound ceremony." I watched his face fall.

"Brie, we have been through this. It's dangerous for a witch, and once you exchange blood in such a way, you are bound forever." The gleam in his eyes left, and not even the flicker of the candlelight reflected in them.

"I'm not any witch. I'm likely the most powerful witch to have lived in centuries, and I want to be bound to you." It was the ultimate commitment I could offer to him to show my trust and love.

"It's a bad idea." He shook his head.

"We mixed our blood for the new lovers' ceremony. You've already had my blood, so this time I get yours, too."

"Are you sure you understand what you are asking? If we're not careful, we could turn you." He searched my eyes.

He was exactly what I wanted, and I would take the risk.

"I trust you." I looked into his eyes. "I love you, and I want to be bound to you forever."

"I love you, and for a vampire, there is no greater commitment," he said, placing a lingering kiss on my already swollen lips.

He looked me in the eyes. Our special connection sprung up. When he found what he needed, he began the ritual by sinking his fangs into my wrist. I moaned as he drank deeply from it. He then opened his wrist in much the same way. I expected my reaction would be repulsion, but it tasted sweet like honeysuckle mixed with a hint of metallic and filled my senses. Pleasure erupted through me with every small touch. I understood the fascination the humans who were part of the vampire world felt. I whimpered, bombarded by the flood of familiar memories of his we had shared during the new lover ritual.

"Brie, are you okay?" Nick asked. I barely heard him. I could only nod, but I wondered if he saw the same memories each time he had my blood or if it was my memories he saw.

He placed a new trail of kisses from my wrist up my arm, never pausing as he sunk his fangs into my neck. I moaned again and shuddered in ecstasy as he sucked blood from me. When it was my turn to drink from his neck, he reached for the knife on the bedside table. He was astride me and flipped us over, so I sat on top of him. With the knife, he cut himself in the same spot on his neck as he had drunk from mine. I leaned into him and drank the sweet nectar pouring from him until the wound closed. My wounds healed with a mix of pleasure and pain. Nick's memories danced through my mind as I eavesdropped on him. He had not overstated his cruelty over the years, especially the way he had treated Ella, but he had shown me a different side to him. The Nick I was bound to now was capable of love.

He pulled my face to him. "Brie, open your eyes." The pleasure mixed with the painful memories flowed in me, and I had to force them to flutter open. I looked up at him through my eyelashes. Our connection engaged, and Nick seemed to find the acceptance he needed.

He positioned me over him, and I moaned as he held my hips still and controlled the motion. Each swivel and thrust built until I was thrown over the edge, and he went willingly with me. I collapsed on him, panting against his neck. With a gentle touch, he moved me next to him so I could lie beside him, resting my head on his chest.

)) ● ((

WE WERE BOUND, and I could discern the difference. His every movement was like an extension of my own. A faint trace of my pink aura covered him, and I wondered if it would remain. He brushed his fingertips across my cheek, and I smiled at him. His smile didn't quite reach the corners of his eyes.

"Are you still worried? Because I'm not," I said, smiling as if I had a victory.

"I'm concerned for you if something should happen to me tomorrow," he said. I felt the pang in my gut, and I understood fully what he meant. Should he die in this battle, I would experience not only emotional pain but physical pain. The choice I would have to make crept back into my thoughts. I accept the risk and would choose the blood-bound commitment to him again if given a mulligan.

"There is no choice, Brie," Nick said, looking me in the eyes. "You save Brandon if it comes to choosing between us." I took a deep breath.

"I don't know if I can choose," I said. He kissed my forehead and pulled me up against him.

"You are capable of much more than you know. You will make the right choice," he said.

We had only slept a few hours when we heard a knock at my suite door. I slipped into my long robe, and Nick had his jeans and t-shirt on from last night before I had it tied. He stood behind me like a guardian. My senses confirmed Brandon waited on the other side of the door before I answered it.

"Hey, Brandon," I said. My groggy, weak voice betrayed my need for sleep.

"Hey, Sis," he said, his eyes passing over me to look at Nick and nod. "Dad has sent Alastair out to meet with another diplomat, and he wanted to know if you two could address the joint army before we move to the farm."

I looked up at Nick, who nodded. "Of course, we can,

but we shouldn't be moving the army until this afternoon if we are going to attack an hour before sunset. We don't want to tip off Stefan."

"We're going to transport to the location Nick marked on the map," Brandon said, keeping his voice low and hushed.

"I can't teleport everyone, Brandon." I shook my head. It wasn't selfishness on my part. The drain of teleporting increased with each person I took with me.

"I said transport, not teleport. Grandmother and Mom are going to do a transportation spell to send us to the correct spot," he said. "Since they are not going to the battle, this was their way to help."

It was good to see them getting along. "They work well together. Nick and I will teleport there first just to make sure all is well before we send everyone." I looked Brandon in the eye as his queen, not his sister.

"Sorin may have a difference of opinion on that matter, but you two can hash it out later," Brandon said, smirking. I smiled at him, shaking my head.

"We'll get dressed and meet you and Dad. Have the armies assemble in the back, and we will need to have the master cloakers there just in case." Brandon nodded and left. Speaking to him as the queen was strange. We both knew when he agreed to the role of my Protector, there would be a time when we would have to fulfill our roles.

Nick and I showered quickly. Nick sat dressed on the couch waiting for me while I stood in my walk-in closet the size of my first apartment, looking at the clothes before me. There were casual and formal clothes. I had what I would call queenly clothes, and there were clothes that were pure huntress. I thought about what the joint armies needed to see from Nick and me to show we were unified for peace. The huntress outfit of all black leather with lots of pockets to conceal weapons wanted to be worn. I held the outfit up, looking it over and inhaling the sweet smell of leather. As much as I wanted to wear it, it wasn't what the vampires needed to see.

Nick had on a blue check button-down shirt with navy blue slacks. It was so much easier for guys. I could see by the look in his eyes I had made the right choice. My navy A-line dress hit just above the knee. The white piping around the neck gave it the perfect contrast. I let my hair flow naturally, and the only jewelry I wore were the diamond earrings my grandmother gave me for gradua-tion and my engagement ring. We looked like royalty.

Nick took my hand and kissed my cheek. "Are you ready?"

"I better be," I said, giving him a small smile as we headed out the door.

TWENTY-FIVE

)) ● ((

We stood before the group looking sophisticated, but I felt anything but. I was nervous to the point of nausea, and my palms were sweaty. I had never spoken to a group this large, and I thought of all those willing to die for peace. There were so many souls standing before us, looking for guidance. I sent a silent prayer for protection, and I felt the tingle of my aura reaching out. It wrapped around Nick and me, and I heard gasps from the soldiers. Thank you. I sent the last prayer up. Nick smiled at me, and I smiled back at him. Show time. Some of the amazing people before me would die today, but it wasn't my job to remind them of that now. It was my duty to give them hope.

Nick went first and spoke about the prophecy and his faith in me. He spoke of peace and what it would mean for us all when we achieved it. I was touched by the way he reached everyone. He had been groomed so well for being a leader. He spoke like a king. All eyes were on him, and I wasn't sure there was anything left unsaid. It was my turn, and I had to say something. Honesty flowed from me in the hope of what we could accomplish.

"If you had asked me a year ago if would I ever consider peace with vampires, I would have said no. I was our coven's fiercest hunter, but I am no longer proud of that accomplishment. A year ago, I didn't know I would be queen. I didn't know my father, and I didn't know the actual history of our people." I paused, taking a small breath. I gazed out at the crowd. Eyes were all on me.

"Today, I stand before you as the Queen of the Witches, the daughter of Sorin Vladislav, and the fiancé of Nicholas Domenico. I choose light for everyone forced into the dark. I love a vampire even though I am best known for hunting them. My tattoo marks me and the Blood Moons call me, but I choose to follow my own path. I will never ask you to fight a battle I wouldn't fight myself, which is why Nick and I will lead you into battle together. We will know victory today." I didn't plan to have the ceremonial candles the elders brought flame up, but it added a nice dramatic touch. I thought I hadn't said enough when everyone remained silent, but then the crowd erupted into cheers and applause.

Nick reached for my hand and lifted our clasped hands. The army shouted louder. Their confirmation was the final encouragement I needed. This path was the right one.

Sorin whisked us away to the library. His anger would be directed at me for my public declaration. He couldn't keep me away from the battlefield now, given I had declared I would be there. I prepared to hear his lecture on how foolish I had been, but it wasn't a foolish choice. I chose to fight with them because the right thing to do called me to take my place there.

"You looked like a queen," Sorin said. With pride in his eyes, he wrapped his arms around me. He caught me off guard, and I almost couldn't hug him back out of surprise. "They would follow you into the fires of Hell."

"Well, let's hope that doesn't happen," I said, hugging him back. "Nick was the polished one." I winked at my man over my father's shoulder.

"You were amazing," Nick said, taking his turn to hug me.

"So were you," I said, squeezing him tight.

"Enough with the pleasantries. We have a lot of work to do." I turned to see Brandon come through the door. He smiled and winked at me as a silent show of support. He could sense how uncomfortable the compliments made me, and I from him.

"When we teleport to the farm, set the timer for five minutes. If we are not back by then, abort the mission. It means something has gone wrong," I said.

"Can you teleport both Nick and me?" Brandon asked, speaking as my Protector.

"I could, but all three of us shouldn't go." I touched his arm, a final protest to his acceptance of his destiny.

"I have a feeling, Brie. I should be there."

"All right then. The three of us will teleport to the farm." His right as my Protector meant he didn't have to divulge his reasons.

"It's going to take more of your strength. Without a full moon, your energy will not rejuvenate as fast," Sorin said.

"I know, but I've got this covered." The timing seemed wrong to tell him I had extra energy since Nick and I bound ourselves through our blood.

"Gentleman, I need some quiet time. Would you mind leaving me here for a while?" I looked at each of them. They exchanged looks. "I'm not running off. I need to focus." I assured them.

"We can adjourn to my study," Sorin said.

"Don't even consider going anywhere without me." Nick kissed my cheek as they walked out.

I walked around the room, running my finger across the spines of the books and inhaling the old leather scent. The strength in our history hummed in my veins. I walked to the middle of the room. Closing my eyes and tilting my head up, I held out my arms. I opened up to the power and let it flow through me. The force could be light or dark, but my conscious choice was light. I breathed in slowly and exhaled, finding my center. I would have to find it quickly during battle and I failed miserably in my attempts previously. I had to find the strength inside for all those counting on me.

I meditated on the choice I faced today, and I didn't know how I would make it. I would rather give my own life than lose either of them. I played out scenarios in my head, and the best one I could come up with involved throwing an energy ball at one weapon while flinging myself in front of the other. With any luck, I would survive the blow. I was not convinced it would work, but I had to try something. A knock at the door interrupted my thoughts.

"Enter," I said.

"Brie?" Cal peaked around the door.

"Hi, Cal." I smiled at him as he entered the room, shutting the door behind him.

"I wanted to see if I could stand by your side at the battle today. When everyone else learns of my father's betrayal, I want no doubt in their minds my allegiance lies with you." His voice, full of pain and honesty, called to the broken part of me from my childhood.

"I would be honored to have you by my side. Nick, Brandon, and I will lead the group, and I will let them know you will stand with us," I said. He hugged me tightly, and his sorrow billowed from him. Today would be a choice for him as well. Neither of us would leave the battlefield as the same person.

)) ● ((

I MADE my way to my suite and smiled as I saw Nick stretched out on the couch. He already felt right, like home. Life would never be easy for us. Nick would have to lead his people at some point, maybe starting today, and I would have to lead mine. We wouldn't always have joined forces, but it did me good to see what we could accomplish by bringing them together. I sat down beside him on the couch, and he wrapped his arms around me, pulling me to his chest.

"We need to get ready," I said, burying my face in his neck.

"You're positive you are needed on the field? It will not be like when you hunt," he said, resting his chin on the top of my head.

"I know, and yes, I am."

We dressed, and I laughed at the contrast. *Apparently, vampires wear black t-shirts and jeans to a battle.* I had chosen the black leather catsuit. If tonight's fate dictated I would die, I wanted to have worn this at least once. I filled every small hidden compartment in the outfit with some kind of weapon. I unzipped the suit enough to show some cleavage. Nick looked at it with a raised eyebrow and zipped it up to my neck.

"You can't give a vampire a heart attack, Brie." He shook his head and laughed. That would be my easiest mission today... to make him laugh.

"I guess not." I shrugged, laughing too. "It might be a first."

Nick pulled me into his arms, claiming my mouth, and I forgot where we were. His arms around me and his mouth on mine were all I wanted every day, but today wasn't the day we could say it was ours. We had to fight for the right to claim a day we wouldn't have to look over our shoulders. We were both breathless when we broke the embrace and reluctant to let go of each other, knowing what lay ahead of us.

"I like the incentives you offer, Mr. Domenico." I smiled.

"Incentives? Those are benefits, Ms. Danforth," he said, returning my smile.

"I look forward to enjoying those benefits." I winked playfully at him.

"Good. I plan on showing you some new ones tonight." He winked back. He gently took my hand, and we walked out to greet our army with our hands entwined. Outside, I portrayed a witch ready for battle, a queen, but on the inside, I wondered who we would lose today. It tore at me, and I shoved it into a neat little compartment.

Rob, the bartender from Club Red, handed me a frosty shot glass of vodka. We exchanged a look, and I wondered how I never sensed the magic in him. I realized he knew all along my status. Nick held his one shot glass filled with blood as we entered the green grassy area where the joint army congregated. I surveyed the group, noting the vampires all had red-filled shot glasses while the witches all had vodka shots. This counted as another first in a long line of them as we marched towards a new future. I held my shot glass up, and everyone, vampire and witch, followed suit.

"To solidarity and our success," I said. My toast came out in a regal voice I didn't recognize as my own.

"To our peace," Nick said. The group repeated both as we all drank together in our historical moment that would surely find its way into our legends.

"Blessed be," I said, and everyone went into action.

Nick, Brandon, and I moved to our meeting point.

"Ready?" I asked. My stomach twisted. The leather catsuit didn't offer any place to wipe my sweaty palms.

"Let's do this." Brandon held out his hand.

"Ready." Nick held out his.

"Sorry about the sweat," I said.

I teleported the three of us to a barn on the farm, and I didn't even feel a lag in my energy. I was different, whether it be the power of my ancestors I carried or Nick's vampire blood flowing through me. We checked all around the enclosure before exiting to check the transport coordinates. Everything looked fine until a smell hit me. The smell of death hung in the air. We followed the pungent, rotting smell to find a dead cow and a trail of blood. The blood led us to a young vampire cowering behind a stack of square hay bales. He looked like he could be a teenager, and he was a new vampire. The blood lust consumed him. The eyes looking back at us were hollow shells.

"What is your name?" I asked. He didn't respond. Nick stepped forward and grabbed the young vampire on either side of the head. "Nick! Don't!" I stopped him before he could snap his neck.

"He could be a spy, Brie," Nick said, setting the vampire down.

The young vampire's eyes were wide, and he shook.

"Nick's right. We can't leave a loose end. He could spy for Stefan," Brandon said.

I walked up to the child vampire.

"I don't think it's a good idea for you to stand so

close," Nick said. He and Brandon moved to positions on either side of me. The young man cowered beneath us.

"What is your name?" I asked again, reaching for his hand. I winced as he grabbed a hold of mine with his vampire strength.

"Christopher." He stared at me. Somehow, the knowledge found its way to me on how to help him. I reached my free hand to his face, letting my aura flow over him.

"Well, Christopher, you will no longer feel lustful over your hunger. It will no longer consume you. You will do what you must to sustain your life, but you will be free." His eyes instantly cleared and were focused. My aura retreated back to me, and he threw his arms around my neck. I waved Brandon and Nick away as they went to pull him off of me.

"Thank you! I wanted to die from the way I felt, but I feel better now," he said, kissing my cheek.

"Our time is up. We need to go back, and we should take Christopher with us," Brandon said.

"Agreed," Nick said.

"Christopher, we are going to take you with us for a little while. It's not safe here," I said, looking him in the eyes. He nodded his head, but I could sense his fear. I took his hand and my twin took his other hand. I reached for Nick's and saw the concern written all over his face. He thought it was a trap, and part of me thought it, too.

We were met with a room full of curious gazes all directed at the young man hurling blood onto the floor. I touched his head and used my aura to ease the discomfort he felt from being whisked across a hundred and fifty miles in a matter of seconds. Grandmother approached us with one eyebrow raised.

"Grandmother, this is Christopher, and he is going to stay with us until it's safe," I said. She nodded and touched Christopher's shoulder. He hugged her like she was his flesh and blood. She led him away as we made our way to join the rest of the army for the final hop. We waited for about twenty minutes for Grandmother to join us, and I could see the concern on her face echoing what I saw on Nick's earlier.

They were right to be concerned, but the peace had to start somewhere. One action could make the difference in the prophecy.

Nick, Brandon, Cal, and I teleported back first to secure the opening of the transport bridge on the other side. Part of my personal guard came through first, and then the army quickly filled the designated spot on the far side of the barn. Once everyone settled, I turned the lead over to Nick. He was more familiar with the territory, and we needed his knowledge to lead us. I felt strange as I looked from Nick to Brandon. Brandon wrinkled his forehead, and I could feel the uneasiness roll off of him. Cal touched my shoulder for support, knowing my visions, and I reached my hand up to his, squeezing it.

I looked up into the afternoon sky, trying to figure out what wasn't right. The sun shone down brightly on us as it should for the time of the afternoon, but there was no wind. Not so much as a hint of a breeze. We crossed the meadow and leapt the small stream running between the two properties. The absence of wildlife drew my curiosity.

Not a bird. Not a rabbit. Nothing. It heightened my suspicions of something being off. We traversed the hard ground under our feet here, which contrasted with the soft soil at the farm. We slowly made our way to the field of my vision with pale green winter grass knee to waist high in places. The hair on the back of my neck stood up as we approached a clearing. It was all too obvious the closer we got. Surprise wasn't ours. Not in the least. We had been fools to believe we had the advantage. It wouldn't be necessary to lure Stefan's vampires to the field. We'd been had, and I blamed myself.

In front of us stood an army of vampires poised with spears and arrows, and their speed and strength would make their rudimentary weapons lethal from this distance. They wore no armor, much like Nick had chosen not to do. Of course, the witches and warlocks had little armor on themselves, and the vampires on our side wore no armor either. Nearly everyone on the side of light had Vampire Death on the tips of stakes or bullets filled with them. We didn't plan on letting them get close enough to need much armor. I regretted not pushing for more protective covering now, seeing the trap laid before us. At least we had the sun to our backs. It was the one part of the plan that appeared to work for us.

I looked at the sea of soldiers in front of us, and it crossed my mind the difference between human wars and our wars. Vampires and witches fought with weapons similar to those used for hundreds of years, whereas humans modernized into mass destruction rarely having the chance to look their enemy in the eye. The nature of both witch and vampire with magic, speed, and strength meant we could inflict the same kind of damage without modern weaponry.

I surveyed the battlefield for Stefan, but I couldn't find him. I stole a glance at Nick, and I could see him searching. "He's not here," he said, without looking at me. "He's probably hanging far enough back where he is hidden. Maybe he has a witch cloaking him."

"Alastair. I am sure of it," I said, taking in the breadth of forces about fifty yards in front of us. I saw Cal wince out of the corner of my eye. The truth hurt him, but it was not a time we could afford weakness.

"We should cut a path straight through to the other side. It's our best chance to get to him," Nick said.

"I'm in," Brandon said, nodding at me as I turned to look at him. The determination in his face gave me strength.

"Me, too," Cal said. He wasn't as confident as the other two. I could feel his pain and the internal conflict raging in him. It reminded how connected we were from the prophecy and of my pain from the knowledge we gained with it. He looked at me and nodded.

"Alright. Straight in like a knife through butter." They all shook their heads, but only Nick and Brandon were smiling. They looked forward to the battle, but Cal didn't want to shed blood any more than I did, especially if it came to his father. I wondered if it came to it, whether his loyalty would still lie with me.

Stefan's army fired first, sending a flaming arrow engulfing one of my guards. He dropped instantly, and a twinge of pain passed through me. The death of each of my subjects would be my pain. I looked at his burning body with the arrow protruding from his chest. I fought the sorrow building in me. The plan was clearly to separate me as the second arrow pierced another one of my guards through the eye. Both kills were instantaneous. Again, the pain came. Each death made my energy dip and would be like a chink in my armor. I nodded to Brandon and Cal as I gave Nick the sign. Nick whistled the attack command, and my skin crawled as I heard it. There was no going back as we advanced.

We stuck close together as the battle began, but we quickly drifted apart. Not so far I couldn't see them, but the distance distracted me as I thought of my visions. They were cutting Stefan's men down easily with their skills, and I could see dust piles in their wake. The huntress in me wanted to take over, but my goal was to not draw blood unless I absolutely had to for life or death. I conjured small energy balls to knock my aggressors out and push them some distance away. I wanted to get to Stefan and capture him, but he didn't want peace, which meant he wouldn't give up. Bodies were falling on both sides, and crimson puddles and piles of ash covered the ground. It was a dismal reminder of what we faced. Each loss for us weakened me. I counted twenty on our side. Their deaths made me a little less focused, and I almost missed the signs of my visions.

It happened fast and slow at the same time. Two arrows and a wooden spear hurtled towards us with pinpointed accuracy. The deliberateness of the aim could only mean they knew Brandon and Nick would want to save me and would die to do so. Sun reflected off the metal tips the same way the moment lived in my subconscious for months. The previous version didn't have the emotion it did today, and I was light-headed, with my brain in overdrive. The spear's deadly aim spiraled toward Nick, and one of the arrow's path took aim at Brandon. What I hadn't seen in the vision was the arrow coming for me. Cal had advanced ahead of us looking for Alastair, and he didn't seem to know we were living the vision behind him.

Nick had caught sight of the arrow barreling in my direction and ran toward me, which put him directly in the spear's way. I couldn't make the decision about who would live and who would die. I didn't feel like it was my choice, but if I did nothing, we would all three die. The sun hid behind the clouds, turning everything gray except for the blood pools. Thunder rumbled from my uncontrolled emotions. I saw Brandon close his eyes. He said he knew his destiny, and he was painfully right. He had accepted his fate, but I refused to concede. I needed a moment. A minute to collect my thoughts. The wind whipped my hair over my face as I closed my eyes.

"Stop." I threw my hands out to the side with my fingers spread wide. Lightning struck the middle of the field, intensifying the smell of blood, ash, and burnt flesh. It sickened me and repulsed my senses. Silence fell on the battlefield. I opened my eyes. I had frozen time again.

CHAPTER
TWENTY-SIX

☽ · ☽ · ● · ☾ · ☾

The armies on both sides were larger than a battalion each. I could feel the drain on me keeping so many people frozen at once, and I wouldn't be able to hold it long. The smell of death assaulted me, making it even worse. An arrow hovered only a few inches from Brandon's chest, one a couple of feet from me, and the spear no more than six inches from Nick. Scenario after scenario sped through my mind as I looked for options to save them. "I can't let either of them die," I said, looking up to the heavens.

"I've got it, Brie," Sorin said. His voice came from over my shoulder, and I thought my mind played a trick on me. He moved in front of me and faced me with tears in his eyes. "My only regret is I was not here to see you grow up, but my solace is seeing you as a magnificent queen. You are a great ruler, and you will lead the world into a new era." He hugged me. I couldn't hug him back or I would lose control of time, and tears blurred my vision.

"Dad, what do you mean?" The blood trickled from my nose. My hold on time slipped. "How are you not frozen?"

"You can't hold time forever, nor can you save all three of you." The truth in his words echoed through the ache in my head and my chest. I sobbed from the pain coursing through my body and from what he asked me to do.

"No! There has to be a way," I said. I fought it even as the blood poured faster from both nostrils.

"There is," Sorin said, kissing my forehead. "I love you, my daughter." He stepped toward Brandon. "This is my sacrifice as the rightful King of the Witches. I caused this by avoiding my destiny, and I am the one who can right it. My sacrifice today is for love and light and will redeem yours by righting my wrong. I choose light, and peace is yours. I give back your life. Blessed be." I felt blood trickling from my ears as I watched my hold loosen and the weapons move closer. My breaths were ragged as I tried to tighten my grip.

"I love you, Dad." My voice was nothing more than a whisper, but he gave me a gentle smile.

"Release it, Brie." Sorin's voice resigned. Soft and quiet. "I will save Brandon. You focus on yourself and Nick."

"I can't," I said, tears rolling down my face.

"Damn it! Release it now, Brie!" His voice jolted me with power, causing me to shake just enough I couldn't hold it in my weakened state. The magic was interrupted, and time once again marched forward in full force.

I went into action, doing what Sorin said. I pushed Nick out of the way, causing the spear to graze my shoulder and the arrow to land in the bloody mud. I held my hands out to the spear and arrow, sending them flying back from where they came. They found their masters and turned them into dust. It was vengeance for them making me choose, and I was angry. Pain radiated in my chest for Sorin's death, and then an unexpected surge of power. I glowed on the battlefield. I glimpsed Brandon kneeling to Sorin. Nick touched my arm, but I brushed it off. It was part defense and part selfishness.

I wanted to fall to pieces in a puddle on the ground, but I had my duty. Anger filled me and rage took over. It was the darkness that had remained in Sorin even as he chose light. I could feel it course through me and darkness hung over me like a storm cloud. The wind blew and thunder rumbled, turning the sky dark. Lightning struck around the battlefield. As my rage grew, so did the storm around us. I wanted to protect us, but there was no doubt it was Hell's Fire when the ring rose around us. The fires were a dark deep red instead of the white light I was used to. My aura changed as the fire grew tall. I walked to Sorin with each step deliberate.

"Brie, this is not what he wanted for you. He didn't sacrifice himself for you to turn dark," Brandon said, his voice in my ear as he laid his hand on my shoulder. His touch and soft words calmed me. I closed my eyes and drew in a deep, cleansing breath. The heat from the fire dissipated, and the storm calmed.

Stefan's troops, what remained of them, retreated for the time being. Even though Sorin's life force now coursed through me, I fell to my knees beside his lifeless body. The arrow had pierced his heart perfectly, and he must've turned into it welcoming a hero's death. I wept over his body until long after the sky returned to normal and the sun had set. I finally had the father I wanted, and he was taken from me over a damn prophecy. My anger flared and lightning struck close to us.

"Sis, stop," Brandon said. I looked up into his eyes. The pain on his tear-stained face reflected my own. "It's getting dark. We need to go before Stefan's men come for us. Step back and let the guards take Sorin's body."

"He's our father," I said. My voice echoed through the air, but he didn't flinch.

"I know," he said, taking my hands and pulling me to a standing position. "I loved him too." He wrapped his arms around me. I cried into his shoulders until his shirt was wet. We were an awful sight, covered in blood-soaked mud.

He passed me to Nick, who picked me up in his arms and carried me to the rendezvous spot. I raised my head to watch them load Sorin's body into the SUV, sent to take him away. I suppose his life force compelled me, but I couldn't stand to see him go alone.

"I want to ride with him," I said, tilting my head up to Nick.

"Whatever you want, Brie." Nick's voice was gentle as he changed direction and walked to the SUV. I climbed in the back and held Sorin's hand as the tape in my head of our last conversation played. Fear waved over me, but it wasn't my own. I looked up into Nick's eyes, taking in his drawn features and wrinkled forehead. He shut the door and took the seat directly in front of us so he could reach me. I looked out the back window to see Cal and Brandon's concerned faces watching me. Everyone was worried about me, and I clung to my dead father as if he was going to wake up.

The ride back to the Great House seemed much longer than it should. We moved slowly and had more than twice the normal guard. I couldn't get my head around how this could happen, but Sorin's words danced through my head like a ballet. It was his sacrifice to free me from mine. He was dead because of me. I wondered if I could bring him back to life, but the only magic I knew would be dark magic. The cost was another life, and the person brought back was never the same. It had never been done with a witch, but I could not imagine it would work since their magic releases back to the earth or their ancestors or both.

My mother ran to the SUV when we finally pulled up to the front of the mansion. She was disheveled and distraught. Her face was stained with tears, and she didn't acknowledge me at all when the SUV doors opened. She nearly collapsed at the site of Dad, and probably would have if Nick hadn't caught her.

"I don't understand," she said, sobbing. "How could you let this happen?" She looked at all of us. "This is your fault. You should have protected him." She pointed a finger at me and walked toward me. The guards restrained her, and she fought them.

"Let her go," I said. "She's right." We stood immobile as they removed Sorin's body from the SUV. I knelt in the old world bow for my father, a fallen King. The guards, elders, and witches all took a knee with bowed heads for respect as Sorin was carried into the Great House. The surprising part was seeing the vampires follow suit. I stood, but the others remained in their kneeling position. I watched the door close. There was a haze over everything as I looked around. My gaze stopped at the back of the SUV. There was a dark spot in the back. Blood. The blood was my father's soaked into the carpet.

Nick stood. "Come on. Let's go get you cleaned up." He grabbed my hand. My gaze was unfocused and frozen in place. I couldn't even move my head to look at him. The loss and emptiness registering inside overwhelmed me. Rain came down to match the tears streaming down my face. The wind howled like the pain in my soul. The hollowness was foreign to me. It was loss.

Nick picked me up in his arms. My body formed to his out of habit. He crossed the threshold of the door, and I looked over his shoulder. The witches and vampires rose in the rain. Nick didn't set me down until we were in my bathroom. He drew a hot bath and removed my battle clothes.

Everything happened as if I was floating and watching from above. I didn't feel present in the moment, but I felt bone-chilling cold. It was the only thing I felt. He picked me up once again and sat me down in the steaming water. The water sloshed around me as he stepped in, taking a seat behind me. He took a washcloth and soap and washed away the blood and mud covering my body. Some of it was my own, which ran down in the suit from my nose and ears, but most of it was Sorin's blood. I shook violently at the thought, and Nick stopped for a moment to hold me tight. When I stopped shaking, he washed my hair, massaging my scalp. The time with him was therapeutic, and I nestled against him when he finished rinsing the shampoo from my hair.

"Thank you," I said, sighing. His lips touched the top of my head.

"You're welcome," he said, tightening his arms around me. "I'm here for you, however you need me." We sat in silence until the pink-hued water cooled. His compassion and patience gave me strength.

Once we were dressed, reality returned to me. I'd be expected to act every part of the queen, not the grief-stricken daughter. I would have to address the coven, but I wanted to see Brandon first. Nick and I found him in his quarters, lying on the couch. He was freshly showered, but he had the dazed look I was sure I had earlier. I sat beside him and grabbed his hand. I gave him a gentle pull to sit up.

"It doesn't wash the pain away, does it?" I asked.

"No," Brandon said. "It's because of me he was willing to die. I had seen my death many times, and I was prepared to die."

"His death is not your fault, Brandon." I swallowed against the fresh knot building in my throat. *It's my fault.* "He was trying to set us free by sacrificing himself." A fresh tear rolled down my cheek landing on our joined hands.

"I want Stefan to pay," he said. The bitterness echoed my own.

"As do I," I said. "And he will pay." Brandon studied me to the point it made me uncomfortable.

"Your aura is different, and I'm not liking it," he said, wrinkling his forehead. "It's still pink, but it's twisted with black." Black auras were not necessarily bad, but with mine, I sensed it was. My pink aura of light battled the black, dark aura, betraying my struggle. "Sorin sent his life force to you."

I closed my eyes, inhaling at his revelation. I turned my head, looking at Nick. Father had hidden his aura for a reason, and when it touched mine, I knew I touched darkness. He was stoic, letting Brandon and I have our time, but he listened and took in every syllable.

When I looked back at Brandon, his eyes looked more like his own. "Yes, and I am choosing light, Brandon. I will not lie to you. I feel the struggle every time I make a decision. Anger makes it harder to control."

"Think of him when the dark creeps into you. Think of his sacrifice and what he wanted for us," Brandon said, sucking in air as our heads leaned against each other. "He wanted light for us. We are his legacy, and his sacrifice was to ensure our survival."

"I understand why he struggled with the dark. It is relentless and strong. If I gave into it, it would consume me like him." My voice cracked.

"It will get easier. Sorin was able to do it. You will too," Brandon said.

"He was able only after he gave into it and then spent years in solitude, not practicing magic to get control of it. How am I supposed to lead our people and find peace when I am struggling like this? Solitude isn't an option for a queen." Frustration oozed from me.

"We'll do it together, Sis," Brandon said, motioning for Nick to join us on the couch. They both wrapped their arms around me in a group hug, and peace filled the air around us. Brandon was right. Our unity was the answer. It gave me the strength to find the light, and I was ready to face the group amassed at the mansion as the queen, with both of them by my side.

I was nervous as stood before the vampires and witches who had assembled. I took Nick and Brandon's hands, and we walked to the center of the elevated area standing behind the half-moon-shaped table where Cecily once stood. It was the first time vampires had been allowed into this room. There was standing room only, and the crowd overflowed into the hall. I glanced at Brandon, receiving a nod, and repeated it with Nick. I was going to have to let go to call the elements to the room, and I was worried I would lose my courage without the contact with them. I took in a deep breath, letting it out slowly before I called the elements one by one. We could feel the air swirling around us. Tonight, I used the truth spell so everyone would know I spoke the truth not to force the truth on them.

"We lost the rightful King of the witches tonight. Sorin was my father, and he sacrificed himself so not only my brother and I would be spared, but a vampire as well." The words flowed freely from me. "We are still bound to the prophecy and must fulfill it, but we will no longer be required to sacrifice what is most dear to us. There were no winners in tonight's battle, and I believe there will be many more to come in the days ahead. To those of you who lost someone tonight, I send you peace and comfort." I held out my hands, letting the soothing energy find those who needed it. The drain was significant on my already weakened stature, and I could tell many needed it. "I cannot promise there will not be more bloodshed as I have seen more, but I can promise you I will lay down my own life to find the peace we seek." I cleared a tickle from my throat as I felt the anger rise. I reached for Brandon and Nick's hands to find strength. "We will avenge Sorin's death, but we will not do it tonight. Tonight we will celebrate his amazing life, and the path he chose so his family could fulfill a destiny they did not choose. We celebrate all those who sacrificed for peace. We will triumph," I said, releasing the elements. Bottles of vodka and blood passed through the crowd with mournful exclamations.

I adjourned to the library with Nick and Brandon in tow. I was relieved to see Grandmother waiting for us there. She patted the seat for me to join her. "You did well, Granddaughter," she said. "Please leave us, gentlemen. Brie and I need to speak in private." She dismissed them, but they both looked at me. I could feel the worry rolling off of them, and it was only surpassed by my own.

"I'll be fine. You two go check on the rest of our people," I said. "Have a drink with them." It was the first time I collectively referred to vampires and witches. It felt right.

"Your dark battles your light." She studied me when we were alone.

"Yes," I said. "I don't know how Sorin ever had control with the dark so dominant."

"You are worried about your strength."

"Yes, but I feel strong and in control as long as Brandon and Nick are by my side," I said.

"They won't always be available for you to pull strength. What will you do to maintain control then?" She asked in a concerned tone.

"I don't have the luxury of choosing isolation and not practicing magic as Sorin did. I'm worried about my ability to control it on my own."

"It wasn't a luxury for him. It was a necessity. You are not like him. The strength is within you, Brie. You have a strength like no other... not even Sorin. You find it in Nick and Brandon because they believe in you. You must believe in yourself, in the same way, to find it within you. It is the only way you'll succeed.," she said, putting an arm around me and pulling me to her. "Meditate. Let the answer come to you." She left me alone in my study. I looked around at the room, and I didn't want to meditate in a room built for business.

I walked straight to the chapel where Sorin's body would be held in Royal State. I took a deep breath before opening the doors. I thought I would have the room to myself, but there sat my mother in a chair pulled up next to where his body was encompassed and suspended by a spell for the dead. He glowed with a silvery white light filling the chapel along with the soft glow of candles.

"Mom?" I said, putting my hand on her shoulder. I

expected her to shun me, but she placed her hand on top of mine and squeezed.

"He always regretted leaving. Even when he was consumed by the dark, he regretted leaving us. He thought it was the only way to save us from his destiny and from yours," she said, her voice tear muddled.

"I know. He made the best decision he could." I paused and swallowed my tears. "He and I had made peace."

"Can you forgive me for lying to you? I only wanted to protect you from this life. I thought if I took your powers, then we could stop your destiny." She sobbed, and I moved around in front of her, kneeling to look her in the face.

"I already have." Tears flowed down my face. She surprised me by leaning forward and hugging me. I hugged her back. The hole inside me healed. Sorin's gifts came even after his death.

We stood up, walking hand-in-hand to Sorin's body. We stared at him for a moment as he lay there in the white royal robes adorned with gold stitching and the purple sash of the king. He looked peaceful and regal. From the darkness around me, I understood he never knew this kind of peace in life. The darkness once tormented him, but no more. I looked from his head to his shoulder and to his fingertips, where I reached to take his hand. I expected cold, but it wasn't. A slight warmth met my fingers. I racked my brain trying to remember if there was ever a time he consumed vampire blood, and I couldn't recall ever sensing it. I used his life force coursing through me to search his memories, and I found nothing. My gaze was drawn to his chest where a wound should be, but it was completely healed. He can't be vampire. He can't.

"Mom, look at his chest." She was fragile, but I needed someone to confirm I wasn't hallucinating.

"What? Brie, what do you mean?" She looked at me with the same arched brow I had when I was confused.

"Where is the wound? Do you see where the arrow pierced him?"

She looked from his chest to me.

"How can that be?"

"It looks like he is healing. Is that even possible?" I asked her.

"I've never seen it before." She took a deep breath. "We should keep it to ourselves and find your grandmother. We need to find her now."

"I can reach her without hunting her down in the mansion." I quieted my mind and thought of her. I could see her talking to Brandon and Nick, but I couldn't hear them. I tried to show her a picture in her mind's eye, and I thought it worked as she excused herself.

TWENTY-SEVEN

>・>・●・C・C

I wandered around the mansion unable to sleep after the talk with Grandmother. The corridors passed by until I ended up on the green knoll in the back. The winter had been kind this year, but it was the magic here keeping the knoll lush and green. I slipped my shoes off, running my bare feet through the grass. The softness relaxed me, and my gaze traveled upward to the stars. My thoughts on Sorin and what his struggles must have been like. I wondered if, like him, I would have to leave to combat the dark now dwelling in me. It wasn't a choice I wanted to make, but it wasn't one Sorin wanted to make, either.

Familiar arms slipped around my waist. I leaned against the muscular form behind me for comfort, welcoming the distraction from my thoughts. Nick enveloped me, pulling me tight against him. His embrace blanketed me in safety, if only for a moment in time.

Safety never existed in a reality, for either of our kind, but we had these illusions of it when we were together.

"Could we have beaten the curse of the sacrifice?" I asked.

"Sorin was convinced his sacrifice was the key, and I trust him," Nick said, his voice deep and melodic. That voice alone soothed the rushes of pain inside me.

"I can't believe he's gone. He blew into my life, and then right out of it. How can the pain be so great for someone I barely knew?" I closed my eyes, pushing back the tears, once again overwhelmed by grief.

"He was with you all along, Brie. Even at his darkest point, he was with you. You will carry a piece of him with you always," he said, his voice soft, a gentle breeze against my ear.

"Literally," I said. The pain in the core of my soul rotting me gnawed to come out, and I didn't miss the look on Nick's face.

"He wouldn't have allowed it if he wasn't sure you could handle it," Nick said.

"Are you sure? I'm thinking there is some other reason all these powers are drawn to me. It's not normal for a witch to possess so many." I paused. "You know what I would really like to do?"

"Enlighten me," Nick said.

"I'd really like to scream at the top of my lungs and throw things. Revenge is calling me to rain Hell's fire down on Stefan, and everyone knows I can do it now. It wouldn't bring Sorin back, but I would enjoy seeing Stefan suffer."

"What's stopping you?" His arms tightened around me

like he thought I really would. Like he thought he could stop me.

"Acting dramatic is going to make me look crazier than I feel, and it is not what the people expect or need from their queen." I sighed.

"You can't keep it all inside either," he said. "The warriors would say you should save it for the battle."

"Let's enjoy the solitude right now. Who knows when we will have peace like this again." I said, avoiding the subject. Being in a moment of peace and quiet had become a truly rare thing. We stood there until exhaustion exceeded my will, and my knees gave way. Nick supported my body with his. When I regained my composure, he released his grip. I pulled away and slipped my shoes back on. The ground shook, jarring me. I looked at Nick. His confusion matched my own.

The earth trembled around us. A loud explosion rained debris in the air. I coughed through the dust, and Nick's hand grabbed a hold of mine, pulling me inside the mansion. My guards jumped into action and separated Nick and me. One guardsman on each side dragged me down the hall. I saw Nick and Cal securing the door. My tattoo became a trusted friend as it warmed and glowed on my arm. It reminded me of my purpose and cleared the fog around me. I struggled against my guards.

"Let me go." The guards stopped but didn't turn me loose. "Now!" I commanded, and they relented. "We're under attack. Sound the alarm and get my mother and grandmother to safety." I ran back to where Nick and Cal were. Brandon and many others joined them. They were ready to fight whatever lurked in the dark for us, and we all knew precisely who had come for battle.

"I should have seen it coming," Nick said. "They were testing us earlier."

"We can debate the should've could'ves later. Right now we need to prepare for battle," I said. Nick grabbed me by the neck and kissed me. "We will definitely discuss more later."

"Something tells me this is my father's doing," Cal said, backing away to where the group congregated. I looked at him and quickly took his hand. I let my instincts guide me.

"May peace and strength always bring you to the light." It came out in a whisper of a voice, and my aura passed over him.

He blinked and squeezed my hand. "Thank you, my Queen."

"We are short on time," Nick said, pulling me away.

He and I dashed to my suite for my stash of weapons. Everyone else ran to the armory. I grabbed the pistol made especially for me and loaded it with the explosive bullets of Vampire Death. I put stakes in my boots, and I took two more from the arsenal. Nick only took two stakes.

"You're going for Stefan."

"I am." He confirmed my fears. We both wanted his father dead, and it was an honor we both deserved.

"What if I get there first?" I asked.

"Then revenge is yours," he said, almost emotionless. I looked into his eyes and saw fear. He never showed fear for himself, only for me. This fear was not for the loss of his maker but for what revenge would cost me.

"Light is my choice. Remember, I made the choice for light," I said, reassuring myself as well as him.

He nodded to me.

"May my love give you strength in your choice," he said, whispering back to me.

We ran down the long hall to find everyone readied in front of the door to the once beautiful green knoll. They all looked at Nick and me and took a knee in front of us. We had to succeed for them. They needed both of us to lead them, a united team.

"Rise," I said. "Victory is ours if we choose light. We fight for peace tonight, not revenge." I was sure I was the only one who heard the sigh as it escaped Nick's mouth. He knew revenge was imminent for one of us. While we would feel the bittersweet taste of revenge, I wouldn't let it be so for those pledged to us. The curse would be ours to bear.

Brandon suggested we use the old escape tunnels so we could flank either side of Stefan's army. His vast army comprised of many vampires, but that was expected. None of us were prepared for the abominations we saw as we approached their army. Stefan had a witch on his side for sure. The grotesque creatures at the head of the army were at least eight feet tall and grossly disfigured, no doubt from the dark spells used to create them. In modern terms, they looked like giant ogres. These poor creatures signified his efforts to recreate the old ways. His failure appeared to have created something he could control and use. The dark aura swirling around them was singing to the dark aura now entwined with my pink aura. I could feel the pull as a wave of nausea passed over me.

The fight would not be fair, and I would have to take lives before it even really began. Stefan stood at the front with his guards on either side and two of the creatures just beyond them. Nick and I nodded toward each other as we led the charge. Brandon and Cal led the group on the other side, right into the middle of the fight. Alastair nestled in the belly of our enemy's army. I stopped in mid-stride. It all came together for me. Cecily had never helped Stefan as he had implied. It was Alastair all along, and it was why Cal had to travel after him. Alastair had already been in the States.

"Now is not the time for hesitation, Brie." Nick took my hand. His touch jolted me from my thoughts. We progressed through the labyrinth created by the two armies clashing. Nick impressed me once again with strength and speed as he ended two vampires to my one. The dust would not have settled from the first when his stake would find the next. As we approached Stefan and Alastair, Christopher came into view. As we got closer, I could see Stefan had his arm around him. The sight made my skin crawl and turned my stomach.

A rush of air drew my attention to one of the abominations. They were smarter than they looked, and it had spotted us. When it ran for us, I grabbed Nick's hand and teleported us closer to Stefan.

"A little warning next time would be nice." Nick gave me a quick smile, warming me from the inside out.

"No time." I shrugged, giving him a quick smile back. We walked confidently toward Stefan. I wanted to throw an energy ball right into his evil smile, but I feared for Christopher's life. Alastair had beads of sweat glistening on his brow, and my only thought for him was he should be worried. Nick and I looked at each other one last time. The attention focused on us. I drew in a deep breath, calming my mind and making my decision.

If ever there was a time to use the dark, it was now. "Hell's Fire encircle us," I said, closing my eyes. I could feel the tug of the dark from the black aura as the flames rose from the ground and surrounded us. The fires burned hot enough that no one on either side could cross. I opened my eyes and focused on the two figures in front of me I wanted to see them pay for my father's death. Stefan only laughed wickedly, but Alastair's eyes were wide with surprise.

"Have you met my new favorite son?" Stefan dug his nails into Christopher's shoulder. Christopher winced. When his eyes reopened, I could see only fear in them. The calm I restored to him before the first battle was gone. I didn't feel anger at his betrayal. Pity flowed from me as I saw the pleading look in his eye. Stefan shoved Christopher forward slightly. "Tell them what you did for me."

"Kill me," Christopher said. His voice was inaudible, but I could read the words he mouthed to me. He dropped to his knees in pain from Stefan digging his thumb into his neck. "I told them about your plan," Christopher said. The words came in a rush as the blood poured from his neck. When the wound healed, Stefan forced his nail through the skin again. He moved to snap Christopher's neck, and there was no doubt in my mind he would rip his head completely off.

I held up my hands and froze everyone in the circle. I couldn't budge Christopher. I held everyone with my left hand and touched his temple with my right, willing my pink aura to untangle from the black and unfreeze him. I sighed with relief and immediately gasped as I felt the black aura fighting against my pink aura as it returned to me. The pain was enough to make me lose concentration on time, and I took Christopher by the arm, running back to Nick. I saw Nick shake the confusion away, giving me a side glance. It was hard to fight the dark when it seemed to lie in wait for any moment to slip into my being.

"You have become quite powerful, Brie. I can see how the dark has a hold of you," Stefan said. The wicked smile never left his face. No freaking shit, asshole.

"Aren't you observant?" I said, letting the condescending tone rake over him.

"Well, little witch, I can command Christopher to come back to my side. Do you intend to play this cat-and-mouse game all night?" Stefan said, settling his eyes on Christopher. "Oh my son, clever boy, you are. Now come to your father where you belong."

Christopher took a step forward, fighting through the pain, forcing him forward. There would be a price, but I sent my aura to surround him without thought for myself. It encapsulated him like an insulated bubble protecting him from Stefan. The shock on Stefan's face made me smirk in delight. Christopher took a step back.

"I've never-" He stopped before finishing his sentence and turned to Alastair. "Did you know?" Alastair shook his head from left to right.

"Aura isn't known for its malleability," Alastair said. He never took his eyes off of me. Dark aura grabbed onto me. Its tendrils stung. Each one explored a weakness, and the battle became more about my battle with the dark versus the battle with Stefan. The sounds of death came from all around me, and the dark aura gained strength from it. The longer I called my pink aura, the weaker it became, and the less likely it could penetrate the dark. I struggled to maintain control. Hell's Fire shot further into the air, heating the space. The dark whispered offers to whisk me away to a place where I would always be in control. To a place where my power would not be surpassed. The desperation in its need to consume me for its own design of the future. I understood so many more things about Sorin now, and I believed the aura was the reason he stopped practicing magic. He didn't want to give into the dark. I wished to the heavens I could tell him. It was just a wish I sent up, not realizing the impact it would have. Am I going to be dark when this battle is over? *I choose light. Light.*

"Light," I said, confirming my choice aloud.

Peace washed over me like I had never experienced. It hushed my mind as I stood there completely focused for the first time since my life changed. My pink aura returned to me, and I felt no pain. The pull of the dark lessened as it retreated. The fires still burned around us, so I still commanded dark in some way, but it no longer had a hold on me. *Is this what Sorin went through?* His strength coursed through me, and I looked at Stefan, wanting nothing but vengeance. Vengeance constituted dark, but I wanted it. I raised my hand and silently called the elements. Thunder rolled around us as bolts of energy streaked their way through the air into my palm. The electricity crackled as it touched my hand, and the power grew. I would end Stefan and end this war before there was any more bloodshed.

"We're done here," I said, directing my words to Stefan as the wind swirled around me, ready to unleash my power on him.

"Stop!" I heard a gravelly voice behind us. Stefan and Alastair both stared over my shoulder, compelling me to turn around. I stood in amazement as Sorin took slow, deliberate steps through the wall of fire surrounding us. His movements were not unlike those I took earlier to his lifeless body. I stood in awe as he passed through unscathed. The dark aura swirled around him, and his eyes were burning like embers.

Sorin looked into Stefan's eyes as if he could burn him from the inside. "Brie is correct. We are done here. Go now if you wish to see another day." He said, holding his hands out palms down, and calming the fire raging around us. He had control of Hell's Fire. Sorin clasped his hands together in front of him and out to a V shape. We watched the abominations turn to dust from his simple gesture. Sorin commanded great power, and even more so than I imagined. His force manifested as equal to, if not greater than, my own. Why the elders thought my powers were greater escaped me as I watched him. I wanted to pinch myself because it was all beyond anything familiar to me.

"Your head will be mine." Stefan eyed Sorin before ordering the army to return to the castle. "Christopher, I command you to return with me." Christopher stood still. My aura had released him from Stefan's control, and he could choose. I put my arm around his shoulder. Stefan's nostrils flared, and his eyes narrowed as Christopher defied him.

"Christopher's choice has been made." I stared at Stefan. He took a step towards us, and a small fire rose between us.

"Don't think I will spare your life if you take one more step towards my daughter." Sorin's voice rumbled. Stefan spat at Christopher's feet.

"Remember your choice when they tire of you," Stefan said. He turned, and with the wave of his hand, motioned his army to leave. I stood still for a moment, watching Stefan's retreat.

"How is this possible?" I ran to Sorin, hugging him tightly. Brandon had found us and stared in disbelief. We hugged each other for a long time. Even though he embraced us, Sorin stood slightly rigid, and the battle he fought now lay inside him. I faced it too. I sent up a silent prayer he could conquer the dark once again and stay with us. I didn't want him to disappear for another two decades. I needed him here.

"You, Brie. Your light. Your aura protected me even in death. I was in death, not with darkness but with light, standing on the precipice of Hell. Your light kept me from going over," he said, looking at me. No one could escape death, and there would be consequences just as resulted when he tried to forgo his destiny. The price would be mine this time for saving him, even if it was unknowingly. I wondered how our destinies would change from my actions, and I sent a second silent prayer up for forgiveness.

"But your eyes?" I asked, staring at the embers, looking at me.

"There are consequences for all our choices, even in death," he said, echoing my thoughts as he hugged me. He held something back with his cryptic answer. I was too happy and held that conversation for another day. I caught sight of my aura as we pulled apart, and a faint trace of the dark aura still wound itself through my own. Sorin took my hand and studied it with me. "This is your darkness, Brie. Even though you professed your choice of light, the dark will always wait to take over when you are vulnerable." I nodded, understanding fully my choices would be difficult, and I would face them from here until we had peace for all.

My tattoo glowed, and I looked down to see the first of the moons pulsating on my arm. The dance entranced me, and it turned white coming to a stop. I looked up at Sorin, who smiled. I had chosen light in the face of darkness fulfilling part of my prophecy, but I would face it again. Confidence filled me as I thought of achieving my destiny. We still had battles to face before the war would be won, but bloodshed from my hands was not the answer. I would fulfill my destiny as queen, and I would do so by continuing to choose light. I squeezed Sorin's hand before seeking out the love of my life.

"Hey, handsome," I said, wrapping my arms around his neck.

"What would you like to do now, beautiful?" he asked, looking deep into my eyes. I relished the connection between us, but his wrinkled forehead did not get past me.

"Well, I'm engaged to this handsome, albeit stubborn, vampire. I guess that means I need to make wedding plans because my family wouldn't approve of me living in sin," I said, winking at him. He tilted his head back, laughing, and we felt normal again. It was our own kind of normal. When he leaned in to kiss me, I wanted to melt into his arms. This was my kind of forever.

To be continued…

)) ● ((

When darkness comes to claim Brie, will she be able to fight her way back to the light?